Pillow Talk

Other books by Lesléa Newman

Novels

Good Enough to Eat   *In Every Laugh a Tear*
                Fat Chance

Short story collections

A Letter to Harvey Milk   *Every Woman's Dream*
                Secrets

Poetry

Just Looking for My Shoes   *Love Me Like You Mean It*
        Sweet Dark Places   *Still Life With Buddy*

Humor

Out of the Closet and Nothing to Wear
The Little Butch Book

Nonfiction

SomeBODY to Love: A Guide to Loving the Body You Have
Writing From the Heart: Inspiration & Exercises for Women Who Want to Write

Children's books

Heather Has Two Mommies   *Belinda's Bouquet*
Gloria Goes to Gay Pride   *Remember That*   *Saturday Is Pattyday*
                Too Far Away to Touch
                Matzo Ball Moon

Anthologies

Bubbe Meisehs by Shayneh Maidelehs: Poems by Jewish Granddaughters About Our Grandmothers
Eating Our Hearts Out: Personal Accounts of Women's Relationship to Food
A Loving Testimony: Remembering Loved Ones Lost to AIDS
My Lover Is a Woman: Contemporary Lesbian Love Poems
The Femme Mystique

Pillow Talk

Lesbian stories between the covers

Edited by
Lesléa Newman

alyson
books
LOS ANGELES • NEW YORK

© 1998 BY LESLÉA NEWMAN.

AUTHORS RETAIN COPYRIGHT OF THEIR INDIVIDUAL PIECES OF WORK.

COVER IMAGE: GUSTAVE CORBET'S "THE SLUMBER," 1866. MUSÉE DU PETIT PALAIS, PARIS, FRANCE. PHOTOGRAPH BY ERICH LESSING/ART RESOURCE, NEW YORK.

ALL RIGHTS RESERVED.

MANUFACTURED IN THE UNITED STATES OF AMERICA.

THIS TRADE PAPERBACK ORIGINAL IS PUBLISHED BY ALYSON PUBLICATIONS INC., P.O. BOX 4371, LOS ANGELES, CALIFORNIA 90078-4371.

DISTRIBUTION IN THE UNITED KINGDOM BY TURNAROUND PUBLISHER SERVICES LTD., UNIT 3 OLYMPIA TRADING ESTATE, COBURG ROAD, WOOD GREEN, LONDON N22 6TZ ENGLAND.

FIRST EDITION: MAY 1998

02 01 00 99   10 9 8 7 6 5 4 3 2

ISBN 1-55583-419-1

LIBRARY OF CONGRESS CATALOGING-IN-PUBLICATION DATA

PILLOW TALK : LESBIAN STORIES BETWEEN THE COVERS / EDITED BY
LESLÉA NEWMAN. — 1ST ED.
    INCLUDES BIBLIOGRAPHICAL REFERENCES.
    1. LESBIANS—SEXUAL BEHAVIOR—FICTION. 2. LESBIANS' WRITINGS, AMERICAN.
3. EROTIC STORIES, AMERICAN. I. NEWMAN, LESLÉA.
PS648.L47P55 1998
813.008'03538—DC21   98-5296 CIP

For all you naughty girls

Contents

Introduction

Well, do lesbians do in bed? Why, each other, of course. We do our lovers, our lovers' lovers and our ex-lovers. We do our lovers' ex-lovers and our ex-lovers' lovers. We do our crushes, our roommates, the girls next door, and our friends. And our delicious doings are by no means limited to the bedroom. According to the stories collected in this volume, we do it everywhere: in the yard, in the car, in the garden, in the bar. At the movies, in a diner, at the office, in amusement parks. Outside at women's music festivals, inside sleazy hotels. Against the wall, on the grass, in the bathroom, on the table. Morning, noon, and night. Whenever two (or more) women meet, there is always a chance we will fall in lust…and maybe even love.

How do we do it? We do it soft and sweet; we do it rough and hard. We do it with fingers and fists and toes and tongues. We do it in boots, bustiers, and boxer shorts. We do it in lipstick, lace, and latex. We do it nice, and we do it nasty. We ride the line between pleasure and pain. We hurt, and we flirt; we tease, and we please. We do it in ways our mothers wouldn't like. We do it in ways the religious right wouldn't like. We do it in ways other lesbians wouldn't like.

We do it the way we like to do it and the way our lovers like to do it, political correctness be damned.

I left no stone butch unturned in my search for the hottest lesbian stories I could find, and it was a great honor and pleasure to read the hundreds of stories that were sent to me for this project. As I read (and read and read and read) I was struck by the fact that lesbian sex is not only alive and well; it is alive and thriving. Whoever came up with the phrase "lesbian bed death" would certainly have to eat her words (and her girlfriend) if she ever took a look in my mailbox! And I have to assume that all the activities described in these pages aren't just figments of our collective imagination. In fact, I like to think that the women who sent me stories did a bit of research as they wrote. I know reading all the stories that came my way certainly gave me plenty of ideas I can't wait to try. Like what? You'll have to dive between the covers to find out.

I invite you to curl up with your best girl or your favorite sex toy (perhaps both) and take *Pillow Talk* to bed. Use both hands to spread it open. Go from front to back or back to front. Or just pick whatever appeals to you and start from there. Let your eyes travel from top to bottom, and lick your lips as you savor everything you see. I guarantee, you won't be disappointed.

Lesléa Newman
May 1998

Pillow Talk

A Friend of a Friend of Dorothy's
by Roberta Almerez

Iwas referred to her by a friend of a friend of a friend.
She worked by referral only. No one in my crowd wanted to admit they paid for it, though prostitution is legal in
our state.

I hadn't been in the women's community long, just since
my divorce. I had a life by then, a real if quiet one. The
"gals" and I played cards or tennis once a week. Like most
women my age, I didn't seem to go out much except for the
monthly potluck. Most of the single women I met were single for good reason. Still, that didn't seem like a good
enough excuse for what my friends were suggesting.

"I really don't think I need this," I said to my friend Mel,
short for Melody.

"Sheila, everybody needs this. Go," she said. "I've heard
she's worth every nickel. Besides, no one's gonna want to
bring you out anyway, so you might as well get it over with."

What a pal.

I finally relented and sent a cashier's check to her business name and post office box along with a brief note. Mel
also said to bring a generous tip with me. M'lady certainly
did not work cheap.

A few days later I received a phone call.

"Hello. You were referred by Mel?" The voice was ever so businesslike.

My roller coaster slipped a gear. I reached to cradle the phone carefully in both hands.

She continued, "I would like you to meet me at the Riggfield, in room 326, 3 o'clock. Go straight up. It will be unlocked."

This was too weird.

"Wait, don't we meet for coffee first or something?"

She laughed, "Not usually."

My God, I thought, *this is really going to happen.*

I hadn't remembered it, but early in my marriage, while vacationing with Nathan (my ex), we had met these two lovely ladies in Las Vegas. One was exceedingly glamorous and well-built, a nightclub singer. We all talked about our travels, and the singer complained about constantly being propositioned by prostitutes in Amsterdam. We laughed and were suitably shocked and amused. But deep below my politeness, some nerve began to tingle.

What would it be like to sleep with a woman? To buy a woman? It was truly a most decadent and delicious thought, told to no one, and quietly forgotten until now. I assumed that it would never happen, not to me. Yet here I was.

I had never in my life done anything like this. Maybe that was reason enough. Mel suggested I not make too big a deal out of it. I had to start somewhere. The women's community was not the easiest club to get into. In short, I had to want to be in it very badly for anyone to take me seriously. It had taken a full year to be as well-settled as I was, with real friends and all. Lord knows, I had done the homework. My bookshelves were chock-full of everything from lesbian softball etiquette to lesbian astrology. It was time to graduate.

The room at the Riggfield was very pleasant. Sort of pseu-do-Victorian. Its glory was the high-posted brass bed. I could see why she chose this place. It seemed warm and comfortable.

A suitcase lay on the stand. She had already been there. Towels and wine sat on the dresser, along with a note:

"Have some wine, shower if you like. When you're ready stand in the window."

This was getting to be torturous. I paced the room and drank my wine in three gulps. Sipping my second glass somewhat slower, I took a deep breath and walked over to the window.

Immediately I saw her, just another well-dressed woman reading in the hotel courtyard. She looked up, smiled, and slowly gathered her things. She wore soft brown colors in well-cut, low-key fashion. She seemed to enjoy my watching as she moved casually and sensually. When she stood and walked toward me, she seemed the perfect blend of vanity and confidence.

The door opened, but I could not bring myself to turn around. I chose to gulp down the last of my wine instead. I could hear her walk across the floor, high and above the loud pounding of my heart and temples. She gently took the glass from my hand and pressed me to her, kissing my neck and holding me firmly. She was taller than I was and smelled nice, of something herbal like lavender. Her full breasts were a revelation to me. It was like the breaking of bread, warm and soft against my body.

Clouds seemed to gather from nowhere.

"It's getting stormy out; looks like it might rain." They were the first words she had spoken.

"I'm sorry, I never got your name."

"Does it matter?"

Her voice now was smooth and exceedingly feminine, which surprised me. She was indeed very feminine, not what I expected. I had been dreaming of cigar-smoking tango dancers and the rough painted women that craved them.

She massaged my chest and squeezed open my shirt. I moved to close the blind, but she pulled my hand away.

In my ear she said softly, "Imagine you are in an ancient city. It is springtime, and you have come to receive your rituals at our temple. No one is too old, too ugly, or unwanted. Nothing is right or wrong. We are in a temple of earthly love."

Next she turned us both around and leaned back into the windowsill. Looking at her up close, I saw that her hair was pulled back into a long braid. She was neither young nor old and was very beautiful, with eyes like daggers—serene, powerful, yet gentle. I think I just stood there sort of blinking wide-eyed. I reached to kiss her, but she held me back.

"No kissing on the mouth, please. Kiss me down here."

She pushed my shoulders down, dropping me to my knees, and waited expectantly while I kneeled. I found myself eye level with her tweed-covered open pubis.

Sweet Jesus, we were to the point, by golly. I massaged her pubis with my face, imbibing her fragrance. The strangeness was most overwhelming.

She uttered her approval and began undoing her shirt and jacket. Her exposed nipples were long, dark, and mesmerizing. My chest sang silent hymns and praises. Above me was…how can I say this without sounding like a giddy lovesick teenager? I can't and won't.

It had begun to rain. She opened the window with no concern for her nudity.

"I love the sound of water, don't you?"

She casually finished undressing both herself and me, placing our clothes on the chairs. She then took my hand and led me to the bed.

"Is this a workday for you?"

I had to think for a minute, work being the furthest thing from my mind.

"I took the afternoon off."

"Good," she replied.

In bed she began kissing and touching my breasts. As if sensing my nervousness, she asked between kisses, "Is there anyone you've always wanted to make love to?"

"Oh, God, lots of women: my neighbor, my clients, the grocery clerk. But I guess I'm shy, and I'd…"

More kisses, more glorious skin against mine.

"Do I remind you of anyone in particular?"

"Well, as a matter of fact, you remind me of a yoga teacher I once had."

"Oh?" Through the thin blanket she began massaging my mons. "And what was she like?"

The feel of her gentle pressure and my own memories stirred together. "She was very beautiful like you and had this vibrant energy. No one was ever late for class. I'm sure it was obvious I had it bad for her. All I could do was stare at her as if she were a feast. Funny, though, I never knew what it was."

"And what was it?"

"Well, lust, I guess."

She paused, laid a towel between our hips, and crawled on top of me.

"Can you imagine her breasts over your face like this? Can you imagine taking one into your mouth?"

"No, really, I—"

"Make love to her breasts, touch them, feel them. Relax and enjoy. Anywhere you want to go, I'll go with you."

Well, what a delirious proposition. She fell to my side and held me till I found my rhythm. *Hmm,* I thought, *yes, I can do this.* I sucked hard on her skin, and soon she was on top of me again.

It was not like being with Nathan. Nathan was a Dodge minivan. This was a foreign sports car careening madly through the French Alps. This was, well...*great!* The more I touched and caressed, the more I wanted to. I felt a grasping aggression that made me want to consume her. She responded by clenching her thighs tight against me.

Outside, the rain began to hammer loudly in a wonderful rhythm. She reached into the nearby nightstand and pulled out lubricant and gloves. She snapped on a glove and gave me one as well. Facing me, she slowly slipped her hand into my slick opening, entering me gently and uttering graphic things in a low whisper.

She silently pulled me up on my knees and penetrated me deeply from behind as if all she wanted to do in the world was please me, be inside of me. It was so different from being with Nathan (the ex) or Vincent (the first), save how much I was there, burning like a cheap candle. So different, so strange, so much better.

Time seemed to stop until I felt her pull away from me. In the growing darkness, I could see her taping Saran Wrap across her belly like a flap. Wordlessly she mounted my face and offered me her dark sex with its silvery veil. I swam in it as she rocked and rolled, sending me to wild, passionate places I had never been to before. She reached for my gloved hand, daubed it with lubricant, and guided me inside her. I then moved about slowly in rapt fascination, letting her body lead.

I was inside of her. Me, deep inside of her. It was amazing, simply amazing; I could do this forever. She bucked harder and harder, then collapsed against me. I bathed in her stillness, loving the weight of her, so real and solid above me.

When she recovered somewhat, she guided me onto my back and taped Saran Wrap low over my belly. She put on a new glove and got down between my legs, bowing before my fevered bush.

"Now," she laughed, "I'm going to show you the lesbian missionary position."

Even through the plastic her mouth seemed incredibly hot and focused. Again, it was very different and much better. This was not prelude, not perfunctory foreplay. She stayed perfectly there until I came in slow rolling waves.

Without pause she laid a fresh towel between us and pressed against me until she orgasmed again, her passion flowing into mine.

As we lay there afterward, I wanted to believe that her passion was real. How could it not be? She certainly wasn't shy about pleasing herself. And I liked that too, that she could please herself so unself-consciously.

We made love once more in the shower, the gloves and fragrant soap so obviously made for each other. What I could not kiss, I drank with my eyes, watching her wet lips and face fashioned into pleasure. I imagined every woman I had ever wanted, wearing that same helpless look of abandon.

We finally sank to the bottom of the tub together. I remember feeling the warm spray of water falling upon us and my crazed brain trying furiously to commit every precious moment to memory, as if I might forget. We stayed like this until the shower ran cold. Our lovemaking had come to its end.

The sky was dark when I was finally dry and dressed. Time seemed elongated and stretched thin, the way a soap bubble floats on air.

I lay on the bed and watched as she sat at the mirror, lovely in the soft lamplight, combing and redoing her braid. When done, she turned to me and said, "It's time for you to go."

"Will you take a coffee with me?"

"Sorry, no. I have to stay and finish up."

The bubble vaporized, I was back in the world again.

I slipped the tip envelope onto the table. She smiled and said thank you, making her way to me.

"You can always make another appointment."

We both knew it would never happen.

She said, "It was fun. You were really great."

"Gosh, I don't know about that."

"No, you were pretty hot. Once you got started, you gave as good as you got. I'm sure when you find someone, you'll do fine. Just don't move in on the second date."

"Move in?"

"It's a joke."

"Oh."

She opened the door and kissed me on the cheek before scooting me out.

I reluctantly made my way to the car. The dark boulevard was wet and shiny with streetlights. The air was sweet. Life was sweet. I took one last look at the Riggfield. I never pass it now without thinking of her.

Family
by Katya Andreevna

"Honey?" I mumbled as I rolled over in the unfamiliar bed and found that Robin was no longer beside me.

"So, are you going to get up?" Robin's voice had an edge to it as if already I had done something to embarrass her.

I sat up slowly. The hotel room scent pervaded my nostrils and made me cough. Robin was slumped in a chair at the foot of the bed. She stared dully at The Weather Channel on TV.

"It's not late," I said.

"I want to get going," she said.

I slid out of the bed, sank into the wall-to-wall carpeting, and plodded to the bathroom.

"Well, when are we supposed to be there?" I asked.

"I don't know," Robin snapped. She flicked the television off. "I need to call Ben."

I opened my mouth to retort but thought better of it. I continued into the bathroom and turned on the shower. *Maybe talking to her brother will cheer her up,* I thought.

I wanted to stay in the shower forever, but I didn't dawdle. I wanted to get this meeting-the-girlfriend's-family stuff over with. We were supposed to go by her parents' apartment on Nob Hill, have lunch, visit the grandmother, have dinner, and see her brother somewhere in there too.

When I got out of the shower, Robin seemed calmer. She said we had to meet some of her old friends before we went to her folks' place. We hit the streets and headed for a café.

The quietness of the Castro surprised me. But it was early. We walked slowly, not even holding hands the way we often did back home.

Breakfast was a blur to me. I was unable to remember the names of any of Robin's friends. Their talk of mutual acquaintances, whom I did not know, swirled around me. I gazed at Robin's handsome face, her capable hands around a mug of coffee, her dark hair slicked behind her ears. Pride and desire swelled in me. But then I remembered our schedule for the day, and I felt cold.

"Here, Katie," Robin whispered in my ear. She smoothed her leather jacket over my shoulders. "Sorry about this morning," she continued.

I smiled and darted forward to kiss her lips. But she moved back so my lips barely grazed hers. I pulled her jacket closer around me.

We left the café and walked numbly through the streets. The surrounding scent of Robin's jacket made me wish that we had no obligations, that we had the afternoon to ourselves.

"Do we have to go see your grandmother?" I asked.

"I'm afraid so," Robin said with the mere hint of a smile. She bit her lip and hung her head.

This was not turning into my idea of a vacation. Here we were in San Francisco, the gay world's mecca, and we were both too anxious to have any fun. I kicked at a bottle cap on the street. Robin shrugged. We kept walking.

"Let's just stop in here a second," Robin said after a few minutes. "Maybe this will relax us." A mischievous grin spread across her face as she pointed at a gay male theater.

"Why not?" I said, although I didn't feel in the mood. Not anymore, at least.

The place seemed amazingly clean, considering it was a jerk-off joint. But the atmosphere was heavy with spilled seed. We stood at the back behind the mostly empty seats. I clutched Robin's arm.

"Do you think it's OK that we're here?" I asked in a whisper. I peered into the dim light, trying to see the scant patrons.

"They're cool here," Robin said, patting my hand. She stared at the screen. "Ben took me here once."

I giggled. "You two really do share everything."

Robin smiled. *I do want to meet this brother,* I thought.

On the screen two oiled, male bodies wrestled. The blond one pinned the dark one, who grinned his surrender. The blond hopped up to reveal his growing erection. The brunet knelt, as if in prayer, then unleashed his dripping tongue. The blond's face contorted as his cock expanded under his friend's eager ministrations.

I clung to Robin. The seam of my jeans began to dig into the tender flesh between my legs. Robin's arm snaked around me. She pinched one of my nipples, and I felt my free nipple go hard. I leaned against Robin's strong torso, me eyes still on the screen.

"Come on," she said.

I thought she wanted to leave, and so I resisted.

"Let's go upstairs," she explained.

In the balcony several booths, all in a row, looked out over the cinema screen. Here you could view in private or with a friend. We slipped into one, laughing at the shocked look of one of the other patrons.

"Women. Those were women," the man said as we disappeared inside.

"You, woman," Robin said. She grabbed a handful of my hair and pulled my head back as she slipped her tongue deep into my mouth. I sucked hungrily as she probed my palate.

I closed the curtain that separated our booth from the hall. On the screen the brunet swallowed the blond's whole piece of meat. Hardly able to breathe, I leaned against the wall and stared at the screen. I could feel my pulse tapping a tattoo in my cunt. Robin undid the top button of my jeans.

"He's going to come," I whispered. "He's going to come in that guy's mouth."

But the man on the screen pulled out. And then he went off like a geyser. Glistening jism shot out of his hot rod.

Robin pressed me close. Her breathing too had grown labored. My knees weak from desire, I let her and the wall at my back support me. The fire inside me was melting my limbs. I was so excited, it almost hurt.

"I need you," I whispered in Robin's ear.

Her hands slid the zipper on my jeans down. The sound inflamed me further. She slipped her hands inside, caressing my buttocks, then pulled my pants down so she could access my pleasure center. My cunt throbbed for her.

"I'm going to shoot inside you, baby," Robin whispered in my ear. Falling to her knees, she rubbed my fur mound and began to part my slick inner lips.

"I wish you had your dick with you," I said.

At that moment I realized that our booth was separated from the adjoining one by a glass partition. The curtain lay open so that anyone entering the booth next door would have an unobstructed view of me and Robin at play. I wanted to close the curtain over the glass.

"Rob, honey?"

"It's OK," Robin mumbled from between my legs. Her tongue traced the length of my clit. Wrapped up in sensation, I forgot about the curtain. I shivered and closed my eyes.

"I want your dick deep inside me," I said hoarsely.

"It's throbbing for you," Robin replied. "You're such a tight squeeze. I can barely fit my meat inside you."

"Oh, do it, baby," I moaned. "I want you to come inside me."

Ever so slowly Robin slid into me. I wanted to buck, driving her deeper and deeper inside, but I stood still. My pussy twitched around her fingers.

"I'm so hot. My dick is going to blow up. I'm gonna fill you with my come," Robin growled.

"Yes, yes, yes." The words poured from my lips as Robin's tongue danced around my love button. She dived deeper inside. I felt I could swallow her up and still have room for more. At the same time, I felt we were flying and each stroke of her fingers and tongue sent us soaring higher.

"Tell me what your dick looks like," I croaked. "I want to know what it's like pushing inside me."

Robin let out a sly laugh. She thrust deep and slow, holding herself inside me for a moment before drawing back for another stroke.

When she didn't reply, I opened my eyes. I almost screamed. I almost came right at that moment. For an instant I saw Robin's dick, hard and erect, straining toward me. Then I realized that the member I gazed upon was on the other side of the glass partition. A voice in my head told me not to look, and yet I couldn't draw my eyes away. My pussy seemed to like what my eyes saw. I felt myself slicker and more yielding to Robin's fingers.

I eyed the man in the next booth. He had the same dark hair, firm jaw, and naturally arched eyebrows that Robin did. The rectangular shape of his face was practically identical to hers, as was his compact build.

His dick, like his body, was thick but not terribly long. Then I realized that the hand of another man had brought his dick to its erect state. The other man worked slowly with his back to me. The presence of this other man eased my mind somehow, and I felt full permission to gaze on their activity. I concentrated on the erection in front of me.

This is what Robin's dick would look like, I thought. As Robin continued to pump into me, I imagined that the sturdy piece in front of me was drilling into my insides. I began to gasp for breath. I had never felt so open and charged.

The other man's hand began to move faster, and Robin's twin groaned loudly.

"Yes, faster," I said, panting. "Faster. Faster."

Robin increased her speed and force. I felt as if my body had dissolved. All that was left of me was my pussy and my eyes, which I could not move from the throbbing penis before me.

Suddenly the man let out a low howl. His come shot out in an arc and splashed on the glass partition. I leaned toward it, licking the glass, trying to taste him. Robin's arms circled my waist, her face and fingers still buried in my pulsing pussy. Shudders of delight crawled from my center up my spine. I let my voice go, and I too emitted a howl of pleasure before giving in to a cackle that rose up from deep within my belly.

Wiping her face on her sleeve, Robin stood up. She pulled me to her and held me tightly. I couldn't stop the great release of laughter that kept boiling over in my throat. Robin giggled into my ear, then nibbled on it. Finally, I was able to catch my breath.

"That was amazing, darling," I whispered. "But—"

"You are amazing," Robin interrupted me.

Gently she pulled my jeans up and fastened them. I sought her lips with my own, and we kissed long and slow. After a few minutes she pulled back, a grin dancing across her face. I smiled back and unsteadily followed Robin's lead out into the hall. There he stood. The man whose dick made me come.

"This is Ben," Robin said. "Ben, Katie."

Ben winked at me, and I blushed.

"My partner, Paul." The other man whose hands I had seen at work smiled and nodded at me.

"So, are you ready to meet the rest of the family?" Robin asked.

"For sure," I said. "And I know I'll have something to think about during lunch."

"Well," Ben said, "like they always say, 'The family that plays together…'"

We all laughed. Robin put her arm around me. I leaned into her strong shoulder. Paul and Ben joined hands, and the four of us left the theater together.

Play Ball!
by atara

Grinning widely to herself, Cassie booted up her Mac, sighed with impatience as the computer started up, then opened her E-mail program.

To: Leah.
Subject: It is a competition!

She wrote:

"Babe—Only about 32 hours until I see you! I can't wait! When I woke up this morning, all I could think about was my tongue circling your nipple and driving you to distraction. I love reaching down and running one finger between your lips and listening to you gasp and moan. Mmm... But to get to the point of this missive: Did you know the Dodgers-Giants game is going to be on TV Saturday night? What do you say we play a little game of our own? The person whose team loses has to do whatever the winner says for the rest of the evening. How about it, babe? I love you, Cassie."

A few hours later, checking her E-mail at work, Cassie spotted a note from Leah, and her heart jumped as it always did. She read,

"Sweetheart—Fine idea. I just love a little healthy competition. But why don't we make it more interesting? At the end

16

of the game, the winner takes all, but during the game, each
time the Giants score a run, you have to remove one item of
clothing so I can play with whatever parts are revealed. If
those losers in blue happen to score some runs (as if…),
then I pay the same penalty. Love you madly and can't wait
to see you! Leah."

Cassie dashed a quick note back:

"I accept the challenge. Let's just hope it isn't a pitching
duel!"

On Friday, Cassie raced home from work, changed into
her shortest miniskirt and a Dodgers T-shirt, ran her fingers
through her shoulder-length mane of brown curls, and
drove to the airport humming "Take Me Out to the Ball-
game." Her stomach performed a complex series of flips the
entire way, particularly when she worried that her detour at
a flower shop would make her late. Clutching her bouquet,
she arrived at the gate a few minutes before the plane from
San Francisco did. For the 134th time she asked herself,
What if she doesn't make it?

Cassie had met Leah while visiting a friend in San Francisco, soon after breaking up with her girlfriend of three years.
She had started going with Suzanne her last year in college;
Suzanne was very politically active and had nurtured Cassie
through her trepidation about coming out. She was a tender
lover, but Cassie always had the sense of something missing.
Suzanne had always regarded Cassie's collection of dildos and
vibrators and assorted toys with distaste; she wanted to make
love, while Cassie felt an increasing urge to really fuck and be
fucked and have fun in the process.

Cassie moved into her own place, bolstered by a raise at the alternative newspaper where she worked, and acquired her cats, Ripley and Vasquez. On a weekend visit with some friends who had moved to San Francisco after graduation from UCLA, she met Leah at a party at their new house. Leah had shaken her hand while looking her up and down with an appraising gaze that made Cassie shiver. Not even pretending not to notice Cassie's reaction, Leah grinned, raised an eyebrow slightly, and said, "Yeah, I'll admit it—I think you're cute."

Cassie had replied, "Tell me more!" and they spent the rest of the party chatting and flirting. When Leah had reached over to trace a light circle on the back of her hand, Cassie felt a quick clutch in her cunt and knew she had to spend the night with this woman. They had been going together for over a year now, getting together every four to six weeks, depending on their budgets and schedules. Leah had one more year of law school; when she finished they would be able to make more permanent plans. Meanwhile, they sent E-mail back and forth obsessively and ran up their phone bills, describing in vivid detail all the pleasures they wished to perpetrate on each other's bodies when they were together.

Cassie watched eagerly and anxiously as the passengers walked up the ramp, and her suspense was soon relieved by the sight of a woman in jeans and a Giants shirt, waist-length wavy black hair falling over one shoulder, and a shoulder bag draped over the other. Cassie ran to help Leah with her bag but instead found herself caught up in a rough embrace, being deeply kissed in the middle of a terminal at LAX.

"Whew," laughed Cassie when she caught her breath, "I'd almost forgotten what an exhibitionist you are!"

Leah grinned and kissed her again, proudly showing off for the crowd, then pointed at their respective shirts, noting, "Have you noticed how we think alike, babe, even when we're on opposing teams?"

"Speaking of teams, I noticed that yours is in the cellar, and the door is locked!"

"True enough," conceded Leah graciously, "but I have a feeling about tomorrow's game. Your boys are going to go down in burning flames, love, and when you pay the inevitable price don't forget this was your idea."

"We'll s-e-e-e," trilled Cassie. "Oh, Goddess, Leah, do you have any idea how glad I am to see you?"

Leah ran her fingertips lightly along Cassie's upper arm and was pleased to see her girlfriend practically melt into the floor.

"Yeah, hon, I have a pretty good idea. And the feeling is mutual."

On the evening of the big game, Cassie and Leah were both wearing shorts, T-shirts, panties, and bras in order to be fair. The pizza arrived conveniently during the bottom of the first inning, while they were working their way through their first beer. When the Dodgers came up in the top of the second, the first batter hit a single up the middle. Cassie forgot to eat, crossing her fingers and hoping. The second batter of the inning was an easy out, a shallow fly ball. Cassie sighed impatiently and focused her attention even more fixedly on the TV. Swing!…and a miss. Leah was smiling to herself at Cassie's intensity, watching her sit up even more. Swing!…and this time the ball was hit out of the park.

"Fuckin' A!" exclaimed Cassie, pumping her fist. "Two runs! Shirt and shorts off, right now!"

"But I'm still eating," declared Leah in a mock whine.

"If you spill anything, love, I'll lick it off, OK?"

Leah complied, making a great show of grudging unwillingness but obediently sitting on the floor in front of the sofa where Cassie directed her.

Cassie was hoping for more runs, but the Giants pitcher got his act together and struck out the next two batters, while the lovers decided they really had wolfed down enough pizza. Cassie took the plates back to the kitchen and came back with two more beers. Sitting down immediately behind Leah, she rolled her icy bottle over her lover's right nipple, causing it to become instantly erect, obviously straining against her bra. Leah sucked in her breath sharply, but Cassie moved on to the left side, remarking with satisfaction, "Now, that's how I like to see them."

She took a long, slow swig from her bottle, put it down, then proceeded to lean over Leah, circling each nipple with an index finger, murmuring, "You have lovely taste in bras, girl."

"Glad you think so," sighed Leah, leaning back. The sensation was tantalizingly frustrating, but she knew she wouldn't be getting any real satisfaction soon. As she watched her team strand one man on base while flying and striking out, she found more and more of her attention drawn to her nipples, one finger of Cassie's still maddeningly and slowly circling around each one.

"Unh," she groaned, "it goes straight to my cunt."

"I know," laughed Cassie triumphantly. So far this evening was going very well. She kept an eye on the game but continued to lavish attention to Leah's breasts, lightly stroking them all over with her fingertips through the silky fabric of her bra and just as lightly pressing the nipples between the tips of her index finger and thumb.

Leah could feel her cunt contracting, becoming increasingly aware of the moisture seeping out. Her beer remained untouched, and she had to force herself to keep an eye on the game. After an inning and a half of continuous light stimulation of her nipples, she felt she couldn't bear it any longer.

"Oh, please, baby, harder, please!" she begged.

"Well, I'd hate to be a bad hostess," mused Cassie aloud and began pinching Leah's nipples harder, pulling on them slightly, then letting her fingers slide briefly off the fabric before fastening on for another pinch. Leah would have been able to come if pinched hard enough, but Cassie wasn't going to give her that satisfaction. After the Dodgers went down in the fourth, Cassie demanded, "Come up here and sit next to me."

Leah struggled to her feet and muttered, "I gotta pee. I'll be right back."

"Good point—I have to go too," replied Cassie, taking her turn when her lover got back. Leah was staring intently at the TV, as if willing the Giants to get some runs, but so far it was to no avail. Cassie sat down next to her, patted her thighs to indicate that she should spread her legs, and began teasing Leah through the thin silk of her panties.

"My, my, aren't we wet?" mocked Cassie, as she slid one finger up and down.

"Like you're really surprised!" snapped Leah, her frustration mounting. Couldn't those fucking dorks just start hitting the ball?

As the Dodgers came up in the top of the fifth, Cassie began alternately slipping her fingertip into Leah's eager opening and stroking her clit. Her panties were soaked through at this point, and Cassie's finger slid around easily.

It was a long inning; the Dodgers managed to strand two runners before the third out.

During the commercial break Cassie had an idea. She grabbed her now-empty beer bottle and began rolling it against Leah's crotch. Shameless with need, Leah strained forward, but it wasn't enough. The bottle wasn't pressing hard enough against her clit for her to come. She was about to start begging when the first Giants batter came up in the bottom of the fifth, took one swing, and hit a powerful home run into the right field stands. "Y-e-e-es!" she exclaimed. "My turn! And I ain't wasting time. Off with those shorts, honey."

Cassie sighed. It was just like the Dodgers to blow a lead; she had a feeling that the rest of the game wasn't going to go her way. Served her right for being complacent. She pulled off her shorts, only to see the next hitter smack a line-drive double.

"Shit," she muttered, flinging herself back on the couch. She felt Leah's hand firmly grasp her mound through her panties and begin a vigorous rolling massage.

"You're not exactly dry yourself, sweetheart," remarked Leah, keeping her eyes on the screen. The next batter hit a single, advancing the runner to third. The next batter fouled off several pitches, while Leah kept pressing her fingers against Cassie's crotch, but then hit a long fly ball to the center fielder. The runner at third tagged and scored, much to Cassie's dismay. Leah tugged roughly at Cassie's panties, saying, "I want these off now! Now, that's better."

Cassie moaned. It was both arousing and humiliating to be sitting on the couch in a T-shirt and bra but nothing on down below.

"You're gorgeous, you know," Leah whispered in Cassie's ear. Then she reached down and began toying with

Cassie's curls, pulling them very lightly or twisting them around one finger while the Dodgers pitcher walked the next batter. The next man up hit into a double play, however, ending the inning. Leah continued to play absently with Cassie's curls through the commercials and into the top of the sixth.

Although becoming increasingly frustrated, Cassie was also deliriously happy: She loved the way Leah would take her time touching her, sometimes just running her fingertips up and down Cassie's back for minutes upon minutes at a time; sometimes stroking her bottom in sweeping circles with only the slightest occasional brushes between her legs; sometimes playing with her with a vibrator inside Cassie and on her clit, drawing it out for half an hour or more before granting her release.

It was a quick and unproductive half inning for the boys in blue. Part of Cassie still hoped they would score so she could resume an active role, but part of her was happy to sit back, legs spread, feeling the always-magical touch of her lover's fingers winding her up ever tighter.

As the Giants came up and Cassie idly noted the Dodgers' pitching change, Leah started stroking the smooth, slick spot between Cassie's cunt and ass with one finger in between her attentions to Cassie's curls. Cassie leaned back and closed her eyes—it was utterly maddening. To feel a finger so close to both openings but stubbornly remaining outside was agonizingly delicious. She loved being wound up slowly and kept on the edge as long as possible.

It was an easy inning for the Dodgers reliever as well. Cassie hoped the end of the inning would jar Leah into providing a little more stimulation, but it didn't happen. Just the same stroking fingertip alternating with gentle tugs and twists of her curls. The only action the Dodgers managed in the seventh was a walk.

As the Giants came up, Leah had tucked her curled index finger against Cassie's cunt while stroking her labia with her thumb and middle finger. Cassie was quite sufficiently slippery at this point, and Leah's fingers slid smoothly around her flesh. The pressure against her clit was enough to distract her from the game, and somehow the Giants scored a run without her quite knowing how it had happened, except that she was being told to remove her shirt.

"What happened?" she asked dreamily.

"Single, sacrifice bunt, and then a Dodgers error, which let the run get home. I can't imagine why you weren't paying attention."

"Figures," sighed Cassie.

"Now," said Leah, "I want you to lie facedown with your lovely ass over my lap. Here's a pillow for your head."

Cassie awkwardly shifted into the desired position. She was draped over Leah's lap with her head resting on a pillow so she could watch the TV. Not that she was that interested. Leah slid a thumb inside her but only to collect some lubrication; a moment later Cassie felt the thumb tucked firmly into her ass. She gasped sharply, feeling the familiar slight ache that gathered in the backs of her legs. Two more fingers slid into her cunt.

For the eighth and ninth innings, which were scoreless, she remained over Leah's lap, the thumb in her ass and the fingers in her cunt occasionally sliding in and out but not nearly enough to provide any relief. Part of her wanted to come s-o-o-o badly…and part of her wanted to stay just where she was forever.

When the game ended, Leah laughed. "I'm so glad you proposed this little competition, darling," she said as she let Cassie get up.

"Actually, so am I," returned Cassie with a smile. "Conceding victory to you is not exactly a hardship for me, babe."

"Glad to hear it," said Leah, getting up and pulling off her underwear and indicating that Cassie was to get naked as well. She then led her prize off to the bedroom, remarking, "Before I have my way with you, I want you to put that lovely mouth of yours to work on me. I'm going to lie back and enjoy the fruits of my victory." Matching action to words, Leah was soon stretched on the bed, her hands clasped behind her head in an exaggerated attitude of relaxation.

"Would Her Majesty like some peeled grapes?" asked Cassie, her eyes twinkling.

"No, just your tongue. Get to work."

Cassie climbed on the bed so that she was straddling Leah's upper body. She began by tracing her lover's eyelids slowly with her tongue, then moving on to suck and nibble on her earlobes. Leah squirmed slightly and sighed happily. Cassie then began kissing Leah deeply, probing her mouth with her tongue, sucking her lower lip into her own mouth to nibble on it, and sliding the edge of her tongue along the shape of Leah's lips. Leah suddenly pulled her down into a long, hard kiss, their tongues wrestling in Cassie's mouth. Cassie moaned, and Leah grinned and winked at her as she let her go. Cassie couldn't help smiling back in shared complicity, then proposed that Leah roll over for some attention to her back.

Cassie had no intention of being a poor loser; she was so ecstatic to have her lover here, in her bed, that she wanted to make the most of this opportunity to give her pleasure. She began by nibbling on Leah's shoulders, working her way with tiny bites down her upper arms. Then she started on a tongue bath, licking her way up Leah's spine and drawing circles and figure eights all over her back and buttocks, pausing for the occasional light nibble whenever she encountered enough flesh to bite. She loved the sound of Leah's increasingly ragged breathing and the way her body shifted and wriggled slightly in a series of involuntary responses.

"Would you care to roll over now?" asked Cassie, and Leah consented. Cassie wanted to lavish attention on Leah's breasts. Playing with her through her bra earlier had been fun, but she wanted Leah's nipples in her mouth. Moving back and forth from one to the other, Cassie traced circles around each nipple with her tongue or quickly flicked the very tips. As Leah began to moan regularly, Cassie would suck a nipple into her mouth, using her tongue on it that way. Finally, she settled down to sucking hard, moving to the other breast when she felt Leah getting close.

When Leah's moans began turning more guttural, Cassie slid down her body, pausing to probe her lover's belly button with her tongue and being rewarded with a sharp gasp. Cassie looked up and grinned, then took her place between Leah's legs. She wanted to make this good. First she fucked Leah slowly and deliberately with her tongue and was gratified to hear sounds like "ungh!" and "a-a-ah!" and "ooh!" coming from above her head. Then she began tracing a circular shape with her tongue, up from Leah's cunt and around the hood of her clit and back around. Cassie loved her girlfriend's taste and loved the feeling of her satiny, dewy flesh under her tongue. The sounds from above increased in volume and intensity, so Cassie began focusing her licks right on Leah's clit.

As Leah got closer and closer, Cassie suddenly sucked her clit into her mouth hard, and Leah shrieked with the impact of her long-delayed orgasm. Cassie then pressed the heel of her hand hard against Leah's clit, rubbing in tight circles while slipping three fingers in her cunt. Leah came again, half sitting up with the surge of energy that poured through her, then collapsing back on the bed in a drained heap. When she opened her eyes, she was treated to the sight of Cassie happily licking her fingers and grinning.

"You're amazing, girl, you know that?"

"I try," replied Cassie, "and I love you."

"I love you too," said Leah, her face softening. Cassie bent over her for a long kiss, then went off to the kitchen for a bottle of water. When they had both had enough to drink and Leah had rested, her head in Cassie's lap, she said, "Now it's my turn. I suspect I've been keeping you waiting long enough."

"I was hoping you'd say that," laughed Cassie.

"On your back, then," returned Leah.

Cassie lay down, hoping Leah would use the new dildo she had introduced Cassie to last night. It was double-pronged, to fuck both openings at once, and once the lovers had gotten over giggling at how rude it looked while waving it at each other and making it say things like "Hi there! How's it going?" in a series of silly voices, Cassie had turned over on her hands and knees. When Leah slid it inside her, she had felt full and satisfied and well-fucked in a whole new way. Leah wasn't getting any toys out this time, however, but she did produce a bottle of their favorite lube.

Cassie certainly didn't need any, but she didn't question her lover. Leah began by slowly brushing her thumb over Cassie's clit, back and forth, then teasing the opening to her cunt by drawing circles without moving inside. As she maintained her light touches, Cassie couldn't help pumping her hips forward—she had been so very frustrated for so long.

"I know I won," began Leah, "but I'll only do this if you want it. I'd like to slide my fist inside you. I've been wanting to try this for a while."

"Oh, yes!" hissed Cassie. "Oh, please fuck me; please open me up."

"It might hurt," warned Leah.

"I'll let you know if it's too much, OK? I've been wanting it too, but I thought you might think it was too much or something."

"Same here," laughed Leah, shaking her head. She squeezed lube all around Cassie's opening, then covered her own hand liberally. She deliberately slid three fingers inside, moving them slowly in and out before adding her little finger. Cassie's eyes were closed, her whole being focused on her cunt, as Leah carefully stretched it with her fingers. Then with all five fingers pressed together, she slid farther inside, stopping at the wide part of her hand.

"You OK?" she asked.

"Yes," gasped Cassie, "fine." She wanted to swallow Leah's hand, take it inside her.

Leah began pushing her hand carefully in, pausing to add more lube and using a finger of her other hand to help stretch Cassie's opening where needed. Slowly, slowly, and as soon as Leah pushed the widest part of her hand inside, the powerful muscles of Cassie's cunt pulled the rest of her hand inside up to her wrist. They both stared at each other wide-eyed and overcome with emotion—nothing they'd ever done had felt like this.

"I can't believe I'm inside you," whispered Leah. "You're so hot and so smooth and so wet, like a cavern enclosing my fist. You're so strong; you're gripping my wrist so tightly. You're so open, and your face...you're just so beautiful."

"It feels incredible," murmured Cassie. "I feel so close to you, so connected...and so full!" Without thinking, she automatically reached down and pulled her legs up and apart, holding them with her arms circled around her knees.

"Yes, that's my beautiful girl!" Leah said. She began moving her fist very slowly, with the slightest rocking motion, her eyes fixed on Cassie's radiant face. When Cassie began tilting her hips upward, Leah started moving her fist just a little faster.

Cassie was almost delirious with ecstasy. "Oh! Oh! It's so full! Oh! Oh, my toes are tingling! Oh! I never want to let you go! Yes! Y-e-e-es! More! Just a little more! A little faster! That's...*it!*" she wailed, thrashing as her orgasm exploded through her. Then in a small voice, she whispered, "One more, please?"

"Of course," replied Leah, transfixed by the sight of her girlfriend's gorgeous dripping body and the sensation of those powerful muscles clamped around her wrist. "I'm going to try something a little different."

She began rotating her wrist from side to side. It didn't take long. Feeling Leah's knuckles rippling along her vaginal walls, Cassie came again, expelling Leah's fist with the violence of her spasms. She almost instantly crumpled into a sobbing heap, gasping breathlessly, "It was so good! I didn't want to let you go! Felt so close to you! So intense!" then finally, in a smaller voice, "I miss you inside me...and I miss you when you're gone. And I don't want you to leave!"

Leah gathered Cassie in her arms, letting her sob against her breasts while rocking her. "I know, baby, I know. I miss you too. I love you so much. I know it's hard, baby, I know. But we will be together when I graduate; I promise."

Cassie nodded as her sobs slowed to sniffles. "I love you," she whispered, then snuggled in closer. Leah pulled back slightly, offering Cassie a breast, and Cassie eagerly latched on with her mouth, drawing in peace and love and warmth and reassurance as she sucked.

"You know, baby," murmured Leah, "the Dodgers are playing the Giants at the Stick again in three weeks. Wanna go to a game?"

Cassie nodded and then, after carefully releasing Leah's nipple from her mouth, smiled and said, "No one else could make me say this, but I won't even mind too much if they lose."

Daffodils
by Sally Bellerose

Iam vainly, passionately in love with my garden. I consider each crocus bud to be swelling by the grace of the
sweat that dripped off my neck while I planted last fall. The
curve of the tulips' leaves are the curve of my back, straining with the pitchfork over the compost heap.

I have an ex-lover, Annie. My old girlfriend appreciates my
vanities. She's a fecund woman of 55. *Fecundity.* God, I love
that word. A word that celebrates the muck and mire we all
spring from, the richness of life. A word you can use without
feeling corny about the filling, swelling, bursting going on
inside and outside of you. A lusty word for lusty women.

Like everything else in nature that's alive and kicking, my
ex-girlfriend and I know a sexy season when we feel it.
Spring is fucking time. Since we broke up, there have been
some years when I didn't see Annie all winter long. But you
can bet your last tube of vagilube she's going to show up at
my front door sometime before and as sure as taxes are due,
smiling like she never ever did one wrong thing. She's the
first sign of spring: soft, moist, and furrowed.

This year Annie came on April first, All Fools' Day. I know
because my present love-her-madly-till-death-do-we-part
girlfriend left for a conference in Erie, Pa., that same morn-

ing. My girlfriend's tracks were still fresh on the driveway when knock, knock, knock, Annie's at my door.

We sit quietly in the living room. I pour coffee. Her body, full on my couch, extravagant, is what my grandmother would have called pleasingly plump. In fact, Annie looks a lot like my grandmother, except her hair is not gray. Annie dyes her hair red—not auburn but red. She looks incredible.

It's one of those days when the light is so bright and the air is so clean that everything seems possible. I look out the window. I see my neighbor's rusty trash cans lying on their sides near the border of my garden. The damned kids have thrown them over the fence again. When I smile at the sun bouncing off the dirty metal barrels, I know that Annie and I are going to end up naked.

It's always the same. We start out polite, acting like we aren't affected by the bulge in the daffodils anymore, pretending we don't have some unspoken pact to celebrate the rituals of spring together year after year. We're dying to find out what has changed and what remains the same, but we start out slow, just in case one of us has decided that we should quit while we're ahead.

Annie and I were born the same year in the month of April. We met in the spring, 22 years after our separate births. We were young together. We were young together until we were 46. Then we weren't together, and we weren't young. Middle age. I've never been able to wrap my mind around that season of life. It's not what I expected. I thought middle life would take over and make me respectable, settled, comfortably bored. Now Annie and I are both 55, on the cusp of old age, approaching old ladyhood as unsettled and wanton as we were 33 years ago. Annie says you're only as old as you feel. Well, I feel 55 springs horny.

I look at Annie, wrinkles deepening around her eyes as she smiles at me. I see old familiar lust forming in the lines at the corners of her mouth. She brings her coffee to her lips. There's a fold inside her elbow that I don't remember from last year.

*Annie, we're turning into old women with desire tucked in the bends and kinks of our skin. Old women—*I like the sound of that. I touch my neck, my skin warm and loose. Old women, sitting on the couch unfolding. I like the feel of it. Especially in spring. Spring has a way of honoring the layers of life that came before. The thicker the blanket of dead leaves, kitchen scraps, manure, and snow, the more succulent the hyacinth's new shoots. I like having all those winters, all those springs backing me up. It's good that I'm still alive. I'm just starting to get the hang of life. It's mostly the dying-at-the-end part that I'm having a hard time adjusting to.

I lean back on the couch and close my eyes. Annie sits quietly beside me. She touches my hand. Softly her fingertips turn over my memory. I think of Annie's hot breath on the back of my neck, her fingers reaching around my waist to unzip my jeans from behind. I don't think of us as any age. I remember how the sweat forms in the small of her back as she moves on top of me and calls my name. I try to remember where we found the guts to take these liberties so long ago. Even youth doesn't give two women license to do these things together. Maybe age stops asking for permission.

I open my eyes and smile at Annie. The older I get, the better my long-term memory gets, and I can't remember Annie ever asking for permission to do anything. Maybe she was old before her time. She never asked me if she could sleep with other women when we were together. We had a deal. We were doing the don't ask, don't tell thing long before the military got the idea.

But sleeping with other women wasn't why we broke up. Our deal worked out fine for the most part. It was good we broke up. It was getting so we weren't being nice to each other on a day-to-day, every-day schedule. It was time to go our separate ways. So we did.

"Let's see the garden," Annie says.

We walk out to the yard. We gossip among the crocuses. They're in bloom, tiny things, only six inches from the ground, but they're full of themselves, screaming yellow and purple. The first to flower, brave little darlings. There's a chill in the morning air. Still, you can feel it's going to be a warm day. The ground is damp. It feels nice to sink into each step just a little as we walk.

Annie compliments my tulips, marvels at how many there are, more than last year, more than the year before. They're all up, awake, out of the ground, seven or eight inches high. The leaves are striated green and rusty red, profuse and pushing. They're not ready to bloom. They have maybe a foot more to grow and gallons of sun to drink before they're good to go.

It's the daffodils that grab us, stop us in our tracks. We stare for a full minute before we walk toward them, our mugs of coffee steaming in our hands. The daffodils are swollen, not one bloom actually open among a hundred. They're straining. They want to get on with it, bad. They're tired of waiting. You can feel their impatience—just a little more time, just a little more light, a little more sun. Something inside them is pushing. Open. This is the time. Open. This is the place. No shame. They stand in clumps, leaves turning toward the sun. If it were rain, they'd be just as ready. They know who they are, what they want.

Annie and I stare at each other and sip. Annie presses the warm mug to her cheek. The coffee steam rises. I brush my own cheek against my own cup and stare at Annie. It's the morning sun, it's the season, it's me that makes Annie's face glow, but it's something else too. Annie's happy. She's happier than I've seen her in a long time.

She's in love, not with me. She has a new lover. I'm not guessing. I've met the woman. Nice woman. She makes Annie happy. I wonder what kind of deal Annie has with her new lover. I don't ask. Annie doesn't tell.

I push Annie's new lover out of my mind. I push my own lover as far out of my mind as she will go—Erie, Pa. The light is at that certain slant that Emily Dickinson doesn't describe. It's the "Fuck it. This is the only moment that ever was or ever will be" slant. It hits Annie full in the face. She really is illuminated. She doesn't blink. She looks me straight in the eye.

"I want you bad," she says.

We walk back to the house. We sit on the couch. It's still warm where our bodies had been a few minutes earlier. This time there's no space between us. Annie pulls my face to hers. She kisses me full on the lips.

I snuggle my face between her breasts. I love her skin, especially the V between her breasts. The skin there is more furrowed and wrinkled than the rest of her. Beyond the V on Annie's breast are the places where the sun doesn't shine, pale, tender. I like those places too.

I trace my finger down the leathery skin of one breast and up the leathery skin of the other breast. I like the feel of her skin on my fingers. I can see through her blouse that the dark mound of her nipple is swelling up, a hard little seed that I want to swallow. Her bra pushes her breasts together. I put my hand between them. Warm. Soft.

"Aah," Annie says and kisses the back of my neck. She slides her hands down my back into my jeans and kneads the muscle of my ass. She always does this. I always want her to do this.

Annie gets on top of me. I feel her full weight. Mouth to mouth, breast to breast, belly to belly. Her hips plant me farther into the couch. My hips reach up to her. She slides both hands under my ass, takes a firm hold of each cheek, and pulls me even closer as she pushes down.

We get a rhythm going, a dance. We move, her belly, my belly, her thighs, my thighs. I can feel the soft fleshy mound between her thighs and the hard bone beneath pushing into me, my own flesh and bone pushing back. We're touching everywhere, pressing every place we're able to press.

The pressure and the movement get more intense. Our tongues are in and out of each other's mouths. Our hands are grabbing, pressing, kneading any piece of flesh we can work except the one spot that wants pressing most.

Our pants are down around our knees. I have one leg completely free. My legs are slightly parted beneath her. She could lift up and slide her hand between my legs. I could reach up and find her hot and wet too.

She's working me. Everything in its time. I'm so wet. I'm so ready to get wetter. *For God's sakes, girl, hit the spot. It's time. Come on, honey. I want it both ways, to be full, completely filled up, and at the same time completely empty, all the way open so it all spills out. Touch me, girl. I want to explode. I'm squirming under her.*

The phone rings. *Ignore it. Keep moving, keep moaning, keep your flesh heaving against mine, Annie.* The phone rings again, unnatural intrusion, blasphemy of the rites of spring.

36

Annie's mouth is on my breast now. She's biting my nipple. *A little harder, baby. Oh, Annie. That's exactly right.*

The answering machine clicks on. My voice: "Sorry we can't come to the phone right now. Please leave a message at the sound of the beep." The machine is on the end table, six inches from our heads. It's turned up full volume because my hearing's not what it used to be. I try to reach for it to shut it off, but it falls to the floor.

My girlfriend's voice comes blaring over the damned thing: "Hey, baby. You out in the garden? Plane's delayed. What a gorgeous day to be stuck in the airport. Hope you're enjoying it. Love you. Call you when I get to Pennsylvania." Click.

Annie makes a valiant effort to ignore the disturbing sound of the busy signal coming from the receiver that's fallen from its cradle. She keeps right on playing with my breast. But for me there's a line where pleasurable erotic pressure becomes "stop right now" pain. It's the point where you hear your girlfriend's voice talking sweet on the answering machine while your ex-girlfriend has her teeth sunk into your right nipple.

I feel a stabbing ache from my nipple to my crotch. My body stiffens up like frozen roadkill. Annie tries to soothe me. She tongues my nipple softly, strokes the side of my face. I try to melt back into her, but I'm chilled to the bone. A shiver runs up my spine.

Annie sits up. She doesn't try to hide her annoyance. "Sandy sounds well," she says.

"Jesus," I say. "Jesus Christ Almighty."

"What's he got to do with it?" Annie asks.

"Sweet Mary," I say.

"Well, that's a little better."

I sit up next to Annie. "Sorry," I say weakly.

"I thought you and Sandy had an arrangement," Annie says in exasperation, rearranging her magnificent breasts in her bra. She glares at the answering machine. "Progress," she says. She picks her blouse off the floor. I watch as her fleshy breasts slowly disappear under checked cotton, button by button.

I stand on one leg, trying to pull the other leg of my jeans and my panties up at the same time. I fall back onto the couch.

Annie stares at me. "Look at you. You're shaking. Poor baby." She puts her arm around me. She's more concerned than annoyed now. I put my head on her shoulder.

"Sandy hates the arrangement," I whine.

"Wasn't it Sandy who used to carry on about compulsory monogamy?"

"That was five years ago when she had the hots for her sister's neighbor. She's decided that open relationships work better in theory than in practice."

"All theory. No action," Annie sighs. "Never mind. I still love you, you sexy thing." Annie knows me well enough to know it's going to take me quite a bit of time to unthaw again.

I say, "Shit."

Annie stands up, pulls on her pants, tucks in her blouse.

"I'm going home," she says, "to finish this business we started together all by myself."

She holds my face between her hands and gives me a suction-cup kiss on the forehead. That's what I like about Annie: She takes life as it comes. She's not angry, still a tad irritated, but what the hell—she's got the right.

"Thanks, Annie, " I say. "I love you too."

I watch her as she moves toward the door. I'm a lump of deflated libido, limp on the couch. I see her through the window as she walks toward the daffodils. I watch her bend at the knees and lean forward. Her sturdy thighs support her. Her butt sticks out. This posture suits her. Her curves perfectly complement the landscape of the garden. Does she know I'm watching her?

She sure does. Beautiful, mellow old girl. She's trying to direct my attention to the flowers, but I'm looking at her. Her smile is upside down. The garden is only a backdrop. Annie's the focal point.

My spirit rises with her as she stands, waves at me, and points to the flower she holds in her hand. Her grin gets closer and closer as she walks back toward the house. I turn the knob. It's warmer outside than it is inside. The warm air spills in my door. Annie offers me a daffodil, fully bloomed, from my own garden.

Good Girls
by Louise A. Blum

Earlene is cutting the hair up around my ears. "Not too short," I venture timidly, but Earlene ignores me. Whack—and my ear is exposed, red curls lie all over the floor. Earlene steps back, satisfaction stamped on her face like a brand. Behind us the women are watching a movie on Earlene's VCR. Earlene guns up her razor, and I try to keep still. One false move and she'll cut my throat. I've never seen it happen, but that doesn't mean anything around here. This is frontier country, small-town rural outback. In this section of America, you don't take anything for granted. The women behind us turn up the sound just in time to hear the lead describe someone as a fucking asshole.

"Oh." One of the women shudders. "I just hate it when they talk like that."

All the women nod in unison. Close to my face, intent on her job, Earlene purses her lips. "I've never understood it," she says, guiding the razor along the edge of my sideburns. "Why can't they just say something else besides *that* word?" The other women cluck in agreement. Earlene leans in closer. "Why can't they just say, 'That idiot asshole!'" she says, "or something like that?" Her breath is hot on my face. Something in the room smells faintly of wet dog. Is it me? Is it obvious that I spent all morning chasing our dog through every backyard on the street after he slipped his collar? Earlene studies the evenness of my sideburns, exhales sharply. I can feel myself wilt before her gaze. A gunshot sounds from the TV set, and all the women wheel to face it. I try to sniff myself, discreetly. I think it's Earlene. Or it might just be the day in general; it's been raining now for what seems like weeks. Everything has the subtle cast of must.

"My daughter-in-law talks like that," Marge says. She sits in the corner, going through her purse. Earlene has just finished her, pushing and pulling at her hair till it frames her head like a helmet. Marge comes in every Friday afternoon for a wash and set. It amazes me that people still do that. I wonder sometimes if when all these women die, wash and sets will become a thing of the past—all the grandmothers will still be spraying up their high hair. "Every other word," Marge says.

"No," says Earlene's mother, in polite disbelief. "Which one?"

Marge looks at her, pathetically. "Cassie," she says. Her tone is funereal. It leaves no hope.

Earlene's mother surveys her. "Get out," she says.

Earlene swivels me around so sharply I nearly fly out of the chair, brings me face-to-face with my image in the mirror, looking startlingly out of place in Earlene's salon, surrounded by pink hair curlers and advertisements for Retin-A cream, all autographed by Earlene's mother—"This really works! Ask me!!" they say. I glance in the mirror at Earlene's mother. Her face is a mass of wrinkles. Earlene lifts the scissors off the counter, spins them around on her fingertips. "I slapped a girl's face once for saying that in front of me," Earlene says, pulling the hair off my forehead with a comb and brandishing the scissors dangerously close to my eyes. "She never said it to me again," Earlene says, closing the blades around a lock of my hair, which instantly turns into history. It was a lock I liked.

Something happens on the television, and there is a moment of silence while everybody registers it. "Have you seen this movie before, Hannah?" Earlene asks me. I tell her I have, as a matter of fact. Cleo and I watched it a couple of weeks ago. "How does it end?" Earlene says.

I hesitate. Is this a trick question? Will I be punished for withholding information? My dedication to art wins out. "I can't tell you that," I say.

There is a moment of silence in the salon. I wonder if it will all be over soon. No one even breathes. Then Earlene claps me on the shoulder so hard I can already feel the bruise. "Good girl," she says, snapping off the apron she's had around me and dusting me off with an old towel that's obviously seen a lot of necks today. She winks at the others. "She's not going to give it away," Earlene says.

"She's a good girl," Marge says, nodding in agreement.

I lift myself out of the chair, awkwardly. I am nearly six feet tall and over 30 years old. As I root around in my purse for my wallet, I wonder for a moment how old I'll have to be before people stop saying things like "Good girl" to me. I glance around the salon before I leave, at the women still intent on the TV. In this area I'll probably never get that old.

"Good-bye, Hannah," Earlene calls after me.

"Good-bye, sweetheart," calls Marge, who's never even seen me before.

"She's a nice girl," I hear Earlene's mother say as I pull the door shut behind me, and I resist the temptation to open it back up again to hear Earlene's answer. I know how Earlene feels about me. I make my way around the puddles to get to my truck. The air is cold on the back of my freshly shaven neck. Every six weeks she cuts my hair. I take whatever cut she gives me. I never complain. Every six weeks we all sit around together, share a warm and rosy feeling deep inside, surrounded by the hair dryers and the television and the many bottles of aerosol hair spray. They all think I'm a good girl. I don't disillusion them.

But they don't know the first thing about me.

They don't have a clue.

I stop at the grocery store on the way home, pick up some cucumbers, a couple ears of corn, a bottle of wine. When I get home, I unload everything, uncork the wine, pour myself a glass, check the backyard to make sure the dog is still there, give the cats some food. It is nearly 5; Cleo will be home soon. I put some music on the stereo, turn up the volume, and light a few candles around the house. I take my glass of wine and head upstairs to the bedroom. I hum a little under my breath. The cats follow me up the stairs, jump onto the bed and curl up, hoping it's that time already and that I'll join them. I run a comb through my hair, which is thick and red and wild and full of curls, all with a mind of their own, all artificially cemented into place now with Earlene's indefatigable spray. Standing in front of the mirror, I unbutton my blouse, slowly, shake it off, and then unzip my pants. The body that emerges is a good one. I open the top drawer of my dresser, pull out a black silk negligee and a pair of fishnet hose, slip my body into them. I secure the hosiery with two red velvet garter belts, slip into my black high heels that make me so tall I tend to duck through doorways. At 5 o'clock, three things happen: The clock downstairs chimes the hour, Cleo's car pulls in the drive,

43

and I slide open the bottom drawer of the nightstand beside our bed and pull out the handcuffs.

The front door opens, closes nearly imperceptibly. I can hear Cleo's step in the hall as she pauses to check the mail, moving through to the kitchen. I wait for her to see the wine, get herself a glass from the liquor cabinet. I count to ten. In a moment I hear her step on the stairs. Then I sit down on the bed and lean back against the pillows, cross my legs suggestively, wait for her to come in the room, let the handcuffs dangle from my fingers, loosely. For a moment, there is almost no sound in the house.

At Earlene's, the women peer closely at the television screen, trying to determine the ethnicity of the characters. "That really is her son, in real life, you know," Earlene says, tugging at a wayward curl at the back of my head.

"No," says her mother, sweeping feverishly at the pile of hair around my chair, a mix of the last three customers, the iron-permed black clumps of Marge's wash and set; the coarse frosted blond and brown of Betsy's no-fuss cut, feathered back around her uncompromising mountain jaw; and the soft red curls from my own head. It is a swirl of colors and textures, a miasma of world views. Enough to stuff a small pillow with. "Who's his father?"

Earlene names another actor, and Marge in the corner, where she is writing the check for her haircut, snorts. "So he got a double dose of it." She shakes her pen to get the ink flowing. "Poor kid." She looks up at the rest of us. "What's her name in the movie?" she asks. "Epstein, Goldstein—it's a Jewish name."

I sit and let Earlene tug at my curls, mist them with the spray bottle and try to comb them out, cut them evenly. I am properly disguised in this community. My name is Hannah Newman. Nothing that would raise suspicion. You could pass a lot of names off here in this little Pennsylvania mountain town as Polish or Czech. Newman probably seems entirely innocuous to them. Anyway, I'm only half. My father's side, so it doesn't even count. Though sometimes I wonder how that can be.

"Look at that nose," Marge says, clapping her purse shut.

I close my eyes and let Earlene cut my hair. It's not my fight, after all. I'm not claimed by any side.

Cleo enters the room like a wraith, like a shadow. She hangs in the doorway, dovelike, her long light blond hair in her face and deep circles beneath her eyes. She is so thin she could be anorexic. Her hands are delicate, the fingers long and slender, knotting with surprising strength at certain moments in our lovemaking. Her skin is dark, her look full of mystery. No one knows that much about her. Not even me.

"Come here," I say, patting the bed beside me, and she walks across the room, stepping like a deer. There is something animal-like about her, more animal than human. Even her smells are animal, full of a raw iron when she is menstruating, strong and sharp and assaulting when I put my mouth on her. It is like fucking in a pile of leaves, deep in the woods, with all kinds of scents swept in on the wind.

She pauses when she is next to the bed, slips her shirt over her breasts. Her hair falls nearly to her waist, cascades down her back, absolutely straight, nearly silver in the half-light coming in through the drawn blinds. She touches my face. Her wrists are so thin I could snap them with one hand. She kneels on the floor beside the bed and spreads my thighs with her hands, presses her face to my crotch, inhales deeply. I touch her head with my hand, close my eyes as she unsnaps the negligee and pushes it back. This is it—this is what I live for. If Earlene and the others only knew. They'd burn us at the stake. There is something tantalizing about the prospect. It makes me feel like I'm getting away with something, like I've got something on the rest of them. It's a double life I lead here in this town. It gives to everything a thin veneer of espionage.

I say little at Earlene's when I go. I never seemed to learn that art of banter that other people have. I work as a teller at one of the two banks in town—you'd think I'd pick it up. It's how people communicate, keep up a running joke, keep the ball in the air at all costs, don't let things get too serious. It's all a shared humor, depends on a shared perspective, a community way of seeing the world. Whatever it is, I just don't have it. I keep my mouth closed and smile at the appropriate times. Sometimes things are funny, sometimes not. I take it all inside me, breathe it in through my skin, reptilian-style, sit and watch them, blinking, never betraying myself.

Cleo is from this town, believe it or not. Her Polish grandparents came here, worked in the coal mines, died at home, at their hearth. Cleo, with her long, exotic silver hair, is entirely Polish, entirely East European. A country with a long history of anti-Semitism. Cleo fits right in here. My father's family died in ovens stoked by her uncles. We have a common bond, a connection that precedes us. When we make love I seize her hair in my hand, pull her head back, expose her throat, slender and pale, her life pulsing through her clear blue veins. I run my tongue along her bloodline, follow the flow all through her body. She lives in my arms, dies in them every night. A little death. Whoever thought to call it that?

Earlene whips out the blow-dryer, aims it at my head. "Now, *shit* I can say," she says, looking around at the others. "And *damn* I can say. But not that f word." She turns the hair dryer on full blast, sends tufts of my hair all over the salon. Behind us, in the mirror, I can see her mother nod.

Cleo looks up at me from between my legs. Her face is wet with my come. I reach down and pull her up till we are both standing. She comes no higher than my chest. I take her head in my hands and tip it back. Her eyes are closed, her breath quick; I can feel her heart pounding deep inside her breasts. I bend and kiss her, probe her mouth gently with my tongue while with my hands I stroke her breasts. She moans just a little as I pull back her head by the hair and push her toward the bed.

Betsy was just leaving when I walked into Earlene's. She studied me as she passed me, appraisingly, from under her bangs. She has a jaw like a cliffside. She had apparently been telling the women inside about some party she was going to, because as she passed me Earlene's mother shouted, "What are you wearing?" You can tell she was raised on a farm, because her voice made the cows across the road look up at us.

"One of my three dresses," Betsy said and stared hard at me, for some reason. Did she think I'd laugh? I'm into dresses—short ones that show off my legs, the one feature I'm confident of. Betsy's someone I thought for sure was gay the first time I saw her, but now I know she's married. Around here, it's hard to tell the dykes and the mountain girls apart. They wear the same outfit—flannel shirt and jeans. Sometimes I think I have someone figured out, and then she shows up on the arm of some mountain man. None of your basic stereotypes really fit this area. Everyone is on their own trip. Which suits me fine.

I spread Cleo out on the bed, fit my body to hers, fill her mouth with my tongue, feel with my fingers for the zipper of her jeans, slowly slide her pants down over her hips, touch the hair that curls so softly and so sparsely between her thighs. She is beautiful, her head tipped back and her throat arched. There are times I think I could keep my mouth on her forever, just tasting her juices with my tongue, smelling the raw purity of her, wolflike and potent with wildness.

Earlene has an account at the bank where I work. She comes in every Friday afternoon with her deposit. She always looks disappointed when she sees me, and I always feel guilty, as if I'm not doing my hair the way she intended. I nearly always wash out her styling the minute I get home, to get my hair back to normal.

She coughs a little when she comes in the door, catches my eye, and discreetly runs the fingers of her left hand along her neckline. I stare at her for a moment, fascinated. Is this a come-on? I must have underestimated her. Then I realize she is trying to tell me my bra strap is showing. People are always trying to put me together, as if I were actually coming apart at the seams, trailing bits of stuffing along behind me. Yesterday a customer all the way across the bank hissed my name and pointed vigorously at the tag on the back of her collar. Everyone in the bank felt the back of their necks, circumspectly. Sometimes I wonder if I'm defective in some way, missing some chromosome in my genetic composition that would enable me to care about these little details. Will the world end if someone sees my bra strap? Would it be better if I just didn't wear one and they saw my breasts instead? It's hard to know what's right. It's like everyone else has a rule book I never got a copy of.

Earlene comes up to my window. "Thought I better let you know," she says briskly, dumping her money out on the counter between us.

"Thank you," I say, for lack of anything else, and reach for her money to count it. She touches my hand.

"Here," she says, in a whisper, slipping a little container of something into my hand and closing my fingers around it. I wonder for a moment if it's a crack vial. "A little supergel," she says. "You might want to touch up your left side."

I fasten Cleo to the bed with the handcuffs. It's a four-poster bed; we made sure of that. And then I go into the kitchen, leaving her with her legs spread, her cunt wet, glistening from the touch of my tongue. I go into the kitchen, taking my time, open the refrigerator door and slide that cucumber out of the hydrator, wash it under the faucet, peel it slow. I take the pot out of the freezer and the rolling papers out of the household drawer and take everything back into the bedroom, where I sit on the side of the bed and clean it slowly, roll it into a joint, lick it sealed with my tongue.

"Come on," Cleo says, "come on," and I light the joint, inhale deeply, and then slide it between her lips. I hold it for her, let her take a drag. She has the mouth of a goddess, her lips full and slightly off-center, as if she'd turned her head at some crucial moment in her creation. When her eyes are closed, her lashes are long and curling; beneath them her eyes are the deepest blue in the world. Her hair is spread around her like foliage—she has never cut it.

She is not like me. She has never been like me. We have been together forever, but the only thing we have in common is our sex.

It's always been enough.

Everything has always been enough.

Earlene has a bumper sticker on the back of her Ford pickup that I can read as she pulls out of her space in front of the bank. It says: BUY AMERICAN. BRING THEM TO THEIR JAPA-KNEES. She tells me her boots were made in America, by American workers. Out of poor, unsuspecting American cows, probably. I wonder what she means by American workers. Which kind of American? The ones with pronounceable names? The woman before me coughs, politely, bringing me back to the present. I remember that I am in the middle of a transaction. "Yes," I say, looking deep into her eyes to settle her. "How can I help you?"

I roll the peeled cucumber between my hands, to warm it up. I straddle Cleo's body. I am huge above her; I tower over her. She fits perfectly into the confines of the bed. I touch her clitoris with my thumb, gently part her lips with my fingers. She reaches for me with her pelvis, the only thing she can move. I reach behind me for the top drawer of the nightstand, pull out a blindfold.

She is absolutely mine.

Earlene was the one who told us about the house where we live when we were looking for a place to move in together. The woman who owned it was only too glad to rent it to us. "It's been empty for awhile," she said as we signed the lease. She tore off the carbon, gave us our copy. "But you don't want to advertise," she said. She pulled her key ring out of her pocket, fiddled with it for the key to the house. "Somebody colored might come look at it," she said, looking up at me earnestly, slipping the key into my hand. "And then you'd have to rent to them."

We all stand still for a moment, barely breathing.

She looks back up at me. "Not that I'm prejudiced," she says, and Cleo closes her fingers on my arm, gently, leads me up the front steps into our house, where we close the door behind us.

I part the lips of her vagina gently, then plunge the cucumber deep inside her till she moans. "Louder, " I whisper. "Let me hear you. "

Cleo puts her head back and screams, laughs, gasps. The windows are open, but I fancy the pine trees muffle the sound. I unlock the cuffs from her ankles; she wraps her legs around me, clutches me with her thighs, thin and damp and full of a strength that makes me catch my breath. I slip the cucumber in and out, reach up and undo the restraints on her wrists just as she comes; she seizes my shoulders with both hands, raises her body to mine and wraps herself around me, all naked, slippery flesh, rides it out till she shudders, exhausted, and falls back against the bed. I drop down on top of her, lower my head to her chest. Her heart beneath my ear sounds like a train. I lie still for a moment, listen to the beats until they slow. "Well?" I say. "Ready for dinner?"

I can feel her heart skip. She touches my hair. "Not yet," she says and pries the cucumber from my grip. "Lie down," she says, and I do.

Afterward, we take a shower together, wash each other's private parts, dust each other off with talcum powder. We fancy that we hide our smell, cover our tracks, but I know we don't. The sex is in our skin, emanates from our glands, mixes with our breath when we exhale. There is no hiding it. Cleo smells like musk, like a forest glen. She turns her back to me, zips up her jeans, shakes out her hair. Her hair is like satin, cascading down her back, damp and smooth and straight as a waterfall. She bends over to get her shoes. She has an ass that could melt hearts.

She glances at me, over her shoulder. "Don't get any ideas," she says. "It's time to eat."

We walk down the street to our only restaurant, a discreet space of air between our hips. We move in the manner of people who have just made love. Our bodies feel liquid, golden, amber drops of water pooling on the sidewalk. I feel like my whole body has been entered, like I am one big walking cunt, gliding down the street for all to see. How could anyone not know?

We sit in a corner table near the salad bar, sipping wine. A line forms alongside us, people from the university, in for a meeting, eager for greens. Cleo and I look at each other.

Her look is melting, touches my stomach, makes it go soft. Her eyes are seawater blue, liquid in the light of the room.

One of the men at the salad bar is joking with one of the women. "He said you were a thes-bi-an. I said: Oh, really? I didn't think she went that way!" The man next to him laughs uproariously, so vigorously he nearly spits up into the chick peas.

The women exchange glances. The one addressed says, "I didn't hear what you just said, but I know it's disgusting." She turns to her friend, smiles archly. "I'll get him later," she says.

I become aware of Cleo's knee, pressing against mine beneath the table. Her eyes on mine are concentrated fire, witchlike in the lighting of the restaurant. "Leave it," she says. The flesh of her knee is hot against mine. I don't know what she thinks I'll do—lunge at them, back them up against the salad bar, and hold them by their ties until they choke in earnest? I am only watching.

But "Don't look," she says. And: "Look at me." As if I could look elsewhere, once she's met my gaze. She lifts her glass in a toast. "To sex," she says. "To going That Way."

. I raise my glass to hers. "To sex," I say, just loud enough to make somebody drop the salad tongs into the lettuce. "To fucking." I bring the glass to my lips. The wine on my tongue is like honey, like a balm. I have worked up an appetite. We eat well, Cleo and I. We never lack for hunger. "*L'chayim*," I say, and clink her glass again, look deep into her eyes as I drink. To take your eyes away while toasting is a Slovenian curse. We try to respect each other's customs. "*L'chayim*," she says, and together we explore the menu, just to see if anything has changed.

I'm sitting in Earlene's chair for my six-week haircut. We are alone in the salon; even her mother is somewhere else.

She finishes the cut and dusts the hair off my shoulders. "So," she says. "How's Cleo?"

"She's fine," I tell her.

We smile at each other.

I don't imagine we're a secret. Probably the truth is that everybody knows. But we do what we do in the bedroom, usually with the blinds closed. What we are is hidden from view, kept deep beneath the surface, an invisible brand, concealed by decorum. No one has to see it. We have an advantage that way. To all intents and purposes, we're good girls. We fit right in in this town.

As long as no one raises the blinds.

Women's Rites
by Rhomylly B. Forbes

"Rowan? Hi, it's Elspeth." *Oh, Goddess, she's home.* Elspeth's gut clenched in sudden panic. *For once in my life, I was hoping to get an answering machine.* "What? Yeah, I got home from the Gathering OK. You? Oh, good."

Pause. Deep breath. Grip phone harder. "Listen, I still have your labrys necklace, you know, and I was wondering if you'd like to come over tonight for dinner or something and pick it up, I mean if you aren't...You would? Really? That's...No, you don't have to bring anything. Well, if you insist, how about dessert? Sounds good! Six o'clock? See you then. Bye!" She hung up the sweaty phone quickly, staring in disbelief. *I did it, I really did it. She's coming here. Oh, my Goddess, what do I say? What do I do?* Then the thought that turned Elspeth's blood to ice water: *What do I want her to say? Or do?*

And for the thousandth time in the last two days, Elspeth's hands strayed up to clasp the warm silver-and-moonstone pendant nestled gently in the valley between her soft breasts, and her mind danced back to the moment Rowan placed it there...

They were standing together in the dinner line the final night of Womyn's Spirit Gathering. Rowan, like most of the other women, had taken advantage of clothing-optional space and was sky-clad to the waist except for a scattering of freckles across her shoulders and a small labrys on a chain that made its home between her round breasts. Simple yet elegant, much like Rowan herself (at least to Elspeth's inexperienced and admittedly biased eyes), the labrys was silver with a polished moonstone separating twin crescent blades. As the chow line slowly moved toward steaming vats of lentil pilaf, Elspeth realized with a nearly physical ache that she envied the pendant, that *she* would very much like to be resting in that soft, smooth furrow between the length of Rowan's breasts, to be the one listening to the slow, intimate rhythm of Rowan's heart.

"Hey, you two aren't supposed to be doing something calm and ordinary like eating dinner tonight!" called out another seminaked woman in friendly greeting. Elspeth knew her vaguely as Athena. "You're supposed to be half crazed with last-minute freak-outs before running a ritual for all us uninitiated types, didn't you know?"

"Oh, we're going completely insane," bantered Rowan in her quiet contralto voice. "Can't you tell?"

"Seriously, though, do you need any help?"

"No, but thanks," replied Elspeth. "We've been working on it for weeks." *Weeks,* she thought, inwardly wincing. *Weeks of seeing Rowan almost daily—planning meetings, trips to buy smudge sticks and onyx chips, small private rituals for just the two of us so we'd be better attuned and working as real partners by the Gathering. Weeks to realize that "perfect love and perfect trust" was what I was feeling toward Rowan* personally, *not some abstract Pagan ideal.*

Athena moved off with her bowl of food, and Rowan turned back to Elspeth. "Well, I feel ready, at least. Do you?"

"Um…yeah. I *think* I'm ready."

"Wear this for me tonight, Elspeth, please?" Rowan suddenly said as she took the labrys necklace off.

"Me? But why?"

"I don't know, because it feels right. Will you?"

Elspeth nodded dumbly as Rowan slipped the thin chain over her head. Her hand immediately reached up to clasp it, to feel warmth in the polished metal, warmth that had come from Rowan's body, Rowan's breasts.

Later, twilight in a large oak grove. A bonfire's flames spiraled their way to the stars. Rowan and Elspeth entered the ritual area side by side, Rowan clad in a flame-bright Indian skirt, Elspeth in a black gauze dress and shawl, the presence of Other already settling over their bodies and minds like a warm, soft blanket.

"Hail, our Lady of Light!" the circling women cried as Rowan bowed her head in acknowledgment.

"Hail, our Lady of Darkness!" was the shout that welcomed Elspeth's veiled form. The dancing, chanting, and drumming began as dozens of women came forward, one at a time, to kneel before the Dark Goddess and the Light for a moment's audience, asking for a blessing, a boon, a word of wisdom. The Light Goddess held her daughters when they wept with joy or sorrow. The Dark Goddess washed their fears away with a sigil drawn with saltwater at feet, knees, stomach, above the breasts, and lips, on bare skin or fabric—long, cool fingers marking them with a crescent, a Venus symbol, a spiral, whatever She saw already shining there.

They worked in tandem, these two faces of the Goddess, so attuned to each other's actions and words that all watching truly believed them to be twin aspects of the One.

After, the two priestesses stood alone in near darkness, solitary in their bodies once more. The high bonfire had simmered down to a slumbering lion of embers. "That was one incredible ritual, my sister," Rowan yawned. "But I am far too tired to go to the Trance Dance." Rowan took Elspeth's hand with a shy smile. "I'm going back to my tent to ground myself. Want to join me? We could...talk about the ritual, and maybe..." Rowan softly squeezed Elspeth's hand, letting her fingers end the sentence for her.

Elspeth wanted to say yes, desperately wanted to say yes, but fear of mysteries unknown overwhelmed her and drowned the spark of courage and desire that was about to light her soul. *What irony,* she thought sadly. *After helping so many of my sisters find their power, I am totally powerless to do what I want most to do—make love with Rowan, tell her I want her, show her how I really feel about her. Goddess, what a mess.*

"No..." Elspeth said. "I...can't." She pulled her hand away.

Rowan sighed gently. "Well, good night then, Elspeth. Pleasant dreams attend you." She turned and, with a colorful flare of Indian skirt and flash of Birkenstock sole, melted into the night.

Elspeth blundered through the darkness to her tent in miserable silence. She slowly stripped off her ritual finery and stretched out naked on top of her sleeping bag, for the weather was far too warm to crawl inside it. Faint traces of the Power she had been channeling during the ritual still lingered in her body, making it tingle slightly in answer to the breeze that found its way through the mesh window. Elspeth began to softly caress her own breasts and torso, her body arching up to meet her own fingers in anticipation and need. The labrys pendant, cooling as Elspeth's sweat dried in the night air, kissed the soft flesh between her breasts, maddening Elspeth with memories and fantasies of its owner. She clasped the pendant tightly in her left hand while her right raked through the thatch of pubic hair at the top of her thighs, then spread her legs as wide as she could and plunged two long fingers into her soaking-wet slit.

A few strokes down her deep opening to collect some of the sweet moisture already gathered there was almost enough to make Elspeth come immediately. But she denied herself release for a time, rubbing her slick, wet fingers around her lips, tickling, rubbing, teasing, the fingers of her other hand prying her labia apart and tormenting her clitoris with light, rapid strokes.

As the tension in her thighs grew, Elspeth increased the pressure on her swollen nub and thrust three fingers into her gushing hole. Her back arched and slammed onto the makeshift pallet as wave after wave of orgasm shook her in its hot grip until she collapsed, panting and sweaty.

Elspeth's body was temporarily sated, but her heart was nowhere near content. She wiped wayward droplets of perspiration out of her eyes and rolled over, quietly bursting into tears and clutching her pillow for lone comfort as she did so.

I shouldn't have said no, she wept softly to herself. *I should have gone after her. I should have called her back.*

But Elspeth did call Rowan when she got home.

After her refusal the night before, Elspeth expected dinner to be rather awkward; it wasn't. She expected Rowan to reclaim her labrys right away; Rowan didn't. She also half hoped and expected Rowan to make her offer once again; and Rowan did.

They were sitting on the couch, each perched cross-legged on an end, facing each other. Brown earthenware mugs of spearmint tea steamed faintly between their hands.

"Look, I'm really sorry if I offended or upset you last night," Rowan began, then took a deep breath and continued. "I never wanted to do that. But I feel like we've gotten a lot…closer in the past few weeks, you know, planning the ritual and all. I like you, Elspeth, I like you a lot. And I think you're beautiful, and I really want to make love to you," she finished quickly.

Beautiful? Me? "You didn't—I wasn't upset," Elspeth mumbled, staring intently into her tea mug, hoping to find the answers to her life in its depths. "I…I like you too. A lot. But…"

"Elspeth. Look at me." It was a command. Elspeth glanced up and was instantly caught by Rowan's intense blue eyes. Rowan smiled gently. "You've never been to bed with a woman before, have you?" Crimson with shame at being found out, Elspeth shook her head no. "Do you want to?" Elspeth nodded. "I have an idea. Do you trust me?" Again, Elspeth nodded. "Good. Go take a nice, long, hot shower and meet me in your bedroom after. OK?"

Elspeth finally found her voice. "OK."

Rowan grabbed Elspeth's tea mug with her own and deliberately set them down on the scarred coffee table. She leaned over and kissed Elspeth, long and deep and searchingly. Elspeth's soul was completely stripped naked by that kiss; she felt a slow melting down the entire length of her body until her mouth and lips and clitoris were fused into one hungry sensation as she began to actively kiss Rowan in return, exploring Rowan's mouth with her tongue and lips and rejoicing in every second of contact. After what seemed like blissful eternity, Rowan gently broke the kiss and whispered, "Go."

Towel-wrapped but still slightly damp, Elspeth left the shower and slowly entered her bedroom, which had been transformed into a sacred Temple of the Mysteries. There were lit candles on the dresser, on her private altar, and in each corner of the room. The soft familiar essence of sandalwood incense tickled her nose. And standing in the center of this Temple was Rowan (or was it the Goddess herself?), clad only in her waist-length auburn hair and golden candlelight. Elspeth dropped her towel and moved to stand silently before her.

Elspeth expected, wanted, needed Rowan to take her in her arms and kiss her, but again Rowan surprised her. Slowly, reverently, her blue eyes never leaving Elspeth's gray ones, she knelt at Elspeth's feet and in a voice filled with awe and wonder began a most ancient rite of consecration.

"Blessed be your feet that walk Her sacred path." Rowan whispered as her lips and hair tenderly brushed the tops of Elspeth's feet.

"Blessed be your knees that kneel at Her altar." Rowan kissed each of Elspeth's knees in turn. Elspeth tried not to giggle, but it did tickle.

"Blessed be your sex, the source of life and pleasure." Rowan's small pink tongue licked in and out of the top of Elspeth's cunt a few times, a feather touch on Elspeth's already-aching clit. Elspeth decided she wanted Rowan to do it again—soon.

"Blessed be your breasts, formed in strength and beauty." Rowan's mouth lingered on each nipple, nibbling tenderly at the silky nub just long enough for it to grow hard.

"Blessed be your lips that speak Her sacred Names." Now Rowan kissed Elspeth again, long and deep and hard. Elspeth had to grab Rowan's shoulders to steady herself. Then Rowan smiled and nodded at Elspeth expectantly. Shaking with need and desire, Elspeth knelt and began to ritually bless Rowan's body in return.

Elspeth never remembered too much about Rowan's feet or knees, except that they were perfect. Rowan's moist slit tasted musky and sweet at the same time, and Elspeth could hardly wait to go back for more. Rowan had the most perfect breasts; soft, with nipples responding to Elspeth's tongue as Rowan moaned softly. Finally, Elspeth kissed Rowan's mouth with a growing feeling of confidence and desire and sacred purpose.

"It's so easy, Elspeth, really," Rowan whispered as she led her to the bed and gently guided her down onto it. "Listen, and do what the Goddess tells you to do."

For the moment, the Goddess was telling Elspeth to stretch back and let Rowan's fingers and mouth explore her body. Rowan found and thoroughly caressed and kissed and licked every sensitive spot: the base of Elspeth's throat, the inside of her elbows, behind her knees. Rowan took her time getting to them too, because every so often she would break off her explorations and tease Elspeth's nipples to erection with her lips and thumb.

But whenever any part of Rowan's magnificent body was in reach, Elspeth's fingers and mouth were busy exploring too. She discovered to her delight that Rowan had a particularly erogenous spot at the base of her spine and another one right above her shoulder blades. Thigh, hip, stomach, breast all blended together in the candlelight to form a wondrous whole. Elspeth could feel the heat and dampness increasing between her legs, though, and Rowan seemed to sense that she needed more. Slowly, almost teasingly, Rowan slid down Elspeth's body, nudging her legs apart, gently spreading her moist, musky labia, circling her clit with long yet gentle fingers, sometimes trading them for tongue and lips in the oldest act of worship and reverence. Rowan sucked and nibbled, sometimes tormenting Elspeth by avoiding her clitoris entirely, instead running her soft pink tongue up and down her nether lips in long, slow strokes. Finally, when Rowan saw that Elspeth's breathing was becoming ragged, knowing that Elspeth could stand it no longer, she began to flick her tongue across Elspeth's throbbing button.

As Rowan increased rhythm and pressure, Elspeth lifted her hips to meet her, nearly wild with excitement and happiness, yet moaning softly.

This is all I've ever dreamed of, Elspeth thought, right as Rowan took her over the edge into orgasm and rocked her soul in joyous oblivion. *Thank you, Goddess.*

When Elspeth could breathe and move and think again, she looked at Rowan, who smiled in an impish way, then stretched out beside her. Elspeth remembered the quick taste of Rowan's exquisite pussy she'd had before and decided she was ready for more, much more. She wanted to plunge her tongue into Rowan's slit immediately.

But first the Goddess reminded Elspeth that she had some discoveries of her own to make. Elspeth wanted to find and feel and taste every small, soft, intimate place on Rowan's body and know them as well or better than she knew her own. Lips and fingers and tongue worked to taste and memorize the nape of Rowan's neck, the underside of her breasts, her hips.

Eventually, Elspeth found herself at that same sacred opening. She gently pulled Rowan's lips apart and stared in wonder. Why had she never dreamed a woman's cunt was so beautiful? Reverently but gently at first, Elspeth licked at Rowan's open, exposed clit and hood, sucking the small knob until it blushed and grew with desire. She nibbled and licked and thrust with her fingers at Rowan's soaking slit until Rowan was clenching Elspeth between her thighs and crying out her name, and the name of the Goddess, in joy and wonder.

Elspeth crawled up alongside her, and they lay there for some time holding each other quietly. Rowan's eyes looked black in the candlelight. Finally Elspeth had to ask. "Did I do all right?"

Rowan laughed gently. "Oh, Elspeth, yes. You did everything all right."

As Elspeth shifted to a more comfortable position, she heard a tiny metallic clink and looked down. "Oh, I almost forgot," she said. She started to pull the labrys necklace over her head. "Here."

Rowan stopped her. "I'd like you to have it."

"Me? Why?"

Rowan must have blushed terribly hard for Elspeth to actually see it in the semidarkness. "I...this is so corny, I know, but I've always wanted to give it to someone I thought was very special. Sort of like an amazon version of a class ring or something. Do you mind?"

"No, I'd like that. I am honored," Elspeth whispered past the sudden lump in her throat.

That night they each slept in the arms of the Goddess. *Not much difference between Her and us,* Elspeth thought later, *not much difference at all.*

Le Main
by Julie Anne Gibeau

L*e main*. The French babe has this desperate, breathy way of saying it that makes me just crazy for her. She says it when I'm kissing on her for a while, on her face and her neck and down into her cleavage. *Le main*. And then she'll want me to put my hands on her down between her legs, where I can already feel the warmth and the wet through her clothes.

Le main. The French babe told me it means "the hand" in French. When she says it she kind of swallows the end of the word up into her nose. They do that with a lot of words. It's like they don't really finish them, and you could wait forever just to hear the end of a word.

She's good with suspense. She knows how to make you wait. One time she called and asked me to come over to her place. When I got to her building, she jammed her head out the window and told me I would have to wait, so I stood outside and smoked cigarettes. It was a cold, damp day, and at about the second cigarette it started to drizzle. I was carrying a strap-on in a paper bag, and even though I put it under my sweatshirt, I got so drenched that the thing fell through the paper. I didn't even notice for a while, because somehow the harness got caught up on my pants and the damn dong was hanging at about knee level. I didn't notice until the school buses drove by, anyway.

When she finally let me in and saw the thing, she just shook her head. "No. *Le main,*" she said. *"Le main."*

You'd know just to look at her that she was foreign. She's so skinny, she looks almost frail, and she wears these pants that fit her real tight around the butt and loose tops that hang real short. When she moves around they slide up so you can see the muscles in her stomach and the tops of her little pointy hipbones. Her hair is real short, and she combs it all down flat. I think she calls the color chestnut.

Patty says she's delicate. That's what she said the first time I ever saw the French babe. It had been a rough day, so I went to the bar right after work to kind of chill. When I sat down by Patty, she put one hand on my shoulder and pointed toward the dance floor.

"Look what followed me home from school," she said. There's no dancing that early, so the dance floor wasn't even lit up yet. I could just see this woman out there dancing in and out of the shadows. It was a slow song, and she swayed back and forth and floated in big circles with her arms up in the air.

"Isn't she delicate?" Patty asked me. "She's new on campus. She's from France."

I couldn't take my eyes off her. She was like an angel out there, and I was afraid she might unfold her wings and fly away. I lit up a cigarette and took my beer over to a table near the dance floor where I could see her better. She saw me right away and came over to the table.

"A smoke for me?" she asked. Her accent put my head in some kind of cloud like I'd just walked into a smoky room. All I could see was the red of her lips and the shine of the sweat on her forehead. I was frozen.

"Please. A cigarette," she said.

I'd never been a slave to a woman, and I was proud of that. I'd sworn to never give up my bike, wait by the phone, or take down the car-chick posters in my bedroom. But here was this tiny thing in total control of me. My mind, body, and anything else she could have possibly wanted were hers. I lit a cigarette and handed it to her. She took a couple of long drags, staring into space, and sat down beside me. I was nervous as hell sitting there, and I'm not used to being nervous.

"I liked watching you dance," I said. She just sat and watched her smoke curling up toward the ceiling. I couldn't even tell if she heard me.

"Are you a student?" I asked her.

"Yes. I am new at the university," she said. She looked me right in the eye when she said it and held me in place like that one little sentence was the most important thing happening on the planet. I had this total awareness of her body right then. I was aware of her tiny little waist and the dampness of her belly and the pounding of her heart. It was like I had my hands all over her, but I didn't.

"And you?" she asked. I just stared back at her. I was all flustered. "You are a student?"

"No," I said. I pointed to my uniform. "Groundskeeper on campus."

She frowned a little and made a crooked line between her eyebrows.

"I work outside on maintenance."

"Ah," she said. She pushed out the cigarette in an ashtray and stood up. "I thank you," she said. "What is your name?"

"Buster. My friends all call me Buster."

"I have never heard of that name," she said. "This is bust?" She took my hand and laid it right on her tit.

"No," I said, and I tried to pull it away, but she held it there. I glanced over to see if Patty or anybody was looking, but luckily nobody noticed my situation. The French babe was smiling a coy little smile at me. There was this heat in my face I remembered from my grade school days as a blush. I knew my hand shouldn't be there, but at the same time I was enjoying the warm round thing I was touching. I cupped my hand around it and squeezed as gently as I could.

"My name is really Sara Brown, but my friends call me Buster because there's a little character called Buster Brown."

"A character?" she asked.

"Yeah. He's like a little cartoon dude or something. Sara just doesn't fit me."

"I like Sara," she said. "You are a good Sara." She loosened up the grip she had on my hand, so I let go of her tit and picked up my beer. "I will see you sometime, Sara. Yes?" she asked.

I didn't want to seem too eager, so I shrugged and took a drink. "Maybe," I said. She went back out to the dance floor and started her dance again. The music was faster now, but she still danced in the same slow slinky rhythm. She reminded me of the way wheat moves in a field when the breeze blows.

I wanted the French babe's waist between my hands so bad, I couldn't take watching her very long. I downed the rest of my beer and took the empty up to the bar.

Patty winked at me. "What do you think, Buster?" she asked.

"I think you should keep an eye on her," I said. "This place is too rough for a girl like her."

"If she gets into trouble, you're the first one I'll call," Patty said. She laughed and slapped me on the ass. She's got a lot of energy, but she never can take things seriously. A lot of young ones are that way.

I left the bar and rode over to Sylvia's. She wasn't expecting me, but she was always in the mood for some, and the French babe had given my drive a little jolt. Sylvia must have been sleeping, because she came to the door in her robe, and her bleached hair was flat in the back.

"Well, look at that," she said. "My dream came true."

I stepped inside, and she grabbed my ass. I was tired from digging up cable all day, but watching the French babe had done something to me. By the time I got over to Sylvia's house, my body was screaming all over to take someone, and fortunately Sylvia was always there for the taking. Her robe dropped around her feet.

I staggered back to look at her. Sylvia was a big, fleshy blond, and it took me a few seconds to take in all of her shining white skin.

"I'm not an art exhibit, slug. Let's get on with it," she said. She reached out and took my hand but let go suddenly. "You feel like a damn alligator," she said.

"I can't help it," I told her. "I work outside."

She took me by the sleeve and pulled me down the hallway and into the bedroom. She stood there naked, begging for it with those big cow eyes of hers. With a quick shove I knocked her down onto the bed.

I'm not even sure how things ever got started with Sylvia. I guess I'd been alone for a while. I was worn out from having my heart broken over and over by a long line of nice girls. They really were nice girls, and I was missing the hell out of all of them when I met Sylvia. I was lonely, pissed, and drunk enough to be curious when she strolled up to me that Saturday night and shoved her hand down my pants.

What Sylvia wanted doesn't begin with a formal introduction. After two years of going at it like cats in heat, we'd probably had all of about 20 minutes of real conversation.

"Did you have a good day?" I asked while I rooted through her toy chest.

"Shut up and fuck me," she said.

Sylvia liked it rough. Rough and rude. She pissed me off to make me meaner. Over the past two years, she hadn't learned my middle name or my favorite color, but she'd become an expert at pissing me off. Besides, it's easy to be rough when sex is just sex.

I pulled on some fresh latex gloves from her stash in the drawer and grabbed some restraints. In a few seconds I had her spread-eagled on the bed. She struggled but only to make me flex a little. In the end she was always easy to subdue.

"You stupid ape," she taunted. "You're not woman enough to make me enjoy it."

My heart started racing, and I was more pissed off at myself than her. She always got to me with that crap. It was just part of the game, but it made me want to do her like nobody else could ever do her. I wanted to be the only fuck she thought of, the only fuck she remembered, the fuck she felt when she touched herself. To be that it had to hurt, because to her that's all that really matters.

I yanked the restraints tight enough to make her squeal a little and slapped her meaty gut as hard as I could. She made another little sound.

"Shut up," I said and bit her inner thigh high up where it gets really sensitive. She moaned, but I liked that sound. I went back to the toy chest, pulled out an incredibly big dong, stretched a condom over it, and strapped it on. I could hear the sound of her heavy breathing overlapping my own.

"Do you want to feel me?" I asked.

"I won't feel you no matter what you do," she said.

I jumped onto the bed and stood over her. "You won't say that after you choke on me, you bitch," I told her.

I knelt down and leaned forward and put the dick into her mouth. She moaned again, so I started humping fast and hard. I pumped so hard, I could feel the rub through my thick work pants. I took myself to the edge, then pulled out and slid down on her body. She was gasping. I started biting her tits while I reached down into the slimy abyss between her legs. She arched her back and let out this long, tortured moan. I slid down again, biting hard on her stomach. Then I crammed my hand into her.

Sylvia was about 15 years past being tight. It wasn't even hard to ball my hand into a fist and ram her for all I was worth. Meanwhile, my teeth returned to her inner thighs and worked their way up to her shaved mound. She came while I was biting there and twisting hard. I rode her jerking body like a wave, then fell back across her legs.

I just stayed there a few minutes, trying to catch my breath and forget the hot need I still had between my legs. Sometimes I got off with Sylvia. Sometimes I didn't. All I could count on was no special treatment for stragglers.

"Undo me," she said. "I'm cold."

I sat up and unstrapped her. She was wet with perspiration. I went back to the living room and got her robe off the floor.

"Thanks," she said when I came back and covered her with it. She rolled onto her side and faced away from me. "Help yourself to some food in the kitchen."

Sylvia's wet skin was glowing in the dim room like one of those albino cave fish. I stood staring at her, amazed that looking at the woman I had just fucked made me feel nothing. I had completely lost my appetite. For anything.

"What do you want?" she asked without bothering to look at me.

"Did I hurt you?" I asked.

"Yeah. Sure you hurt me," she said. She still didn't look at me. "Now let me sleep, Buster. I've got a date tonight."

It was still light out when I left the apartment. It was one of those nights when you just have to do something but can't think what it is. I had this itch way down inside me to ride on into the soft pink of the sunset just like I was riding into some babe's tender snatch, pressing with every inch of my body into the warm velvety cushions of her flesh. I pretended I wasn't thinking about the French babe the whole time.

I spent the next week doing a whole lot of pretending, but at night the lights would go out in that little movie theater in my head. I would lie alone in my wide bed replaying her damn dance about a thousand times. In the day I worked my ass off, trying to make my body ache enough to keep out the thoughts of her that crashed like waves inside my skull.

When Patty called on Friday and told me that the French babe had been asking about me, I realized I had two choices. Swim or drown.

"So what did she say?" I asked.

"She wanted me to tell you she'd be at the bar tonight. She said she liked your eyes. They spoke to her."

I thought at first that Patty was pulling some idiot prank on me, but she never really went this far out of her way. A sick joke like this wouldn't have been Patty's style.

"I'm too old for her," I said. "There's almost 15 years' difference."

"I didn't say I understood it," she said. "I just wanted to let you know."

I had just got out of the shower that night when Sylvia called.

"I haven't heard from you," she said. She didn't wait for me to answer. "I have a couple of free hours. Come over."

I pictured her again the way she had looked the last time: a faceless wad of bitterness. I wondered what had come first, her being struck or striking back. Then I asked myself the same question.

"I don't think so," I said. There was a long pause, probably like the shocked silence just after an execution.

The corpse jerked just once. "Should I call again?" she asked.

"No," I said.

She hung up. No sign of life. No more fucks with my shoes on.

I dug around in my closet till I found a blue silk shirt I hadn't worn since way before Sylvia. People used to say it looked good with my eyes.

The bar was just starting to crowd up when I walked in. I found Patty on her usual stool at the bar.

"I had a feeling you'd be here," she said.

I ordered my drink and stood leaning against the bar. The dance floor was packed already, thick with coeds back for the fall. I couldn't have found the French babe out there if I'd had a crowbar. Patty took a drink of my beer and laughed.

"Nothing dresses up the old place like a whole herd of hot young things," she said. It was a good show but not the one I was there for. I took my beer and started walking around the place, squeezing tightly between women as I went. From the hungry looks I saw, I knew the action would be hot and heavy all night. I didn't know if I'd ever find the French babe.

It took me about 20 minutes to get back to the bar. I bought another beer and went back to talk to Patty, but she'd already found another victim and closed in for the kill. She was a sporty little redheaded number who looked like she'd just stopped in from the tennis club. I watched Patty's eyes wandering, purposely obvious, up and down between the girl's tits and eyes. The girl chattered on and on. She looked excited and nervous, as if the attention of the lusty, drunk grad student was some prize she'd just won.

The redhead's tits were magnets for my eyes too, so I lit up a cigarette to distract myself. I smoked with my eyes closed. I could still see the light of the pulsing strobe through my eyelids. My whole body vibrated with the beat of the music and the tension of anticipation.

"A cigarette for me?" a voice said with an accent dark and sweet as a chocolate bar. I opened my eyes to the French babe. She was standing beside me with a tiny little smile on her perfect lips. I handed her a cigarette.

"Merci," she said, brushing my hand gently as she took it. I lit it for her, and she took a long drag and looked out toward the dance floor. Then she looked up and watched the lazy trails of her rising smoke. She said something I couldn't hear, but I was sure I saw a familiar word roll off her lips. "Sara."

It was too loud to talk even if I'd known what to say. I just stood and stared, but just looking at her made me crazy. I put down my beer and wrapped my hand around the side of her slender waist. She tilted her head back farther and closed her eyes. I could see her heartbeat in the blue veins of her neck. I rubbed the silky, smooth skin of her belly. My breath caught a little in my throat, and something quivered way down deep in my gut. Her lips made the word again. "Sara."

I could have been inside her right then for all I knew, but a slap on my ass jolted me back to the bar. I turned around to see Patty, grinning and holding the redhead's hand.

"My work here is done, Buster," she said. "Good luck."

"I'll see you later," I said. Patty disappeared into the crowd pulling the redhead behind her. The French babe was looking out toward the dance floor again. I leaned over and put my lips very close to her ear. Close enough to touch it with my tongue.

"Would you like to dance?" I asked her.

She shook her head and pushed her lips into a little pout.

"Would you like to go then?"

She put her hand on my shoulder, pulled me close to her, and said into my ear, "Not yet." She held me there with her warm, moist breath tickling my ear and the side of my neck. An old sensation cut between my legs, and I felt a tender fullness there. She slid her hand up to the back of my neck and took my earlobe in her teeth for just a second. "Soon," she said.

The French babe let go and kept smoking her cigarette while I steadied myself against the bar and drank my beer. I stared at her, watching the outline of her nipples move up and down as she breathed. She smoked like she was making love to her cigarette. Long hits, eyes half closed. By the time the French babe was done, I felt so swollen, I could hardly walk.

She looked me square in the eyes. "Now," she said.

I took her hand and pulled her through the mass of bodies to the door. I must have nearly pulled her arm off trying to get her across that dark parking lot and into my car. I fought off the need to kiss her. Instead, I drove like a maniac to get her back to my place, where I could kiss her long and deep. Where I could kiss her like a girl like her ought to be kissed.

We didn't talk, even when I got to my building and led her up the painfully long flight of stairs to my apartment. After I let her in, I meant to get her a drink and put on some music—seduction by the numbers—but all I could do was pull her close to me and slide my hands up under her shirt and bra.

"Sara, I want to be yours," she whispered.

The light from the street slashed through the darkness of the room straight into her eyes. They glowed blue with a burning that seemed to come from someplace inside her. I kissed her. Her lips felt steamy hot. My tongue wanted to feel everywhere on her satin-smooth skin, so I traced a path down over her chin and into the hollow of her neck.

"Le main," she whispered. She took my right hand in both of hers and put my middle finger in her mouth. She sucked on it, moving it gently in and out. I slid my other hand down into her pants and played with her fluffy hair.

"You want to?" I asked.

She moaned quietly. I slipped my hand out of her mouth and led her to my bed. Laying her down on the edge, I pulled her shirt off and unhooked her black lace bra. Her breasts were full and round, with soft, pink, upturned nipples. I took one into my mouth and teased the nipple hard with my tongue. The French babe's skin was sweet, with a tang like warm spiced cider.

She sat up and unbuttoned my shirt while I slid off her boots and pants.

"You also, Sara," she said. She reached down and unzipped my jeans. With our eyes locked together, I stripped and stood naked in front of her. She took my hand and pulled me close. I knelt and kissed between her legs.

"Le main, Sara," she said. Slipping on a clean glove, I put two fingers inside her and thrust in and out slowly and gently while I kept massaging her clit hard with my tongue. I felt her shudder and lean back, steadying herself with the fingers she dug into my shoulders.

She leaned forward and rested her cheek on the top of my head.

"Merci," she whispered. I stood up and helped her lie back on the bed.

"No," she said. "Now you."

"You can relax if you want," I told her. I ran my hand along her cheek, and she turned her head and kissed it. Then the French babe got out of bed. I panicked.

"I'm sorry, babe," I said. "Did I do something wrong?"

I started to stand up to grab her, but she reached out and pushed me back down. "You must wait, my Sara," she said. She was smiling that puzzling little Mona Lisa smile again. She made a quiet, breathy sound way deep in her throat and rocked her hips around in a slow, graceful circle. She raised her arms above her head and danced the way she had in the bar that first time I ever saw her, except this time she was naked. And this time I could be sure it was all for me.

My eyes had adjusted to the darkness, and I could have sworn my other senses were sharper too. She was on my lips and in my nose, and the sound of her soft humming filled my ears. She came back to the bed and touched me all over with the lightness of feathers before she finally let me kiss her again. Then she kissed my shoulders and my tits and my knees and wrists and any other part of me before that sweet kiss came to rest between my legs. All it took was a few quick strokes with her tongue and I surrendered to her body and heart.

We've stayed together, me and the French babe. Next month when her lease runs out, she's moving in with me. It's not that I own her. She always does her own dance to her own song. Maybe it's not owning her that's special. When we make love and I hold her in the dark, it's a strange heart I feel beating in my arms, but it's one she keeps bringing back to me.

She's different from all my nice girls. The nice girls just want to be nice, and everything they do is as much about them as it is about you. They don't have the guts to be anything but nice. Sometimes my French babe isn't nice at all. Sometimes she makes me wait so long, I feel like I could bust into a million pieces that hit the wall at a million miles an hour. Then I'll feel her breath on my ear.

"Le main," she'll whisper just above the drumming of my pulse. *"Le main."*

The Carousel
by *Mary Diane Hausman*

The parking lot in front of the amusement park was empty except for the security guard's truck. The rides were quiet, the park lit only by an occasional streetlamp along the bordered paths.

Jasmine said good-bye to Donna, the security guard, and watched as she pulled the gates closed and snapped a padlock through a huge iron chain that linked the gates together. Donna, a longtime friend to Jasmine, had easily agreed to let her stay in the park for a while after closing time. Donna knew she could get in big trouble if anyone found out. But Jasmine had been so troubled lately, and she rarely asked any of her friends for favors. Besides, Donna was on duty all night and had to be at the park anyway. She would study inside her guard booth till Jasmine was ready to come out.

Jasmine thought walking around the park after hours with no one else around—no kids yelling, no barkers calling—was just the thing to help her think through some big issues. Well, really just one big issue: Greg Hinkson.

Three months ago Greg had joined the software-testing team Jasmine coordinated at Dynamic Data Systems. Greg was tall, muscular, effeminate, even feminist (though Jasmine thought a male feminist was an oxymoron), and very straight. He seemed to break all the stereotypes Jasmine had about men.

It took only a few days for Jasmine to fall into a comfortable working routine with Greg. Then, because of an imminent project deadline, they began to meet after work and on weekends to go over test results, streamline reports, and attend to the usual work-related stuff. Jasmine felt an increasing tingling sensation when she was with him. He must have felt it too, because finally he asked her to dinner. For a "real date," he called it. She had no qualms coming out to him. She laughed as she said to him, "Are you blind? Can't you tell I'm a major dyke?"

He calmly looked her in the eye, flashed incredibly white teeth against creamed-coffee skin, and said, "So?"

Jasmine accepted the invitation.

Over the next few weeks, she became more disconcerted about her attraction to Greg and where it might lead. She had never before questioned her sexuality: She was a die-hard lesbian. Period. She never even considered the possibility of being bisexual. But these days the lines got more and more blurred. She wasn't sure what she wanted to do about Greg or why she needed to do anything. She did notice that she seemed less drawn to women. That scared her.

She had spoken with Greg about her feelings. He was open and sensitive and never pushy. He seemed to feel that whatever happened would be OK. His easygoing manner made it even harder for Jasmine to deny she enjoyed being with him. He simply said, "Sometimes it's good to take a risk. You never know if you don't try. I'm here if you're ever ready."

Part of Jasmine wanted to be ready. She wanted to take the risk with Greg. It didn't mean she had to change her life.

Just add something to it. She had never been with a man sexually. She had been attracted to women from the time she was a young girl. *Maybe I need to find out. Make sure it's what I don't want,* she thought but never said aloud to Greg.

She felt comfortable with Greg about a lot of things. They swapped ex-lover stories as easily as Jasmine did with her women friends. With any other straight man, she would have said he was only getting off on hearing about lesbians being together. But she couldn't say that about Greg; somehow he was different. There were some subjects she was more comfortable talking about with Greg than with her other friends. Like fishing and Renaissance literature. She had never felt such emotional intimacy with any man. There was a trust with him that she had felt only with women. If he would just do something really prickish or something really gross, something that would make her say, "See. All alike. I can be friends with a man, but I could never sleep with one."

Still, Greg was a nice guy with a great body, and there was a chemistry between them that they both felt. Jasmine tried to understand the risk to her own emotions, to her own identity, that she would be taking by having sex with Greg. She felt torn and berated herself for not just going along with what she felt. But she wasn't really sure what she felt, other than lust. That seemed strange enough in itself: lusting after a man?

Another issue for her was the fact that she viewed herself, basically, as butch. She always went for the most feminine women. Jasmine liked a woman who wanted to be escorted down the street when they went out; a woman who wore lace and silk stockings and who painted her nails and lips bright red; a woman who wanted a tall, handsome dyke to lift her legs around a slender, dark-skinned waist and carry her to bed.

So what the hell was she going to do with a man who could almost be her androgynous twin? Maybe that was the attraction. Sort of like falling for herself. It was all too confusing. That's why she wanted to be here in the park, alone.

When she was a kid and her parents took her to the amusement park in her hometown, she would deliberately get lost when it was time to go home. She'd hide in the carousel pavilion and wait till the lights shut down. Then she'd climb onto the carousel and walk around the platform, touching each gorgeously curved animal: horse, giraffe, elephant. She was mesmerized by how beautiful everything looked in the dark. Some kids might have thought the animals looked ominous. Not Jasmine. Far from being frightened, she felt an excitement at being alone with such a huge toy. And at the same time, a kind of peace, like she belonged. The shadows played along the curves of horses' backs and elephants' trunks. They cast a softness to the bright colors that was less garish than in sunlight.

She knew she made her parents frantic, and finally after a couple of times they caught on and stopped taking her to the park. They said it was less trouble than trying to make sure she stayed with them till they left.

Tonight the empty park seemed the perfect place to mull over taking a risk. Amusement parks were made for risk. Isn't that why people came to them in the first place? Children and adults liked being taken to the limit, pushed to the edge, in the name of fun.

"Amusement parks are a socially acceptable risk-taking environment," Jasmine philosophized as she walked away from the gates into the eerie silence of the darkened park.

She shoved her hands into the pockets of her jeans and walked toward the carousel pavilion. Her mind couldn't stop tossing around the pros and cons about Greg. She hoped that tonight would give her a chance to clear her head and think about her relationship with him with less emotion—or at least less lust.

As she neared the carousel, she shivered—not from the cool May night but with anticipation. This carousel was one of the few restored originals left in the country. The animals wore bright coats of paint over smoothly carved wood. Remembering the details of jewels, bridles, and saddles on the animals' bodies made Jasmine smile. The black horse with the red saddle and gold mane and tail was her favorite.

She turned right and headed down the flower-bordered path to the carousel. Glancing behind her she realized she cast a shadow on the path. But there was no moon tonight. She looked up to see the lights lit brightly on the carousel.

"What the hell?" She hurried toward the pavilion. Only the top of the carousel was lit. The red and white stripes on the canopy glared in light, while the animals, forms circling in shadow, danced beneath.

Jasmine stopped abruptly, just out of reach of the light.

Who else is here? The words raced in her head. Her mouth opened to call out, but something stopped her. She fumbled for a cigarette, then decided it was better not to draw attention to herself.

Caught by the strangeness of the circling carousel, Jasmine felt her nervousness slip away. She watched as the animals moved rhythmically up, down, around. As the carousel turned, she found herself looking for the black horse with the red saddle.

There it was. Its golden mane flowed back, frozen, caught in an invisible wind created by the carver's tools.

"Oh!" Jasmine caught her breath. There, astride the black horse, sat a woman clothed only in a shimmering, sheer white bodysuit. Auburn hair flowed down her shoulders, and her hips slightly rose and fell across the hard red saddle. Her breasts, small and round, brushed against the curves of golden mane.

Jasmine sucked in her breath. She felt a twinge, a pinch, an ache between her legs. She stood watching, absorbed in the beauty of the improbable scene. The black horse came into full view. Jasmine was close enough to see the unfamiliar face. The woman on the black horse leaned forward, eyes closed, mouth slightly open. She loosely held the brass pole that rose out of the horse's back. Her neck arched back; the horse rose and fell. Jasmine watched as the carousel turned till all she could see was the horse's golden tail flying stiffly behind the woman's back. Then the music began. Carousel music, light and merry, dancing through the air and across the park.

Jasmine turned and peered into the dark; nothing out there, she was sure. All movement, all sound centered around the carousel. A feeling of worry flitted through her, then quickly left. She was curious, awed, mesmerized, yes, but not really worried. She thought briefly of why she had come here in the first place. Greg seemed worlds away.

The horse and its rider disappeared as the carousel circled into deeper shadow. Jasmine took a few steps forward, not wanting to be seen yet wanting to be closer. She stood just at the edge of the light and waited for the black horse with the red saddle to circle into view. Finally, she could see the pale body of the woman; now she had wrapped her legs around the horse's neck, leaned back, held herself with her palms pressed against the horse's rump. As horse and rider drew closer, Jasmine could see the muscles in the woman's legs and thighs as she pulled and pushed herself against the brass pole. Jasmine heard the woman's moans beneath the carousel music as the black horse rose up, came down. With exquisite control of her body (her bottom quivering above the saddle, her legs hugging the horse's neck), the woman thrust her pelvis against the glistening pole.

Jasmine breathed hard. A rock sat on her chest. She hadn't been this aroused by a woman in a long time. She wanted to step forward, jump onto the carousel, slide up on the black horse, behind the woman, and slowly move her hands along those breasts, that stomach, those thighs. She longed to press her fingers into the hair between those legs, the soft, curly hair that must surely be soaked with sweet juice and wanting long, slender fingers sliding inside.

The black horse was gone again by the time Jasmine realized she had just exercised one of her greatest moments of self-control. She needed a cigarette. *No,* she thought. *I need that woman.*

Jasmine stood, waiting in the darkness, as the carousel turned. The music began to soften. A different tune played into the night. The dark horse continued to circle in and out of shadow. Each time it came into view, the woman held a new position on its red saddle. In one turn she lay on her stomach, her head arched up against the pole, her pale bottom moving up and down in syncopated rhythm against the horse's gleaming black flanks. Another turn and she sat backward, pumping against the rim of the saddle, holding tightly to the golden tail.

With each breathtaking sight, Jasmine stopped just short of walking into the light and onto the carousel. As much as she wanted to go to the woman, she felt the scenes were too beautiful to be interrupted. So instead of moving forward, she moved her right hand to the waist of her jeans. The zipper slid down, and a low moan rumbled up her throat as her fingers found her own wetness. Her left hand crept up under her tank top and found a nipple. She pinched, lightly at first, then harder, as her other hand played softly around her clit. Her teeth bit her bottom lip; she sucked in her breath and focused all her energy on not crying out as she moved inside herself. That was no easy task.

All the while Jasmine kept her eyes on the carousel, searching out horse and rider with each turn. The other animals, their colors muted in shadow, rose and fell in a protective cadence around the black horse.

Just then, unable to control her desire to come, she stumbled forward into the circle of light. And in that moment the horse rode into view. This time the woman sat sidesaddle, legs spread apart, one hand slowly pumping up and down on the brass pole, the other rubbing, circling slowly between her spread legs. As the horse rose up, the woman opened her eyes and looked straight at Jasmine. She grinned. Not a surprised grin but a grin of acknowledgment. Jasmine started to speak but couldn't. The carousel circled on.

Jasmine pulled her hand from her pants, dumbfounded. She thought for sure the woman would get off the horse or at least wave, now that she had acknowledged Jasmine's presence. But she didn't. As the horse danced away, the woman peered out into the darkness, legs spread, still moving her hand over herself.

Jasmine lost all self-control. She had no idea what was going on, why this woman was here, who was operating the carousel, or if anyone else was around. None of it mattered. She had to move now.

Her long legs swiftly crossed the short distance to the circling platform. Beads of sweat glistened on her dark skin as she jumped up onto the platform; her arm shot out, catching the hind leg of a yellow lion to get her balance. Carefully, she moved forward between the animals, searching for the black horse. The music was louder here but still slow and melodic.

Soon she caught sight of her horse, its tail flying out from behind; the red saddle, empty. She quickened her step and grabbed the golden tail. Jasmine anxiously peered into the shadows. The darkened animal forms rose up and down, oblivious to her. The carousel kept circling; the music kept playing. Where could the woman have gone? Jasmine slid her hand along the still-wet saddle, then pressed her cheek against the brass pole and breathed in the musky female smell that lingered. She had to find her.

With each movement of horses and giraffes, lions, and ostriches, Jasmine turned, straining into the shadows. Finally, she came full circle around the carousel. Nothing.

Jasmine began to feel a little foolish. The woman was probably standing in the darkness at the edge of the circle of light right now, laughing at her. Just then she heard a movement, not the now-familiar squeak of oil-hungry brass poles but something soft: the light swish of legs sheathed in nylon rubbing against each other. Then came a deep giggle. Jasmine turned. The black horse was just behind her. She hadn't even realized she had stopped near it. There on the horse, leaning against the golden mane, knees up, hands holding on to the pole behind her head, sat the woman. She smiled.

Jasmine allowed herself a hungry look, then stepped forward. As she placed her boot into the carved stirrup, ready to lift herself up, she asked, "What's your name?"

"I'm the one you want," came the low reply.

In one swift movement Jasmine was astride the horse, the luscious woman right up against her thighs.

Jasmine curled her fingers into the auburn hair that flowed out from the slender neck. She leaned forward and brought a fistful of hair to her face. "Mmm." She inhaled the wild aroma that emanated from this woman.

"What are you doing here tonight?" Jasmine, still curious, whispered.

"Shh. Don't talk." The woman brought her lips to Jasmine's ear. "Just come here." A pale hand found Jasmine's dark one and moved it deeper into shadow, to her breast. "And here. And here."

The woman moaned. Jasmine slowly ran her hands over the diaphanous fabric. She followed a path on the inside of the woman's thigh and found the moist center. Forcefully yet carefully she pulled at the sheer crotch till the fabric gave way. Slender, dark fingers glided in.

Jasmine let her own body flow into the rhythm of the rising horse. She moved her face forward and pressed her full lips against small, firm ones. Their mouths opened and danced to each other as naturally as the light flickering and dancing with the shadows in the circle of the carousel.

The woman tugged at the edge of Jasmine's tank top and pulled it up and over her head. She found the fly at Jasmine's waist and unzipped it. Jasmine lifted herself, pulled one leg and then the other out of the jeans, and tossed them down on the platform.

Then in a quick, graceful movement, the woman repositioned herself, her back against Jasmine's breast, her buttocks pressed into Jasmine's crotch. Jasmine reached out to hold on to the pole to steady herself, glancing up as she did. There, hanging just above the black horse, was the carousel's brass ring. She hadn't noticed it all night. She smiled and grabbed it. Her other arm encircled this strange being, who brought her hands up to Jasmine's face and felt the smile there.

The carousel circled. The animals danced up and down around the platform, and Jasmine and the woman made love: to each other, to the horse, to the shadows, to the night.

Later they lay in the dark on the grass across from the carousel and told each other about their lives. Jasmine thought only once of why she had come to the park, and in that thought she knew what her decision would be. She was amazed at how easy it was to take this risk with an exquisite, strange woman and how difficult even the thought of it was with Greg. She pulled the lithe body closer to her. The woman reached up, stroked Jasmine's face, and curled her fingers into thick, raven hair.

Jasmine breathed deep, filled herself with the smell of this woman, the night, herself. She lifted her head and caught sight of the black horse with the red saddle, standing sentinel in the shadows on the platform. The music was silent, the animals still. Only the stars wheeled above, a giant carousel of women, dancing.

Petal Sweat
by Susan Kan

Rhonda Nickels never considered herself a poet, but lately she was drawn to the magnetic poetry kit on the refrigerator in the staff room at the women's health clinic where she worked. The lunchroom was a difficult place for her, she being shy and newly hired. Instead of trying to talk with the other nurses, most of whom spoke about their weekend escapades, dating dilemmas, or children, she would stand at the refrigerator, sipping from her milk carton. Rhonda was interested in their conversations, she had to admit, but she didn't know how to participate comfortably.

A recent graduate from a nursing school in a small Midwestern town, Rhonda's move to Boston had been a big change. Her family back home had been opposed to her leaving, but Rhonda felt the pull of the ocean, the salt spray, and the warm dunes calling out to her. Timid as she was, a kernel of adventurousness was burning inside her. At 31 years old, she felt it was now or never.

At the clinic she was efficient and well-versed in the language of the body, but she interacted with the patients as though they had brought their cars in for tune-ups and repairs. She could say the words *breast, vagina, cervix, fallopian tubes,* and *Pap smear* as easily as *mountain, elevator, door, subway,* and *lunch.*

Rhonda pulled the tiny magnets around the refrigerator:

sit there and I can cook eggs and meat

Not very poetic. The next day she made a list of rhyming words:

make lake steak bake fake take

One day, about a month into her new city life, as she searched for words, she noticed on the side of the refrigerator facing away from the room a line of words all by themselves:

we am love by doing

Rhonda looked sheepishly around the room to see if anyone saw her. The others were absorbed in the latest *People* magazine, the one with *The First Wives Club* actresses on the cover. Turning back to the five simple words, Rhonda thought, *Bad grammar.* Then after thinking a moment, she wondered, *We am love by doing* what?

Obviously, as a nurse, she knew. She knew what the books said. But as much as she hated to confess this, she had never been in love, and she had never done it. All day long she talked to women and girls, sometimes as young as 13, who said they knew love by doing. Rhonda coolly educated and examined them, but always a little tug wore at her soul. What was it like?

At night, lying in her bed, she tried to imagine. She had learned about masturbation but never cared much for touching herself. She tried, back when she was 17 and dating a boy named Jeffrey Wolf. In fact, it was Jeffrey's idea. When Rhonda had refused to go all the way with him, he suggested that she watch him jack off and then he would watch her. The idea had been compelling enough that she had tried touching herself when she was alone a few times. But instead of letting him watch, she decided to break up.

And since she'd become a nurse, she spent a good bit of time looking at other people's private parts, and the whole concept had lost its allure.

We am love by doing. We am love by doing. Rhonda tried to guess who might have written that.

Every day, after that first discovery, Rhonda nonchalantly checked the refrigerator. A week later the sentence was gone, replaced with this:

> **worship a woman**
> **picture her luscious bare fiddle**
> **those easy moons**

Rhonda Nickels blushed and scurried out of the lunchroom. In her haste she ran into Naomi Golden, a physician's assistant, in the doorway.

"Oh, I'm sorry," Rhonda apologized.

"No problem." Naomi's smile was so big, Rhonda thought she could see her molars. "What's your hurry? It's lunchtime." She gave Rhonda a little squeeze on the arm as they headed in opposite directions.

In the hallway Rhonda touched her arm where Naomi had touched it. *Odd,* she thought, *I haven't been touched in an affectionate way by anyone since I arrived in Boston.* Then the thought, which at first had seemed rather exciting, drooped like a wilted flower.

That night when Rhonda changed out of her uniform, she thought again of the poem. *Those easy moons,* she repeated, running her hands over her butt cheeks. Her skin was pale like the moon's face, she noticed as she inspected her body in the mirror. Then she looked herself in the eyes. Who could have written that? Everyone who works at the clinic is a woman. Who would be worshiping another woman?

As she drifted off to sleep that night, she held her arm where Naomi had squeezed it.

A few days later the words from the poem were pushed into the corner all messed up, and replacing them was this list:

tongue
hair
honey
lust
ask
for
it

Rhonda got her milk out and, hoping her nervousness wouldn't show, went to sit at the round table with the other women. They were talking more seriously today about an antiabortion episode at another Boston-area clinic. Rhonda didn't like to think about the politics of abortion. The men who debated the issue seemed completely removed from the medical procedure and the women who came through the doors wanting services.

Naomi was very passionate about the issue, though, and Rhonda rather liked watching the way Naomi's hands flew up like birds around her face when she spoke.

"Our lives are at risk here," she invoked. "We can't just be passive."

The other women nodded agreement.

With the heightened tension around the abortion safety situation, the list of words stayed up for longer than Rhonda's patience lasted. She had memorized it, and every night in bed, she recited it: *tongue, hair, honey, lust, ask for it.* She touched her tongue and hair as she said those words, and as she repeated the words, they became like an incantation. One night her hand drifted toward her vulva when she said honey. *Ask for it, ask for it.*

During her break the next day, she lingered in the lunchroom after everyone else had left. It was very hard to work fast with all the words randomly scattered across the door of the refrigerator, but she wanted to write something back, something to let the writer know that someone was reading her poems. Something also that would ask for more. She wrote:

elaborate a moment as if you
are a blue lake sweating diamonds
gone enormous with beauty

Rhonda stepped back from her words. *What does that mean?* She considered replacing *sweating* with *drooling* but only because that word was right there. But *drool*?

Just then the door swung open, and Naomi strode up to the fridge. Rhonda quickly smeared her words out of order.

"What are you up to, Nurse Nickels?" Naomi smiled her big grin. "A little poetry writing on the side, eh?"

"Oh, nothing," Rhonda lied. "Just trying to relieve a little job stress, if you know what I mean." Her armpits itched from the instant sweat she had broken.

"Me," Naomi winked at her, "I'm not much of a poet."

But the next day Rhonda found these sentences shaped into curving waves:

whisper a lazy trip to the pink place in my forest
let me sing on the breast of your dress as we go
our cry a drunk light flooding after

Reading these words made her wet between her legs, a sensation new and lovely. She looked over her shoulder with a guilty rush. Here under the fluorescent lights, there was something both illicit and delicious about her feelings. She ran to the bathroom and hoped no one noticed her pink face.

Later that day when she was writing up reports, she found her mind wandering to the words on the refrigerator, again wondering who wrote them. She looked down at Grace Sheehan's chart and found that she had been doodling round shapes that looked remarkably like breasts with hard nipples. When Naomi breezed in, Rhonda sprung up, startled. Had Naomi always made her so jumpy?

She was eager to get home, to get undressed, to stand before her mirror and think her new thoughts. *Pink place in my forest.* She touched her tongue, swishing her finger in her mouth and over her lips. Then she lifted her hair high off her head and slowly let it drop. *Honey. Lust. Pink place.* She began to take *a lazy trip* through her *forest,* opening herself, stroking. Just before she closed her eyes, she saw in the mirror how flushed she had become. *Let me sing.*

But Rhonda Nickels stopped herself. Let who sing? And she didn't like the idea of a drunk light. That was not very good writing. Then it dawned on Rhonda that two women were probably writing these things to each other, that she was a voyeur, spying, in a sense, on their flirtation. She vowed she would stop.

The next day she did not look at the magnetic poetry.

The following day and all the next week, she stood at the window instead. Sometimes she would sit at the table, especially if Naomi was there.

"How was your weekend?" Naomi asked on Monday.

"Oh, fine, thanks," Rhonda answered, wishing desperately she had better conversational skills, that she could remember for the life of her what she had done over the weekend. All that flashed through her head when Naomi smiled and touched her shoulder was how she had opened her pink place and reached deep inside, how she had smelled her fingers, then quickly washed off the scent.

"How was yours?" she managed.

"Great! I went roller skating along the river with a real cutie." She clapped her hands together. "Too bad I don't have time to tell all the details; I've got to get back to the health care biz. At least for now." She patted Rhonda's back, threw out her lunch trash, and went back to work smiling.

The room empty, Rhonda couldn't help herself. On the side of the refrigerator she read:

    a
  thousand
   fast
  waters
  tongue
   like
   wind
    on
  winter

essential
as
storm
to
flood
as
woman
to
power
as
you
to
me

Rhonda's patients did not get her usual efficient and competent attention that afternoon. She kept thinking about one word in that poem, one word right in the middle of it: *essential.* She was feeling more and more intensely that she was missing something essential, something she didn't even have an inkling about back in her hometown.

That night she went to a movie alone in order to distract herself. But *essential* followed her, ranted in her ear as though the word itself were a force or had a voice. *As storm to flood. As woman to power. Storm, flood, woman, power.* Over and over.

She left the movie before the end, walked home in the rain, and arrived at her door drenched. She stripped off her clothes right inside the doorway, leaving them in a wet heap, and went to bed. She made herself put her hands under her back so they wouldn't move on her body, but even as she did this, she felt her own easy moons of flesh.

The weather was misty and close to the ground when she woke up the following morning. She felt groggy, and her hand was in her pubic hair, her fingers combing it out before she realized what she was doing. She dressed quickly, had some toast and jam, took her vitamins, and was out the door.

rain girl raw with beauty
your skin sea honey and swim
lets boil petal sweat together
and cry a moon symphony

Whoever was writing the poems was having a more and more interesting time. And Rhonda realized that she had begun to associate the poems with Naomi. Maybe it was the word *raw*. There was something raw about Naomi. Or was that how Rhonda felt around her?

Rhonda was puzzled by the idea of boiling *petal sweat*. What could that mean? Throughout her day, the words *petal sweat* ran around her mind. *Petal sweat. Petal sweat.* The clinic was backed up because Naomi had called in sick. Curiously so, given how well she appeared the day before. Her absence left Rhonda again to ponder who the poets were. If one *was* Naomi, who was the other one?

There was Samantha Graves, but didn't she always talk about her boyfriend, Joe, during lunch? There was Leslie Durante, but she had kids. There was the older doctor, Nikki Johanssen, but Rhonda couldn't imagine, for the life of her, her standing at the fridge moving magnets around. She couldn't think of anyone. And maybe she didn't want to know.

She liked the mystery, the distraction, the intrigue, and when she was completely honest she loved the way she felt after she read the poems. She loved how her body flushed hot and sudden, how the moisture gathered in her panties, how her nipples pressed against her bra. Today she imagined that she was the rain girl; after all, it was just last night when she walked home through the downpour.

The thought of possibly reading another installment of poetry lifted her right out of bed the following morning and into the shower. With the hot water streaming over her hair and shoulders, she recited the bits of poetry that had stayed with her. *Tongue, hair, honey. Fast waters like wind. Essential. Bare fiddle. Pink place in my forest.* She stuck out her tongue and let her mouth fill with warm water and dribble out in rivers over her breasts. She tempted her nipples into hardness by teasing them with her fingers, both breasts at the same time. *Rain girl raw with beauty.* One hand kept up the nipple play while the other stroked up and down her belly, into her navel, down to her pubic hair. *My forest.* She was gushing between her legs, and when she touched there, opening herself, the slick wetness was not shower water. *Your skin sea honey and swim.* Rhonda, her face upturned into the spray, tugged and massaged her lips. *Oh,* she thought, *this is it, this is it. Here are my petals. Let's boil petal sweat.* More fingers exploring, stroking, now her clit. *The pink place. Drunk light.* She swooned and caught herself, held the shower wall as her body shook and delighted and pulsed from the explosion of that kernel deep inside her. *Cry a moon symphony.*

After she came she stood there, eyes closed, letting the new feeling in her body work its way out through every pore. Then she started to shiver. What time was it?

The rest of the week was a blur of work and refrigerator and private touching. She hated to admit it, but her patients' bodies took on new meaning; she looked at them differently. Not as parts made up of just bone and blood but of sensation and vitality.

Grace Sheehan was coming in again, and Rhonda was nervous to be in the examining room with her. Grace's breasts were shaped in such a come-hither way, like those portraits with the eyes that follow you around the room. Grace's nipples pointed straight toward Rhonda, it seemed, no matter which way she turned.

By the time Friday afternoon rolled around, Rhonda found that she had been getting great pleasure from stringing words together in her head. And even more pleasure from letting the words form pictures and sensations in her body. *Tongue. Peach. Mist. Smooth. Ache.*

Before leaving the clinic for the weekend, Naomi alarmed Rhonda by walking up behind her and saying in a low throaty voice, "I hope you do something nice for yourself this weekend."

Rhonda jumped from both her voice and the suggestion. Did her new explorations show on her face? She managed to reply, "Yes, thanks, and I hope you have a good weekend too."

"Oh, don't worry. I plan to. Life's too short, honey. You've got to get it while you can." She laughed as she flew out the door.

Within ten minutes everyone had gone, and Rhonda sat staring at the refrigerator. Then she walked over and began pushing the small magnets around. She stood back and read the arrangement of her words:

to feel you finger
my peach from behind
then swim around
lie on top
urging my bed springs to moan
my petals to sweat honey
take me please
I want a heaving vision
frantic as a summer storm

She was breathing hard and smiling at her bravery. Then she quickly gathered her things and walked out to the parking lot. There were only a few cars left. She noticed the one near hers in the back row. Two people were sitting close together in the front seat. As she neared the car, she realized that they were kissing, so she lowered her eyes. She had to pass right in front of them to reach her own car, and it was then that she turned to look. Someone was waving hello. It was Naomi, and pressed against her was Leslie Durante looking flushed and tousled. Rhonda surprised herself by smiling broadly at the two women. She felt that they had let her in on a secret, had answered a question they didn't know she had, and she felt a rush of relief and pleasure. In fact, she responded as if she knew what they felt when they touched each other. Well, she almost knew.

That night, after relaxing in a hot bath, Rhonda crawled between her soft flannel sheets. When she closed her eyes and stretched out her legs, she imagined Naomi standing naked at the foot of her bed. She saw her warm smile and easy posture. Then Rhonda opened her eyes. "Wait," she said out loud as if to Naomi, and she scampered out of bed in search of a candle. "Wait, wait, wait," she repeated as she opened drawers looking for matches. Eventually, she was back in bed with the shimmering flame, and, yes, Naomi had waited.

Naked from the waist up now, Naomi pulled down the covers and slowly ran her strong hands from the soles of Rhonda's feet up to and along her thighs, around her belly, across her breasts, and down her arms. Naomi stopped at Rhonda's hands and gently lifted them up to her own breasts. They were smaller than Rhonda's, with silky curves around the bottoms and sides. Then Naomi took one of

Rhonda's fingers and led it on a journey over the map of her body: nipples pursed and heedful, neck sleek and pulsing, armpits hollow and tangy. Rhonda looked at and touched and tasted this new territory, so like her own and yet not. Her own breath, panting and reaching. Her own rocking, on her back, glistening with sweat. Her own sweet, slick petal sweat. And as all the sensations heightened, her own words washed over her. *Take me, please. I want a heaving vision.*

And that night she had one.

Fantasy Vacation
by Sara King

We're driving together on a winding country road. The windows are down, and the evening air, though it carries a memory of the scorchingly hot afternoon, is cool and sweet. We're a few hours away from the city and finally starting to relax. I'm behind the wheel, driving barefoot, my light cotton sundress pushed up above my knees. You're sprawled beside me, dozing, your seat back as far as it will go to make room for your long legs. You're wearing faded, tattered jeans, and I'm longing to slip my fingers into the holes and stroke the brown skin showing through at your knees and thighs. Or to press my lips to the tattoo on your shoulder. But for now I'm concentrating on maneuvering the dips and curves of the road, pretending not to notice that you've turned your body toward mine, pretending to ignore your right hand, which has just landed on my knee.

Without looking away from the road, I can see your long, strong fingers, with their short, carefully tended nails, your smooth knuckles, the rings you have to remove before you fuck me. The first time I really looked at your fingers, I wanted to feel them inside me. We were in a public place; I had to look away from your gesturing hands. Now, as your hand starts to move up my thigh, I still avoid looking down. Instead, I catch your eye as you start to wake up.

"Hi, honey," I say, all innocence. "Did you have a nice nap? Are you hungry? Should I start looking for somewhere to eat, or do you want…"

I don't pause to let you answer until your fingers find me, already so wet for you. (I'm not wearing underwear.)

"What I want," you say, "is to get you out of this car and into bed, the sooner the better. Do you want me to fuck you tonight?"

I don't answer you—I'm too busy trying to keep the car on the road, but my hips rise so you can touch me more.

"Is that a yes?" you say, stroking me. "Yes, you want me to fuck you? Because I need to fuck you. I need to fuck you hard."

With a moan, I push your hand away and straighten my skirt.

"I'll stop at the next place I see," I say, trying to catch my breath. When I glance over at you, you're lighting a cigarette, smiling to yourself.

We don't have to go far before we reach an old-style motel, separate one room cottages, each with a parking space in front. There's an old pickup truck parked next to the lighted cottage marked RECEPTION, but otherwise the place is dark and deserted. You look skeptical.

"C'mon," I say, laughing. "What's the matter? Can't you live without room service for once?"

"Room service?" you say. "We'll be lucky if they have indoor plumbing."

Inside the reception cottage, we have to ring a bell. After a few minutes a mountain of a woman with short gray hair stumbles out of a back room wearing men's pajamas. "What?" she says, squinting at us.

"We'd like a room," I say.

She looks at you, looks at me, and looks back at you with an almost imperceptible smile. She opens a cabinet and selects a key.

"Here," she says as she hands it to you. "Number 7. It's the one on the far end. If the air conditioner ain't working too good, just pound it a couple of times." She demonstrates by moving her fist through the air. "You're gonna need it tonight too."

I'm still digging through the knapsack on your shoulder for some money when I realize the woman is leaving us.

"Don't we need to register?" I call after her.

"Nah," she says, glancing at me but then addressing her remarks to you. "You can do it tomorrow. I'll be up early." She smiles. "Though something tells me you won't be. Have a good night."

The path to our room isn't lit, and we stumble along in the dark, hanging on to each other and laughing. The insects are deafening. As you turn the key in the lock, I'm remarking about how I love the sound, and you say, "Just so long as they stay outside." It's stuffy inside, but once we get the light on we're relieved to discover that it's clean. When you turn on the air conditioner, it roars like a dinosaur, but it works without being pounded, and right away the small room starts to cool off. After confirming that there is hot water, I announce that I'm going to take a shower, and you go out to the car to get our stuff.

When I come out of the shower, there's a wrapped box perched on the sink. I open it and find a white silk teddy with soft lace at the breast and nothing at all at the crotch. When I come out wearing it, I can't find you. The only light in the room is a candle flickering on the nightstand. Then I see you sitting in a rocking chair in the corner, still in those tattered jeans that I love, but shirtless. I go to you, climb on your lap straddling you, bury my face in your breasts. Your hands circle my waist, pass over my hips, squeeze my ass so my cunt is pressed to yours. When you start to rock me, I can feel the dildo strapped between your legs.

You pinch my nipples and suck them through the lace, while you touch me between my legs. You bring me close to the edge of coming and keep me there, rocking me, kissing me.

"I want to fuck you a new way tonight," you say.

I almost dissolve at the words.

"Come on." You push me gently from your lap and lead me to one side of the bed. You place a pillow on the floor.

"Kneel here," you say. "And put your arms out in front of you on the bed. Don't move until I tell you to."

You kneel down behind me, separate my knees wide. I'm so wet that your fingers slide right inside me. You move them slowly at first, in and out, rotating, opening me wider.

"Don't move," you say. "Just relax. Let yourself open for me. I won't fuck you hard till you're ready."

Withdrawing your fingers you raise my hips and spread my cheeks and fuck me with your tongue. It is exquisite torture for me to try to stay still, but now you slow down even more, licking and sucking me till my juice flows freely.

You tell me, "I love the way you taste." Reaching through my legs to touch my clit, you say, "Now move."

Instantly I start grinding into the bed, pinning your hand to the mattress with a circular movement. I feel the sweat pour between your breasts and my back.

"I want to make you come," you say. "Are you ready for me to fuck you until you come?"

Waiting for my reply, you sit back, away from me. I'm still moving slightly against the bed. I hear you unbuttoning your jeans, and then I feel the cool, smooth dildo rubbing against me. You are holding it, opening me, moving the tip inside me.

"It's OK," you say. "I won't hurt you. I'm going to fuck you really slow at first."

You push into me, inch by inch. It does hurt a little. I try to breathe deeply. Then I think of a way to make things easier. I sneak my hand down between my legs. To my surprise, this delights you.

"That's right, baby. Touch yourself, and tell me how you want me to fuck you."

"Fuck me," I say, quietly. Then, "Fuck me harder."

I feel you moving faster and deeper. My hand moves faster too. Then I feel your little finger pushing at another entrance, and suddenly you are fucking me in two places at once.

My toes start to tingle, and my own hand drops away. I move wildly on your hands, breathing hoarsely and then not breathing at all and then screaming, sobbing, and nearly fainting dead away.

Later, I wake up to find myself naked, spread-eagled on the bed, bound by my wrists and ankles to the four corners of the bed frame. When I glance over at the rocking chair, I see my teddy, your jeans, and the strap-on. You're adjusting one of the silk scarves at the foot of the bed.

"You're a sound sleeper," you say.

You stretch out on top of me. Your warm skin feels wonderful in the cold room. You kiss my mouth and face and neck for a long time, and I almost relax and forget I can't move. Then you start to suck on my nipples and move your hips just slightly.

When this has already gone on longer than I would've thought I could stand and we're both so wet that you're in danger of sliding off me, you whisper in my ear, "I'm going to lick you until you beg me to stop."

Then with excruciating slowness, you work your way down my body. You kiss the backs of my knees, my inner thighs. You prop your chin up on one of my thighs and look at me, breathe on me, and inhale me. By the time you lower your mouth on me, I'm lifting my hips to meet you. You're driving me insane with your tongue and lips, flicking quick and hard, licking tenderly, sucking, probing, tasting, swallowing—the silk scarves are soft but tight. With one hand you reach up and squeeze my nipples until they burn. Every time I'm about to come, you sense it and start to move differently.

"Please," I hear myself say, very quietly. You come up to hear me better.

"What do you want?" you ask gently.

"I want…"

"Yes?" you say, kissing me, your mouth wet and soft.

"I want you inside me," I say.

I expect you to laugh, to insist that I be more direct. But your look is as tender as it is passionate.

"I need to be inside you," you say.

You move back down my body. With your mouth again between my legs, your fingers poised to enter, you look up at me. You thrust into me so hard I cry out and then fuck me so fiercely that I start to shake.

"Stop," I say. "I can't."

You do stop, but only long enough to say, "Take it! Let me fuck you. You can handle it."

"Then untie me," I say, starting to struggle against the ties. "I need to hold on to you."

"Not yet," you say. "Not until you come."

You move more slowly now, just licking me, barely moving inside. I'm a little angry, but it starts to fade as my hips move under your mouth. This time you wait till I'm about to come before you start to fuck me hard, but then you rise up on your knees to give it every ounce of your power. Without my hands I can't make you stop when I want you to, and through my pain I come again and again, screaming loud enough to wake the dead.

Minutes or maybe hours later, I remember where I am. At some point we must have gotten under the covers. You're sleeping with your arms around me, your cheek against my chest. When I move, you murmur "I love you" without opening your eyes and roll over on your back. I try to balance my desire to plant wet kisses from your neck to your knees with my perceived duty to let you rest. Desire wins. I lick along your collarbone, trail my tongue between your breasts, flicker it over your nipples. You start to stir. I press my lips lightly along your belly, dip into your navel, rest between your thighs. Now it's my turn to whisper "I love you" as your beautiful smell envelops me. I lick you softly until you start to awaken. I put my tongue inside you and suck you, wanting to fill my mouth with your taste. Only when you start to call my name do I let my fingers go where they want to be, and your body welcomes them and holds them long after you're quiet.

Finally, you pull me up and kiss me. When you lay your head on my breast and wrap your strong arms around me, I'm not sure if I'm giving or receiving. My last thought before I drift off is that probably I'm doing both for once and this is the real thing. At long last love.

When I wake up for good, I realize that it's nearly noon. I throw on some clothes and run to the reception, hoping to pay before we get charged for a second night. There's no sign of the woman, but there's a folded bill taped to the desk that says "Number 7." I open it. It says, "Won't be around to say good-bye. Come back and see us again." At the bottom next to amount due, it says, "No charge." On the counter next to the bill is a large Thermos. I open it, and the second most wonderful smell in the world—fresh, strong, hot coffee—greets my nostrils. I take the Thermos and run back to you.

Down at Shug's
by Catherine Lundoff

I was driving my rig down the interstate, you know, that real boring stretch up north. So I started spacing out a little, thinking about the new waitress down at Shug's, 'cause there wasn't much to look at. Shug's is that restaurant in Cramerville where I always stop at when I'm on long hauls. I pretty much just do short hauls, natural foods, rice cakes for yuppies, that kind of stuff. Every now and again I step in and do one of the longer routes 'cause someone's sick or on vacation or whatever. Started driving when I lost my job at the factory, and it's good work mostly.

Anyway, this new waitress was hot. Asian gal, name of Amy, with this long black hair that she puts up in one of those "French rolls," I think they're called, real pretty face and the most gorgeous bod I've seen in a long time. Believe me, I've seen a lot. After all, I've been out for about 20 years, and she's just as femme as I like 'em. Since my wife and I split a while back, 'cause she...never mind.

Well, let's just say that it wasn't a pretty breakup. Nope. Hurt like hell, still does. Still not really up for looking or meeting anyone new. Why the hell else'd I'd be sitting around this fleabag bar, telling you my latest road stories?

That sound like a butch with better things to do? OK then. You get the next round.

So what happened was this. No sooner did I start thinking about that gal than I just had to stop by Shug's and check her out again. Wasn't even sure if she was family or not but figured what the hell? No harm in looking. I'd talked to her a little last time I was in, and flirting with a pretty gal, even a straight one, is better than nothin'. Plus Shug's a good 'un, and I like talking to her too. Life on the road's kinda lonely, and I didn't have nothin' to return home to 'cept the cats.

I was on my return from my run, so I wasn't in a big hurry, not so long as I had the rig back by the next afternoon. Stopped off to help another trucker with rig trouble on the way. He about shit when I got out of the cab and he realized I wasn't a guy. Figured he'd take my help anyhow, seeing as how there wasn't much of a choice. The point is that I was late getting into Shug's, like after 11 or so.

Thought my luck would have run out on me and she wouldn't be working, what with the place closing around 3. But since I like Shug OK and she makes one hell of a pie, I figured it'd be worth it. Good woman to talk to. I know 'cause she always works late nights, and we talk a lot. Pity she's straight. Anyway, I pull the rig into the lot, look through the window, and damned if Amy wasn't working the night shift. I checked my hair quick in the mirror and reckoned I looked as sexy as I was gonna get, at that hour anyhow. Quit laughing.

Well, I went struttin' across the parking lot. Had on my shit-kickers and that big old belt buckle and Levi's like I always wear. Yeah, I know I look like one of them Western wear ads— so what? Can I get on with the story? Least I don't chew.

I saw Shug working the counter, serving the couple of good old boys and whatnot that're hanging around at that hour. She gave me a big grin when I came in.

"Hey, Pepper! Long time no see. Want some joe?"

So I said hey and sat down at the counter to start shooting the breeze with my pal. The rednecks were giving me the eye, but then a few of them remembered me from other runs and nodded to me. Not like some places where I'd have a hell of a time getting served, let alone leavin' in one piece.

Got to be careful on the road. I carry a blade, but I don't carry it into diners and such as a rule, 'less I think I need it. Plus I trust Shug. She told me one time that her sister was a dyke. Got thrown out of the house when she was just a kid, and they ain't seen hide nor hair of her since. Shug figures she might still be around, so she's nice to any dykes she meets, 'cause she figured her parents fucked up once and she ain't gonna do it again. 'Sides, one of them might be her sister. So we know each other five, six years now, since I been driving, and I know from past experience that anyone at that stop who messes with me messes with her.

I had my eye on Amy, who was waiting tables, so I figured I was in for some time before she could sit down. No big deal, though. As long as I crashed by 3 or so, I could make it home pretty easy, and I had a sleeping bag in the truck so I could catch a few winks locked in the cab. Cramerville ain't big on hotels.

I am getting on with it. What's your rush? Got a hot date or somethin'? No? All right then.

Half an hour or so goes by. It'd been a few months since I was through this way, so Shug hadn't heard about me and the wife.

"Oh, honey, I'm sorry. She couldn't have been any good for you. You gotta find you someone steady, like my Fred." Fred's her boyfriend, the one she won't marry 'cause she's got no use for marrying. Always says, "You done it twice, you done it a thousand times. Why throw good years after bad?" So she said this, then followed my eyes. "And she ain't it! What'cha want with a young 'un like her? She's OK, mind you, in spite of what folks around here say about her. Kinda wild, used to run with a bad crowd, but smart, you know? I gave her a chance 'cause she's cleaning up her act. But she ain't gonna be around here long. No, ma'am. Cramerville ain't big enough for a smart one like her. She'll be somethin' big-time. Hell, this is her last night working here 'cause she's taking off for college next week."

Shug's warning was fallin' on closed ears, 'cause if there's anything I like it's a gal who's been around a little.

Amy swung by after the place started to clear out and sat up at the counter with me and Shug. She was even cuter up close and relaxed. So I asked her how she ended up in Cramerville, and she started talkin', telling me about how her family moved here from the Philippines 'cause her dad organized students at the university and the government didn't like it, so he had to leave in a hurry. Her uncle ran a store in a town nearby, so they worked there and saved up money to start their own place in Podunkville.

She told me about college and how happy she was to be gettin' out of this one-horse town. "If one more yahoo tells me how goddamn exotic I am and how he hears Oriental gals make fine wives who know their place, I'll shoot him," she said. Then she looked me dead in the eye and said, "You don't have any ideas 'long those lines, do ya, Pepper?"

Ya ever snort coffee out yer nose? I don't recommend it.
I sat and thought for a minute, 'cause a question like that
deserves a good answer.

"I don't think yer cute just 'cause yer Oriental or 'cause I
think we're gonna get married and yer gonna play housewife for me. Can't say I don't notice you here more because
of it, 'cause it's pretty damn clear that there ain't too many
other folks like you around here."

"That's for damn sure," she said and laughed, kinda sarcastic.

I went on, pretty slow. "Plus, you remind me of my ex
about ten years or so back. And that's meant as a compli-
ment, 'cause I think yer real pretty. I'm just kinda lonely
since my wife and I parted ways last month. I didn't mean
nothin' by checkin' you out, didn't want to offend you or
nothin'. I'm real sorry if I upset you."

She just looked at me, like she's thinkin' on it; then she
had to go wait on a table. So she came back after that and
said, "I guess I'm not too offended, just so long as you're
not a full-time rice queen. I hate someone makin' me feel
like I'm interchangeable with any other Asian chick they
could pick up or hittin' on me just because I'm Asian. Not
like pickings aren't a little slim around here, if that's your
thing." So I shook my head and tried to look innocent and
sincere. She laughed and said, "You look like a basset
hound. Give it up!"

So she started tellin' me about life in Cramerville, in between waitin' on the last few tables. She used to run with
the wild kids, drinkin', drugs, the whole deal, 'cause it was a
way to get out of meetin' everybody's expectations, and she
wanted to fit in. Last couple of years, ex-boyfriend went to
jail, friends got into harder drugs, got killed in accidents,
that kind of stuff, so she got sober 'cause she didn't want to

go out that way. By then, of course, she had a rep around town that wasn't too pretty, and she was sick of it. Plus a big break with her family 'cause of it all. She was figuring on moving to the city where there'd be more of a community for her, and she could start over, do somethin' with herself.

To lighten up the mood a little, I sorta leered at her and asked how come she's so comfy chattin' up an old war-horse like me.

She shrugged and said, "Well, my cousin used to live here, but she moved to San Francisco. You know, bright lights, big city, Sodom by the Bay. Went there a few times to visit and meet her friends. Some of them are even butch. I ain't your average hick, ya know." And she kinda tossed her head back, goofylike, just to show how cool she was, and laughed. "Plus I like butch girls. I think they're hot. And Shug vouches for you, says you're as close to a real gentleman as you can find these days." She winked at me, and I could see she was feelin' better, so I relaxed a little too, but I wasn't takin' any hints, even the ones you could see a mile away like those. I liked this girl. Didn't want her thinkin' I was another yahoo, and hell, now I had a rep to live up to.

She went off and picked up the last of the dishes, 'cause the place had cleared out. Shug was finishing up with the last of the counter customers and shakin' her head at me. But she was smilin', so I figured she didn't mind too bad. Amy came back by and tossed me a rag.

"Why don'tcha help me wipe down some tables. I'll get done faster that way."

And she grinned back over her shoulder at me, makin' my stomach do flip-flops. I was a goner, and I knew it. Just tryin' to salvage the last of my cool for the night by then, but I didn't want to leave just yet, ya know?

So I started wiping down tables. Amy and Shug talked for a couple of minutes, too quiet for me to hear; then Shug threw up her hands and headed for the kitchen. I wondered what was up but didn't hurt myself worrying, if ya know what I mean. Amy walked by, smacked my butt, and grinned at me when I looked surprised.

"Good work. Maybe you can start moonlightin' here. I wouldn't mind watching your butt for a while."

Shucks.

The coffee hit home after a couple of cups, so I put down my rag and headed for the john. I heard the door open while I was in there, but I didn't think nothin' of it. I finished up and stepped out. There was Amy, looking in the mirror, watching me watch her with a little smile on her face. Quick, I figured to act like I wasn't drooling and swaggered over to the sink. She sat on the edge of the counter, and I couldn't help but notice that the dress of her uniform slid way up when she did that. Nice thighs in black hose. Hmm. She let down that gorgeous hair and started brushing it and kept looking at me. I hate when my ears start blushing, but I ain't used to pretty young things in rest rooms checking me out. Usually they think I'm a guy and they freak.

Well, this one wasn't freaking. She knew she was getting to me, and she looked like a cat about to catch somethin'.

"Shug went home. She said good night and don't be such a stranger. You gonna be a stranger tonight, Pepper?"

I was still gaping when she stood up and held the brush out to me and said, "Would you like to brush my hair? I like having it brushed for me, and I bet you've had lots of practice."

Never one to turn down a lady's request and blushin' like nobody's business, I picked up that brush and went to. Her hair was all the way down to her very cute butt, and I was going for long, steady strokes. Let me tell you, it felt as good as it looked. Hell, I figured the odds on a gorgeous woman—straight, lesbian, whatever—asking me to play hairdresser were pretty damn long, so I might as well go with it.

So I was working away on brushing her hair when I glanced up in the mirror and caught her eye.

She said, "You know, I like you, Pepper. You got a nice honest face and the sexiest hands. I like butch girls. Not like I see many around here."

Then she looked kinda thoughtful for a minute and smiled and then, I swear to God this is true, reached up to the top button on her dress and undid it. She moved on to the second one, and by now I was breathing a little heavy.

"Interested? Unless you just like to watch…" she laughed a little, seeing the look on my face. Hell, I could see it myself in the mirror over her shoulder.

Needless to say, I turned her face around to kiss her before she could change her mind. She had the sweetest lips…and neck…and shoulders… I slid my hand along her thigh, up those nice silky stockings. There's something about hearing a real femme moan when you're gettin' to her. God, I love that sound! I was licking my way down her neck 'fore I remembered the restaurant and the fact that we were in the women's john.

"I locked the door. Shug doesn't mind too much, and she locked the place up. I promised to clean up. She didn't like my last boyfriend too much anyhow!" She laughed one of those deep throaty laughs—made me quiver in my boots.

Almost enough to make me ignore that one word.

"Boyfriend?" I whispered as I removed my tongue from her earlobe.

She just grinned at me.

"Don't worry. He's out of the picture, and we always did safe sex. It was the one thing I made sure I didn't fuck up, back in my wild youth."

Then she reached over to a bag on the counter, one I'd missed 'cause it was behind her, and I sure wasn't seeing past her right now. Damned if she didn't pull out some of those gloves and latex and stuff. "I come prepared."

I must have started to back off a little.

"Not interested, Pepper? Or afraid of a little ol' bisexual like me?"

She flipped her hair back and licked her lips. Right then, I wasn't afraid of nothin'.

"I ain't scared. Just never done it like that before, that's all. My wife and I were together about ten years. Didn't see the need. Bi, huh?" I was stuttering, I was talking so fast.

She grinned at me. Her hand went up to the top button on my shirt.

"We'll do it the safe way, I promise. That is, if you're still interested." Her palm grazed my nipple through my shirt, making me groan. "I'll take that as a yes."

Her shirt was unbuttoned so far, I could see the black lace bra she wore underneath. I'm a sucker for black lace. She sat up on the counter again, put her hands on my collar, and tugged me forward so I was between her legs. Then she started kissin' me, slow and careful-like, her tongue running around the inside of my mouth. I put my hands up to those top buttons on her dress. Man, more than anything, I wanted my hands on her black lace–covered breasts. Shit, I'm getting hot talking about it!

So, I got her dress unbuttoned down to her waist, and I run my tongue down to her boobs. You ever run your tongue over a nipple covered in black lace? Hmm. She was having my favorite reaction, arching her back and moaning, running her fingers through my hair.

I got my teeth on her nipple and started nibbling, just a little.

"Oh, yes! Just a little harder," she groaned.

Hadn't had an effect like that on anybody in a while. My one hand was around her back, so I started to run my other one up her thigh.

Damned if she wasn't wearing garters! No stocking on the upper thigh, just nice, smooth, silky skin. *Rrowrh!* My hand got a little higher, and she stopped it.

"Gloves first, honey."

"Oh, I don't need—" I started to whine.

"You aren't sure of that, and neither am I."

She looked determined. I picked up the glove and pulled it on with a snap, trying to look like I went to a safe-sex-for-women workshop some time in the last decade.

Back I went to that pretty mouth. Made me glad I don't smoke anymore. Woman tastes so much better without all that old ash—nothin' personal, mind you. And her kiss, mmm, sent hot flashes through me, and I ain't at that certain age yet, you know. Right about then, I was wetter than I thought I could get, and it felt damn good. I figured I've got the stupid glove on, might as well use it as intended. Plus, no bullshitting around, I couldn't wait to get inside her. So I went back to licking my way down her neck, and the way she was breathing and moaning, I knew I had her full attention again.

Real slowly I started moving my hand up her leg again. Her pubes were soft through the glove and probably nice and silky like the rest of her hair. She groaned and spread her legs a little farther apart. Never one to refuse an invitation, I slipped one finger into her crack. 'Course I couldn't feel how wet she is really, but the glove got all slippery, so I knew I was on the right track. I was sliding my fingers around her crack; then I slipped one up inside her. She started riding it, so I went for two, then three. Then I went for it, one finger up her ass and my thumb on her clit, and I had all I could do to hold her up with the other arm and keep driving. Ooh, that girl, mmm, mmm.

She started coming with a yell. I got her nipple between my teeth again, and she was holding my head so hard, it hurt. She came again, two, three times, then again, soaking the glove and edge of my sleeve.

"Damn, you're good," she whispered coming down, and she kissed me hard again, just to prove it. Well, I was feeling pretty good myself right then. Lot of times I just get off getting them off anyway, but I got the feeling this one was going to be different.

Amy looked up at me under those long dark lashes, then pulled me close as she slid off the counter.

"Now, what can I do for you?"

I started to tell her she didn't need to do anything. She put her hand on her hip and looked at me like she don't believe me.

"Yeah?" she said and started unbuttoning my shirt and kissing my neck. "Think you're about to get flipped, hon."

She started leaving a line of little hickeys down my breastbone to the edge of my bra, then slipped the shirt off my shoulders. She ran her tongue over the edge of the bra, then scooped out my tit. I groaned. So much for the tough butch act.

"Like that, honey? Me too."

She scooped the other tit out over the top of the bra and started licking and biting her way around. *Whooey!* I've had breast exams that were less thorough, and I was lovin' every minute of it.

I was leaning against the wall by this point, 'cause it was gettin' hard to think about standing. She slid my bra off over my head and then started undoing my belt buckle. Her dress was still unbuttoned, so I reached out and started playing with her nipple while she slid the belt out of my pants, real nice and slow. Once she got it out, she moved the belt slowly against my skin up to my nipples, then slid the leather over them. Never felt anything like that before, and believe me, this was wilder at this point than anything I've done in a long time! Standing kept getting harder 'cause my pants were soaked.

She reached up and unzipped them slowly, kissing me the whole time. I reached back to cup her ass and pulled her up against me for a long smooch. She spread her dress open so those nice lacy nips were rubbing against my bare chest, and I was gone. Right then, if she said she wanted to do stuff with razor blades, I probably would have gone for it. My pants were getting dropped down to my boots, so she pushed me up onto the countertop and bunched everything up around my ankles so I couldn't move my feet.

Somehow I missed the part where she got the gloves on, but she was wearing 'em. Plus, she had this piece of rubber, plastic, somethin', I don't know, in her hand.

"Wha's that?" asked the duke of smooth.

"It's a dental dam. It's so I can do this."

Then she planted it over my crack and started running her tongue over it till she found my clit.

"Oh, OK," I went between gasps. Didn't know a little piece of rubber could feel that good, let alone smell like bubble gum. She kept licking, and I started coming, and I never came like that before. It started deep in my crotch and just took over. This gal was the best.

"Where'd you learn to do that?" I managed to get out.

"Here and there. I wanna get you nice and wet for what I've got planned." She went back to work, and I came again, 'cause you know it gets easier after the first one. Then she pulled something else outta the bag, something that looked like a dildo, and stuck a condom on it.

"I don't know about that…," I started chickening out.

"You wanna try it? I'll stop if you don't like it."

I looked at this beautiful young gal, who wanted to fuck me, of all people, in a public john, and I was gonna say no? Not likely. To hell with my image.

So she slipped her fingers inside me to get me warmed up, not like it took much. Her fingers started driving in, couldn't tell how many, and I just hauled out the welcome wagon. Then came the dildo. Hurt just a bit at first, then damn, it felt good. She drove it in and out slow and steady, like the way she was kissing me. It was like gettin' filled up, pretty wild if you never used one. My hips were moving along it like they belonged to someone else, Elvis maybe. I gotta get me one of these things!

I came so hard, I was seeing lights. Hope Shug had gone home by this point, 'cause my yell was pretty damn loud. Amy rubbed me and licked me some more for a while; then we just held each other for a little bit. Sure has sucked not having someone to be close to, after all this time.

She gave me this real sweet kiss and said, "You're the best, Pepper. Thanks for being with me tonight. I've been pretty lonely here, and I really wanted to be with someone tonight."

Anytime, lady, anytime.

So I stayed and helped her clean up, get the dishes into the washer, do the floors and all. Figure it's the least I could do after the night of my life. Couldn't go back to her place 'cause she lived with her parents, and my place here was the truck cab, so I offered to walk her home, and she said yes. Let me kiss her good night in front of the house, just like in the movies.

I was practically doing a jig back to the truck. Couldn't sleep, so I drove some more and got most of the way home before I needed a nap.

You know, I don't feel so bad about the wife now. Maybe the world's just full of beautiful young things dying to hop into bed with me. Well, OK, probably not. But one was, and I figure that'll have to last me awhile. Hell, I got jill-off material for at least a month out of a couple of hours.

Do I think I'll ever see her again? I wish. When my ex dumped me for her guru, teacher, whatever the hell she calls her, she said I wasn't flexible enough, too boring, too dull. And maybe I am. But for one night I was wild and crazy, cute even, and a hot lover, and it was helluva lot of fun. Maybe I'll even try it again sometime.

Come Friday
by Judy MacLean

The afternoon sun warms Daria's arm, and the scent of ripe mango drifts up from the little *supermercado* two stories below. Daria is wearing her most sensual shirt, the crinkly smoke-blue one that grazes her breasts, bare underneath the shirt, when she moves. She washed her short khaki hair this morning. It's at its best.

Daria is lanky and broad-shouldered, almost six feet tall, with a habit of slouching to keep people from being intimidated by her size, of speaking softly so she doesn't come off too loud. Now she's hunched over her worn green metal desk, surrounded by stacks of unfiled papers, finishing a grant application. She's alone in the small office, amid battered gray file cabinets and cardboard boxes filled with papers. Behind her desk are two bright posters saying FOOD NOT BOMBS and WALK FOR THE HOMELESS. It's Friday afternoon, the hour of lazy sunlight and of least-favorite tasks that can't be avoided anymore.

Her mind keeps straying to Janine's heart-shaped face, sprinkled with freckles the exact copper-brown of her hair. This grant form is the last obstacle before tonight when, after dinner, Daria will take Janine's hand, turn it over, kiss Janine's tender inner wrist and say—nothing, perhaps she'll

just lead Janine silently to the sofa?—or the bedroom?—
maybe the sofa first, kiss that sweet spot where Janine's delicate jaw melts into her neck, bury her fingers in Janine's
copper-brown curls. It's going to be long and slow.

When Janine invited Daria to dinner at 6 o'clock tonight,
she added, "Cody will be spending the night with his dad,"
which leaves the possibility of Daria staying over at Janine's
tantalizingly open. Daria has not made love for more than a
year, and that was only one night with a long-ago ex-lover
who was in San Francisco for a convention. Daria is pulsing
with anticipation.

Daria is a head taller than Janine. The last time they were
together, something about the way Janine's polo shirt
tucked into her jeans, the sweet angle from Janine's round
breast to her waist, made Daria want to untuck that shirt,
right in the movie lobby, and run her hands there, feel the
softness…

The phone shrieks.

Daria answers but hears a dial tone. She realizes it was
the fax, now spitting out a two-page message. Daria rips the
paper off and scans it. "Alert…disastrous bill in the State
Senate…put thousands more homeless on the streets."

Damn. She punches numbers on the phone. Sister
Michaela's voice mail. Daria leaves a quick message. *Those
assholes in the Senate!* Bernice isn't there either. Daria leaves
another message. *There are pitifully few low-income housing
programs as it is; do they think poor people are just going to
evaporate?* Arturo isn't at his phone either. Or the Reverend
Otis. She might as well just leave a group message, tell them
to meet on Monday, or should she just call a press conference? But there isn't time to get people's input; better wait—
the senate won't do anything over the weekend, that's for

sure. Daria sends out a group voice mail and knocks out a quick E-mail, just to make sure everybody gets the word.

Horns honk on Mission Street, below Daria's office. Rush hour is starting. There's still just enough time to get to Janine's by 6 o'clock, even if the bridge traffic is crawling. The grant will have to wait. She locks the file cabinets and turns off the lights.

Daria kissed Janine just once, a good-night kiss after the movie last weekend. The kiss had a long finish, giving off sparks for three days, coating reality up to this moment with a sweet sexual glaze. Janine's skin smelled of vanilla, earth, jasmine…

There's an insistent banging on the frosted-glass outer door. Daria opens it to two bedraggled teenagers.

"This Homeless Action?" asks one.

"Yes, but we're an advocacy office," Daria answers. "We lobby for better services, but we don't have anything for you here. I can give you a list of shelters and soup kitchens." Daria holds out the yellow flier.

"Are the shelters far?" The girl's voice gives a little catch, like she's trying not to cry. Her hair is spiked, dyed neon red, and she's drawn dark circles around her eyes with eyeliner. She's dressed in a frayed maroon velvet halter top and a matching long skirt. Against her bare stomach she holds a tiny gray kitten.

"We're kinda tired. We hitched all the way from Fresno," says the other girl. She's huskier, dressed in jeans torn at the knees. She's got a grimy bedroll under one arm.

Daria sighs. "Come on in."

The girl in velvet takes a timid step inside. "Do you have a bathroom?"

"Through that door over there."

Daria finds a Power Bar in her desk and hands it to the larger girl, who rips off the wrapper, breaks off half for her friend, and bites into it greedily. Daria moves a box off a chair so the girls can sit down, takes the sponge she uses to seal envelopes out of the glass dish, rinses the dish and fills it with water for the kitten. Then she goes back to her desk and calls the youth shelter.

It's full.

Daria tries three more places with no luck, then calls back the youth shelter and this time asks for Aileen.

Aileen says no, explaining her agency's policies patiently, citing regulations.

Daria interrupts. "Screw the regulations, Aileen; these girls'll probably have to sell their bodies if you don't take them. They look about *13*."

"Fourteen," says the girl with the kitten.

Aileen's voice on the phone is Friday-afternoon weary. "You know we see about a hundred kids like that a day. If we take too many, how're we gonna help any of them?"

"Oh, come on. Just for tonight. Just this once. They'll sleep on the floor in the hall if that's what it takes."

The two girls nod their heads vigorously in agreement.

Ten minutes later Daria wears Aileen down and extracts a promise that the girls will be squeezed in somehow. Daria bangs down the phone.

"OK," Daria says briskly. She can almost feel what it will be like to stroke Janine's waist. "You two just need to take the Mission bus in, right downstairs, get off at Tenth, walk a block to Market, transfer to—"

The girls look like deer caught in car headlights. The small one strokes the kitten and clutches it tighter against her bare stomach, which is scratched with tiny claw marks.

"Do you have a dollar each for the bus?" Daria asks, her tone kinder.

The girls mutely shake their heads.

Daria reaches for her wallet. She starts going over the directions again, more slowly. *Janine's smile when Daria arrives, their first sensuous kiss…* The kitten mews a little complaint. The smaller girl has such terrified eyes.

"Oh, never mind," Daria says. "I'll drop you off on my way out of town."

Daria met Janine an hour before the opening of the Walk for the Homeless. Daria had been up since 4. She was trying to talk the police into letting the T-shirt guy park his truck, find the missing components to the sound system, soothe an irate volunteer who wanted to register people but couldn't be trusted to handle money and so instead was stuck giving directions to the portable toilets, and decide what to do about the portable toilets themselves (she'd ordered 100 more than had been delivered) when Janine, dressed in a green first-aid volunteer T-shirt, appeared at Daria's side and waited, calm and contained, until Daria finally turned and spit out the words, "You want something?"

"Well, I wanted more cold water for the First Aid tent, but it looks like you can use some help. What should I do?"

Janine stayed at Daria's side, capably smoothing things out, smiling up at Daria with her warm brown eyes. The crowds surged through the meadow. Daria and Janine talked about details of the walk, their bodies doing a separate dance of their own. In Janine's gaze Daria's feet planted themselves in the grass more confidently. It felt good and right to be tall, to be in charge, to have broad shoulders. Beside Janine, all curves and curly hair and adoring smile, Daria became the dashing captain of the meadow.

People kept coming up to Daria with questions. The mere tone of her voice inspired them to immediately do exactly what Daria suggested.

Street musicians were playing in a nearby tunnel. A sinuous saxophone melody drifted their way. Janine's hand brushed Daria's, and fog-kissed air currents caressed the back of Daria's neck. Then Janine went off to settle a dispute about booth location between the Thai noodle stand and a long-distance phone company, the meadow became jangly and congested, Daria herself harried and hunched. At last Janine returned, her curves rounding out her jeans so simply and beautifully, holding even her clipboard and pen in a sensual way. Daria felt herself standing taller, and the charm of the day returned. Later, Daria sat down to go over the papers and money. Janine stood behind her, gently massaging Daria's neck.

"Is this OK?" Janine's voice was silky.

"More than OK."

Then someone came over and said the first-aid tent was filling up with people suffering from foot blisters and dehydration, and where was the volunteer nurse, anyway? With a regretful brown-eyed smile, Janine turned and vanished. The crowd closed over Daria's last glimpse of Janine's sweetly curved buttocks, and when Daria tried to find her later she was gone.

The following week Daria combed through the volunteer lists, exasperated that Janine's name and number weren't there. Then Janine called Daria at the office. "I've still got your pen," she said.

They've had two dates since.

Dropping the girls at the shelter is not exactly on Daria's way. In fact, it's the other way. *I shouldn't have offered to bring them over,* Daria tells herself as she pushes her way through the traffic. *They got here all the way from Fresno on their own, they could get to the shelter. This is my time, weekend time, and I'm entitled to it. I'm too quick to give in to other people.* Janine's curving buttocks, Daria's hand about to run along the side of that thrilling curve. *Why am I making myself late? What could be more important?* Daria glances in the rearview mirror, at the girls huddled in the back seat around the kitten. *Well, what kind of person would I be if I could have sent them away?*

At the shelter Daria calls and leaves a message on Janine's message machine, saying she'll be a half hour late.

Back in the car Daria swings onto Van Ness Avenue. Heat shimmers up from the pavement. Daria imagines Janine's breasts, the bottom of each one nestled against Janine's ribs, their weight and texture, how it would feel to slide her thumb between breast and rib, to linger there. Janine's arms are golden brown, sweetly freckled. The curve downward from her elbow swells beguilingly. Daria has on black silk boxer shorts under her workaday tan slacks. Janine's full upper lip will be so tempting to nibble…

Bicycles.

Bicycles in front of the car, bicycles barely missing the sides of the car, bicycles swarming across the intersection, a regiment of bicycles in her rearview mirror. Sunlight glints off hundreds of whirling spokes. A thousand people in bright-colored helmets are filling up the street with their bicycles.

Traffic crawls. Traffic stops. A blast of irritated horns.

Daria rolls down her window. "What's going on?" she asks the nearest cyclist, who is only inches away.

"Critical Mass," he yells.

"What's that mean?"

He brakes. "We're riding to raise consciousness! If more people commuted by bike, there wouldn't be so many traffic jams."

He has a ponytail, a hot-pink and neon-green shirt, and a belt full of orange fliers. He hands her one.

"But you guys are causing this traffic jam," Daria points out.

"We need more bike paths," says the man. Dozens of cyclists detour around him, chattering to each other.

"Well, I support your cause, but your timing sucks. Look, I've got a bike myself, but—"

"Then join us! We do this the last Friday every month! Help educate the public!" The cyclist pedals off among the throng.

"Did it every occur to you that the public might be trying to get to a hot date?" Daria calls after him.

It takes 15 more minutes for the bicycles to disappear. But traffic stays frozen. Large concrete buildings loom on either side of the street. A gritty wind flaps a stray orange flier against the windshield. Daria inches her car forward. She rakes her hand through her short hair, switches on the radio, punches buttons, then jams an old k.d. lang tape into the player.

A half hour passes. Daria travels six blocks. She wriggles in her seat, trying to rearrange her legs. One of them is going to sleep. She's still not on the freeway, and once on it will be impossible to call Janine.

Daria sees a phone booth on the other side of the street. To lose more time calling or have Janine wonder where she is—which will it be? *Janine's generous upper lip, her scent of jasmine, earth, vanilla...* Daria pulls over, parks, crosses through the traffic. Exhaust fumes billow around her.

This time, Janine answers.

"I'm stuck in traffic," Daria tells her. "I'll get there as soon as I can, but it'll probably be at least an hour. I'm really sorry."

A semi truck rumbles to a halt.

"What? I can't hear you," Daria shouts.

"I said, that's OK," Janine shouts back. "We're running late too. Cody's dad hasn't picked him up yet. Relax and get here when you get here."

"OK. Got to get back in line. See you soon."

Cars ooze onto the freeway ramp, Daria's among them. She creeps along the curve onto the skyway. Gold-tinted afternoon fog strokes the hills on her left. A sweet breeze brushes her cheek. Janine's fingers on Daria's shoulders, that day of the Walk for the Homeless in the meadow, were small and strong, reaching deeper than Daria's stiff muscles. Daria felt a pleasant stirring, a zing between her legs. But even more, Janine's fingers reached some core within Daria, with a wordless understanding about the lone-cowboy feeling of an organizer's life, the dozens of phone calls every day, the anxiety about raising her own salary, the tension, the details, always having to be up, always on, all the people Daria knows only slightly who turn to her for direction, encouragement, validation, how it's worth it to hear of the people who were once out on the streets who are now building new lives, but you can't live on only that, and how no one, for the longest time, has really looked at Daria, not as someone who will solve a problem, not as someone who will do the next task, but for who she truly is, and said to her, "I know what you have been longing for, and here it is, for you." Until that day, in the crowded meadow.

Traffic speeds up to around 20 miles per hour on the Bay Bridge, then slows around the curve. San Francisco Bay is a deep blue. Across it, she can see Angel Island. A grove of dark green trees nestles between two swelling mounds covered with golden grass, like pubic hair between a woman's generous thighs.

Daria has a change of clothes and a toothbrush in the trunk of her car. Should she just openly walk in with them, confident she'll stay? That's what she wants to do, but four years ago, sure she was going to make love with Madeleine, she walked into Madeleine's apartment with her duffel bag. Madeleine accused her of "killing off the spontaneity" and didn't want to make love after all. Safer to leave things in the trunk.

What would be the most romantic way to arrive? What should she say? Kiss Janine right away? A kiss on the hand, or is that too corny? Daria wishes she had bought a single, perfect rose.

Twenty-five minutes later, Daria pulls up at Janine's little house on Cedar Street in Berkeley. It is now 7:24.

Daria has to pee so badly she decides to scrap the idea of making her arrival romantic. She walks quickly up the front path. Janine meets her on the porch and steps forward to give Daria a hug and a friendly kiss, which, in spite of Daria's need to pee, sets off a quiver in Daria's inner thighs.

In a low voice, Janine says, "I wanted to warn you. Cody's dad was supposed to be here at 5:30. He's real late. He hasn't even called. Typical. I'm really sorry. I meant this to be just the two of us."

Daria hugs her, tells her it's OK, asks for the bathroom. She passes through the living room with its homey worn furniture, a crocheted afghan across the pillowy sofa, a half-played Chinese checkers game on the coffee table, toys scattered around.

Ah. Relief. A long pee.

In the warm yellow kitchen, Daria tells Janine about the disgusting bill in the state senate while Janine dishes up food. A definite current moves between them, but most of its crackle is quenched by pudgy, dark-haired Cody, slouching over the kitchen table, a 7-year-old lump of misery.

Janine puts a plate in front of Cody.

"I don't want it," he whines. "Dad's taking me to McDonald's."

"Just eat a little, so you don't get too hungry."

"I'm not gonna get too hungry. I'm gonna wait for Mc-Donald's. And stop bad-mouthing Dad."

"I'm not bad-mouthing Dad."

Janine throws Daria an apologetic smile and sits down across from her. Daria's hungry now. She helps herself to pasta with artichoke hearts, prawns, pine nuts, mushrooms— "Wow, this looks really good," Daria says. "Cody, you're missing out."

Cody glares, snorts, and kicks the table with a steady rhythm.

Daria plucks a black shitake mushroom from her plate. The first time she bit into one in a Chinese restaurant, she looked around, embarrassed, marveling at how much their taste resembles a woman's taste, but no other diners seemed to notice. Now she looks at Janine, smiles, and, in a tone that will carry her meaning if Janine tastes black mushrooms in the same way—and cooked them tonight possibly for this reason—softly murmurs, "Delicious."

Cody knocks over his juice.

Although Daria doesn't usually believe the universe sends messages, she's wondering if the universe is trying to tell her this isn't the night for her and Janine.

Once Janine finishes cleaning up the juice, Daria tells her about the runaway homeless girls, the bicycles, the bridge traffic. Cody stares moodily at nothing, picking at his straw placemat, making Daria self-conscious. He's a little human black hole, sucking energy and lust from the conversation.

The two women finish eating. Cody glares. Janine starts to clear the table. Daria gets up and helps.

Janine turns to the boy. "OK, Cody, it's 8:15. If Dad isn't here by 9, you can keep waiting for him, but in bed."

"I'm not going to bed."

"You don't have to go to sleep. You can just lie down. I'll wake you up if Dad comes."

"Dad's gonna come! I'm not going to bed!" Tears and snot run down Cody's molelike face. "He'll come. You never believe in him," the boy hiccups.

Daria decides he'll probably stay up all night, seething, sitting between her and Janine. His eyes are the color of stagnant swamp water.

Then Daria feels for a moment what it would be like to be this unappealing small person, who is obviously not the most popular kid in his class at school, waiting over two hours for a late dad, evidently not for the first time. She sighs. She softens. Through the kitchen doorway, she sees the Chinese checkers game half finished in the living room.

"Cody, want to play Chinese checkers while you wait?"

He sticks his finger in some spilled sauce, intently smearing it around the table.

"Let's see," Daria says. "I think I know how to play. You shoot the marbles across the board with your thumb, right?"

Cody's head bobs up. "No! You have to jump them."

"Jump them? Hmm. I can't remember how to do that. Can you show me?"

"Well, OK."

"Then maybe we can play a game."

"But we have to stop when my dad gets here."

"It's a deal."

Janine gives Daria a soft-eyed, grateful look. Daria and Cody settle on the sofa while Janine washes dishes. Daria lets Cody win a game. Janine comes in and stands behind Daria, gently and promisingly rubs Daria's shoulders for a moment. Then she sits beside Daria. An inch of warmth separates their thighs. Daria lets Cody win another game.

They're setting up the third game when the doorbell rings.

"Dad!" Cody cries. He runs over, throws open the door, lunges at his father, butts the man's bulging stomach, and stretches his arms around the large waist.

"Hey, Pun'kinhead."

Cody plants his feet on his dad's big work boots and grabs at the big leather belt, so that as the man walks into the room Cody walks backward, in tandem.

Janine introduces him to Daria as Slater, keeping her voice carefully neutral. Then she turns to him. "When you're going to be this late, please call. Cody gets so worried."

"I do *not!*" Cody yells.

Slater says, "I was on a dive."

"You could call as soon as you come up," Janine says, willfully calm.

"Yeah, but there wasn't a phone booth handy. I thought the best thing was just get cleaned up and get over here as fast as I could."

Cody grabs Slater's hands, walks up Slater's leg, flips himself over backward, lands with a bounce. "Dad, we're still going to McDonald's, huh?"

"You bet, Slugger."

"Yay!"

"Get your knapsack," Janine says to Cody.

To Slater, she says, in the same neutral voice as before, "Please bring him back by 6 o'clock Sunday, but if you get held up, call, OK? You won't be on a dive then."

"We'll be back on time."

"Yeah, but two weeks ago—"

"I *said* we'll be back. Ready to go, Big Guy? Nice to meet you, Debra."

Cody kisses Janine good-bye. To Daria, Cody says, "Thank you for playing Chinese checkers. You'll get better if you practice."

Then father and son are gone.

Janine's face is red. She walks around the room, picks up toys, and slams them into a plastic bin in the corner. "It takes everything I've got not to fall back into a fight with that man."

Daria stands by the door, feeling tall and bulky. "He's a skin diver?"

"Oh, he works underwater construction for the port." With a crash she hurls some toy trucks into the red plastic bin. "It's just another excuse for being totally undependable. And did you see how unhappy it makes Cody? But somehow, he never blames the Great God Dad. We've been divorced five years, and Slater is still finding ways to mess up my life."

Janine throws a pillow onto the sofa. Her cheeks are flaming, her body taut. Daria almost says, "You're cute when you're mad," which is true, but she's afraid it will sound like she's not taking the situation seriously. She can't think of anything else to say to turn the evening back where she wants it to go. She crosses over and deflates onto the sofa.

Janine strides up, bounces down next to Daria. "I'm sorry. I didn't want tonight to be this way at all. I didn't want you to have to play games with Cody or listen to me complain about Slater. I wanted it to be about you and me." With a lunge she kisses Daria.

The kiss is hard. Daria has climbed over traffic to get to this kiss, over runaway girls and bicycles, over the Bay Bridge and Chinese checkers games, but now something's wrong. She feels nothing. She's thinking, *I have to change the oil in my car on Monday.*

After a long minute, Janine pulls back. "You seem...stiff," she says.

Daria takes a deep breath. "I think I just got a little wound up back there when Slater came." And when Janine got mad just now, though Daria doesn't mention this part.

"Ah." Janine smiles. "I think I know what we should do." She stands up, takes Daria by the hand, pulls Daria up, leads Daria silently to the bedroom.

It's small and neat, with a calico quilt on the bed, some daisies in a vase. A candle flickers in a glass bowl. It's been burning the whole time. "Lie down on your stomach, OK?" Janine says softly.

Janine begins to rub Daria's shoulders in a firm rhythm, reminding Daria of ocean waves breaking on the shore, washing clean the sand. Janine's thighs are warm and solid against Daria's hips, like sunlight on a lazy summer day. The memories of Janine's argument with Slater, Cody sulking, traffic, slowly leave, the way shore birds take flight for the far horizon. Wind rustles in the tree outside Janine's window.

Janine's breath is close to Daria's ear. "I could do better with your shirt off."

Daria turns over, sits up. Janine unbuttons the crinkly blue shirt slowly, with concentration, pulls it off. Daria turns back on her stomach. Janine's small hands press Daria's shoulders, and Daria again has the sensation she had that day in Golden Gate Park, of Janine's fingers tuning in to places deeper than muscles. She gives herself up to the rhythm of the massage.

Janine's hands work slowly down Daria's back. At the waistline, Janine's fingers encounter the upper edge of the black silk boxer shorts. "Mmm, yes, I see you had a plan or two for tonight," Janine says.

The massage stops. Daria rolls over a little. Janine is about to untuck her own polo shirt.

"Wait." Daria takes Janine's hand from the shirt and slowly, slowly pulls the shirt out from Janine's jeans. She strokes Janine's waist. So warm. Just the softness Daria was expecting. Candlelight dances on the walls. Janine raises her arms, and Daria pulls the shirt off, catching it on Janine's chin.

Daria fumbles taking off Janine's bra. They both giggle softly. "I'm not used to these contraptions," Daria whispers. Her own breasts are bare. Janine releases the clasp.

They sit facing, jeans still on, legs curving around each other's hips. Daria lifts Janine's hand, sucks each finger languidly. Janine's other hand explores Daria's small, firm breast, and Daria's breast comes to attention, points longingly back.

Daria releases Janine's hand, and her own hands roam over Janine's lush breasts, lifting them a little, sliding her thumb into the sweet fold between breast and rib. She raises Janine's round chin and kisses her full upper lip, just a quick butterfly kiss.

She reaches down for Janine's waistband, pops the metal button from the denim buttonhole, pulls down the zipper. She moves back, pulls the jeans down over each small foot, pausing to caress each instep. She tosses the jeans on the floor. Then she slides her hands up Janine's legs to pull off lacy red underpants. When she feels how damp they are, an electric thrill heats her own thighs.

Still in her jeans, Daria gently pushes Janine back until Janine lies nude beneath her, freckled all over, honey-colored. Doves coo in the eaves outside. A car passes. Headlights filtered through curtains brush along Janine's plush curves and Daria, lanky and angular, leaning over her. Daria buries her fingers in Janine's copper-red curls, the longest ones at the nape of her neck. Daria lowers her body down against Janine's, her face against Janine's breasts, her rough jeans pressing Janine's thighs. Daria catches the warm scent of vanilla, earth, jasmine.

Daria moves her head up, nibbles Janine's collarbone, licks her neck, then kisses that sweet spot she's dreamed of, where Janine's jaw meets her neck.

Janine sighs.

A long, full kiss on Janine's mouth, tongue probing, teasing. The taste has complex undertones, like a well-aged wine. Then Daria pulls back, sits up, begins at Janine's wrists, kisses her way along Janine's plump, tender inner arm, lingers at the golden crook of Janine's elbow. Janine's freckles are like spots of brown sugar. Daria leans back down, lets her small breasts graze Janine's larger ones.

Janine pulls Daria down against her and wraps her bare thighs around Daria's jeans-clad hips. Janine kisses Daria, her tongue insistent. "Off with these jeans."

Janine tears open the zipper and tugs off Daria's jeans. "Could you leave these on a while?" she asks, lightly touching the moist crotch of the black silk boxers.

They lie back on the bed, side by side, facing. Janine's thighs are satin against Daria's. Daria enfolds Janine's body with both arms and legs, feels a pleasant surge of being larger, stronger, a big, golden, short-haired goddess in the candlelight.

Janine's hand reaches around to play between the black silk and Daria's solid lower buttock. There's nothing in the world but the progress of that small hand, working its way around Daria's muscled thigh, brushing damp tendrils of hair between Daria's legs. After days of dreaming of pleasuring Janine's body, now a wave of desire to be pleasured herself knocks Daria over, and she's lying beside Janine, helpless, needy, greedy, wanting only Janine's hand to continue, powerless in a way that's almost shameful, she wants Janine's hand there so much, wants it so badly she'd do anything, she'd beg, she'd grovel, and Janine slides her hand under the silky shorts between Daria's legs, and her fingers understand, it's like the massage, Daria doesn't need to fear this vulnerable core, this place seldom cared for, seldom touched, she moves against Janine's fingers, shows them her rhythm, and Janine follows, thrusting her fingers inside Daria, Janine's breath hot on Daria's neck, and Daria heaves, she moans, Janine's fingers slide and slip, and Daria presses herself against them, insistent, urgent, Daria rides, she rides those fingers, panting, and it is all right, the fingers tell her, here in this bed it is impossible for Daria to be too tall, too much, too loud, she can move, she can buck, bellow if she wants to, and she does, she's bellowing with the triumph, the power of her own pleasure and then, fast, hard, Daria comes.

Daria rolls on her back. Janine rests her head on Daria's shoulder. She nestles her body along Daria's side, lets her fingers idle in the delta of Daria's thighs.

"You have kind of a short fuse," Janine says.

"Too short, you think?" Daria asks, wary.

"Oh, no. I admire you. What a lusty woman." Janine kisses Daria's cheek.

Daria rises up on one elbow beside Janine. Their eyes meet. Janine's are dark, with little reflected candle flames near the center. Daria runs her fingers over Janine's round cheek, kisses her mouth tenderly. Daria nibbles once again that sweet spot where Janine's jaw meets her neck, then runs her tongue down to tease Janine's nipple.

"Oh, *yes*." Janine presses Daria's head closer, and Daria stays, nibbling. Then she runs her tongue down, down, inhaling the scent of vanilla, earth, jasmine, and now ocean, but Daria moves on, down Janine's thigh.

Daria nibbles the inner fold of Janine's knee, then kisses her way up Janine's inner thigh. Janine sighs, urges Daria's head up, but Daria will not be hurried. Her tongue idles at a silky place, midway. Daria's fingers tease the springy hair where Janine's thighs meet. She moves her kisses closer. Janine is moaning, thrusting her whole lower body down, toward Daria's fingers, Daria's lips.

Daria rolls onto her stomach between the gateway of Janine's legs. Her tongue explores Janine's rosy folds and swellings, probes her hollows. Daria tastes again, at last, the taste like black shitake mushrooms. Her tongue slides and seeks, then finds the sweetest spot. Tongue and lips placed with art on a flute can fill a whole hall with music and cause the hearts of all present to beat together; Daria feels her tongue and lips set Janine's every cell pulsing to her tongue's stroking rhythm, and Daria's body too, the room, the world, everything turns around that small point where rough tongue meets wet silkiness, Janine's breath coming shorter, shorter. Janine tenses, silent, taut, still, and then bursts into a crescendo of gentle jolts. Daria slides up. Their slick skin is golden in the flickering candlelight.

They lie quietly, tangled.

Janine buries her face in Daria's neck, eyes closed, and shyly says, "I thought I blew it, getting upset back there in the living room."

Daria pulls back, tips Janine's face up so she can look into Janine's eyes. "I thought I might have blown it, being so late."

"I was thinking, if Slater didn't come, I could hide your purse and then you couldn't leave. Then I thought, uh-oh, she didn't bring a purse! You walked in here with nothing."

Daria raises Janine's hand and kisses her fingertips, sucking on the last one. "Only a woman made of stone could leave after that massage. And even then, probably not."

Janine's eyes are dark and soft. "When I get nervous, I fall into this hypernurturing mode. The more nervous I am, the more I massage."

"Don't fight it. That's a great trait. Don't call it overnurturing. It's wonderful."

"Oh, thanks for saying that."

"Trouble is, now I'm worried."

"About what?"

"Is making you nervous the only way I'm going to get another massage?"

Janine licks Daria's chin. "I think you'll be able to come up with some other way."

"I've been waiting for this since that kiss last weekend," Daria says.

"I've been waiting since the homeless walk."

"Really?" Daria strokes the satin curve of Janine's waist.

"Yes."

"*That* long?"

"That long. I thought, oh, I want those long legs and that take-charge manner in my bed. And tonight there was a point you looked so sexy, you were driving me crazy."

"And when was that?"

"When you were playing checkers with Cody. So sweet. Turned me on. It's a mom thing."

Janine wraps her leg around Daria. A warm wind stirs the tree outside Janine's bedroom window. Daria breathes in Janine's scent of vanilla, earth, jasmine, a scent already a little familiar, one she will smell all through the night. Janine's coppery hair is like raw silk encircling Daria's fingers. The women whisper, fall silent, and whisper again, exploring different ways to intertwine their bodies. The candle sputters. Outside, the tree gently rubs against the house, as tree, house, and women rest secure in the accepting embrace of the black and starry night.

Shadowboxer
by Mary Marin

I want to tell you a story. I want to tell you about what happened the year I turned 40. It was during that year that I met a woman who begged me one night to teach her how to box.

We were on our third date, and on this particular evening I had been bragging about my boxing lessons. I went on and on about how I had taken up boxing on a whim one day and discovered, much to my surprise, that I not only loved the sport but was actually quite good at it. Of course.

With each date I was becoming increasingly more attracted to Illana, and her glances and accidental touches led me to believe that she felt the same way. There is nothing more exhilarating than an accidental touch that isn't accidental. Turning 40 had coincided with my meeting Illana, and for the first time ever I was beginning to feel a sorrow for my 20s and 30s: For whatever those years had been worth, they were gone forever. Illana, with her youth, was a double-edged sword. I felt younger around her at the same time that I felt a terror of being unable to keep up with her.

I remember that we were in a restaurant that night, the dimly lit kind where relationships often begin and decisions are made, usually impulsively, that will haunt you the rest of your life. All dimly lit restaurants are haunted houses, and though you may never return again to that place, a part of you stays forever fixed in that time, a ghost hovering over new lovers sitting where you once sat, making the same familiar promises:

"I will love you forever."

"I will never leave you."

"This will never die."

And actually it doesn't die. It remains a part of a place and time, a reminder of your past, even as it floats invisibly into the beginning of someone else's future.

I didn't know any of this then, but I think Illana did. A spark of amusement in those beautiful black eyes of hers seemed to hint that she had been here before and would return again in the not-too-distant future. In fact, her past was already crossing into her future at that very moment while she sat there drinking me in, orbiting me closer to her with every question she asked.

She was a struggling photographer, a student at a nearby art institute. I was a struggling writer, also a student at a nearby university. I was months away from receiving an advanced degree in some field of complicated research. It all escapes me now, because what I most remember about that night and that time was the feeling of being fully alive and holding this beautiful, sensual, and gypsylike woman enthralled by my story. It would not be until later that I would come to my senses, stunned and dazed, with a Ph.D. in psychology, of all things, with Illana gone, and without a clue as to where or why or how this had happened.

But that was in the future, which had no value as currency. This night, however, did, and I had a story worth its weight in gold.

I talked seductively to her about the softness of my black leather boxing gloves, which were back at my apartment. I

didn't mention in what part of the apartment, but by innu-
endo I left no choice but the bedroom. I lingered over the
image of those gloves, velvety and padded, and encouraged
her to imagine what it would feel like to wear them. And to
use them. I could already feel those gloves against my flesh,
and I shivered with desire.

By the time dessert came, I was beyond stopping. I was
regaling her with vivid descriptions of the brightly colored
boxing shorts that looked like candy wrappers, the thin undershirt tops that quickly soaked through with sweat and
then clung possessively to a woman's body, outlining her
nakedness, making her an easier target to hit. And then back
to the leather again, this time the skinlike leather of boxing
shoes that were made to fit the foot like a lover's caress, firm
yet molded to its shape.

I don't remember what I had for dinner. I ate as an af-
terthought. All that mattered was Illana's smile and the intentional way she had of pausing to place a bit of food into
her mouth, chewing slowly with pleasure, then swallowing
and softly asking another question. I was jealous of everything she ate because it was inside of her and not outside,
seated across the table from her like me.

I'll never know, but I think it was this conversation, with
its hidden undercurrent of curiosity and lust, that made
her decide she wanted to come home with me. Much later
I remembered that I had avoided any mention of hitting
or punching or getting knocked down. How had I managed to separate boxing from blows? Punching from pain?
Getting knocked down from not being able to get back
up? Did I want her so badly, I could simply ignore all that
just to have her? Where on earth was I that night? Illana
and I left that moment so quickly to move on to what

awaited us that I can't remember anymore and probably never will.

I paid the bill, and we left. I actually smiled to myself in the car on the way home as I began to plan which of my boxing outfits I would dress her in. This was taking on the air of a fashion show laced with desired danger. Illana sat quietly by my side, a little closer than before, and at one point lightly touched the side of my face with her fingertips.

"Is this where I get to hit you?" she asked me playfully. I nearly ran the car off the road and could only nod. Then her hand drifted to my heart, which promptly stopped at her touch.

"Or can I hit you here instead?" she asked.

The best I could manage was to croak out that that was a body blow, and I didn't really know the rules about that kind of contact.

"Then we'll make them up as we go along, and the first rule will be that hitting anywhere we want is not only allowed but encouraged." She said this teasingly as her fingertips lingered lightly over my heart, jump-starting it with every touch and stroke.

I have no idea how I got us home, but suddenly we were there. Once inside I opened a bottle of ice-cold wine, crammed it into a bucket of ice, and jokingly put a straw in it so we could sip during our lesson. I also cleared the living room of any obstacles by moving the coffee table to one corner and the love seat to the other. In effect, I created a boxing ring for us, albeit small in diameter. But then I wasn't concerned about small. I wanted to be as close to her as possible. While Illana sat on my couch, with an ease that suggested she owned it, I brought out several boxing outfits and laid them at her feet like a sacrificial offering. After looking at them and touching the fabrics, she chose the turquoise undershirt and the bright cherry-red shorts with the yellow stripes down the side. I chose the bright lavender undershirt and the black satin shorts with the pink stripes. We decided to box barefoot since she had no appropriate shoes, and then we each took off to change in separate areas of my apartment: she in the bathroom and me in my closet. I had never dressed so fast for anything in my life.

I found her waiting for me in the living room, and I stopped short. There she stood, a secret candy brightly wrapped, more sexual and alive than if she had been naked in my bed waiting for me.

"Please teach me," she said. My knees buckled, and I almost fainted with pleasure. First came the hand wraps, gauzy and elastic. I wrapped her hands, explaining that this way her knuckles wouldn't bruise and she wouldn't sprain her wrists. Her hands were so soft, and the closeness to her made me dizzy. Her eyes burned into mine, distracting me, yet somehow I finished wrapping both of her hands. I had a small moment of panic when it dawned on me that I might accidentally hurt her.

I go back frequently to that moment and each time realize again with deep sorrow that that would be the first and last time I would ever worry about accidentally hurting Illana. How could I have known how malignant our blows would become?

Next came the gloves. Slipping them onto her hands and lacing them up felt almost sacred, like the ceremonial dressing of a warrior. With the tightening pull of each lace, I brought her closer into me and this drama of desire. Since I had given her my boxing gloves for this lesson, I quickly yanked on my sparring gloves, which are thinly padded and require no lacing.

There was a sudden stillness between us. Illana raised her glove and lightly tapped me on the shoulder. "Well," she said, "now what?"

Suddenly embarrassed, I launched into a mini boxing lesson. First I showed her how to stand and how to hold her hands. I showed her the semicrouched weaving stance a boxer takes so she's always at an angle, which make her a smaller target. I showed her how to place one leg slightly behind the other to give her good leverage to turn or back away quickly. She loved the weaving part, how a boxer never stands still, how she sways and bounces lightly, a constant dance before your eyes. I told her that boxers always kept in motion because a moving target was hard to hit, that the sudden stillness of a boxer in the ring was a sign of exhaustion or defeat, and that in either case a knockout blow would follow from the opponent, who, seeing the weakness, would lunge for it instinctively to deliver the final crushing blow.

I also taught her about the gloves, how a boxer always holds one up high, hiding her face except for her eyes, ready at a moment's notice to ward off any upper blows. I taught her how the second glove trails slightly below the first one, only more to the side, to protect against uppercuts and body blows.

Like Rock Hudson teaching Doris Day to play golf as an excuse to put his arms around her, I used every maneuver I had to stand close behind Illana, showing her how to stand and how to hold her gloves. I could feel the heat emanating from her body, and I answered it with a thin sheen covering my own. When we stood face-to-face, weaving together in a slow hypnotic way, I was lost, already in a world where words could not enter, where only sensations mattered. Our perfumes mixed in the air between us: hers a musky cinnamon with traces of sandalwood, mine a more biting citrus with hints of lime and spice and traces of an ocean breeze.

Quickly I demonstrated a few preliminary punches, a left hook, an uppercut to the jaw followed by a weighty blow to the ribs, a series of left jabs and then the surprising crush of a right hook to the temple. And finally the whole series as a kind of ritualistic dance of movement and blows.

Finally we were ready. We each took a sip from the wine, which was cold, crisp, and intoxicating. And then we faced each other. She stood apart from me, weaving slightly, lips apart, waiting for me to say the words this whole evening had been leading to. And I had no intention of disappointing her.

"OK, Illana," I said softly. "Hit me."

For a moment, nothing happened. I think I shifted slightly and looked down briefly. Then everything began to happen. The first blow took me by surprise, and I staggered slightly to the left from the unexpected force of it. But Illana had somehow anticipated this, and she caught me neatly with a right hook. I was dazed, yet my eyes had never left hers after the first blow, not even for a second.

I lifted my glove to uppercut her, but again she stopped me with a heavy blow to my kidneys. I was reeling. Again I felt the soft leather of her glove graze my chin, but as I spun away from that blow, I delivered a nasty right hook that momentarily stunned her.

That was when I saw it. The look in her eyes. They darkened quickly to a black that was impenetrable and furious. A fleeting but shocking thought crossed my mind: Illana was no novice. At anything. I stepped back with the intention of stopping the fight, but Illana didn't give me a chance.

I never even saw the left hook. It crashed into my temple, and I went down hard onto my knees. Then I must have passed out, because after that I remember nothing.

I woke up slowly to a sensation that made no sense. Pleasure was coursing through my body, shooting off in every direction. My shorts were gone, and I was spread-eagled on the floor, drenched in sweat. I raised my head to look up, and then I understood. Illana was between my legs, slowly licking the sweat from my thighs, moving up with every stroke of her tongue. She still had her gloves on, but she too was naked below the waist.

"Do you want me to stop?" she whispered.

"God, no," I moaned. "Please don't."

She continued with slow upward licks that were driving me wild with their approach. "What will you do if I stop?" she asked between long stroking licks that were edging closer and closer to my center. I could feel her face brushing against the thick tangle of my hair.

"Please, Illana," I was pleading now. "Don't stop, don't stop, don't stop."

She stopped. I nearly screamed from the sudden lack of her tongue as well as from the throbbing between my legs that had transformed to a deep ache that pulsed, and would continue to pulse, until she reached me with her mouth and brought me home.

"Beg me," she said quite simply and clearly. "Beg me to make you come."

And I did. I begged until I was hoarse. I begged with words I had never used. I begged with every movement of my body. I begged with shouts of laughter because it was the most delicious game I had ever played. I begged and begged until finally her tongue closed around me furiously, and I came with a shout that echoed within the four walls of the room.

Illana was pleased. I saw it in her eyes, in the curve of her lips. Then slowly she mounted me until her dripping sex was inches away from me. I begged her again, and when she lowered herself onto my hungry mouth and eager tongue I gave her the raw sucking she wanted. And I kept giving until her shouts joined the echoes of mine, where they continue to exist even today, intermingled, one indistinguishable from the other.

On quiet nights I can still hear them. Sometimes I go to the place on the floor where this happened, and I stand on that same spot. I remember the passion we created, and I am struck with how empty that space is now. Except for my memory and the echoes that only I can hear, it's just a plain gray patch of carpet, no different from that of any other apartment. Someday someone else will live here, and their experiences will overtake the traces of mine, and this apartment will again bear witness to the passage of time and what it does to lovers.

Oh, yes, Illana and I became lovers. I was obsessed with her, couldn't get enough of her, would sit by the phone waiting for her to call and would agonize when the phone didn't ring. And Illana? Initially she seemed to want me incessantly, craved being with me, came to see me constantly. It was an excessive love that was exhilarating and terrifying at the same time.

And there was the sex. It grew more passionate, more daring, more violent. I threw myself into fantasies that arose from a part of me I had never even known existed. There was nothing we wouldn't do. We threw caution to the wind and probed and explored each other's bodies with total abandon. We bit, sucked, and chewed on each other, then joyfully licked up the blood we drew. We took turns handcuffing each other to the bedposts so that we could own and be owned. It became a contest to see who could be the most politically incorrect. I discovered that when I was tied down and unable to walk away from an orgasm, when I couldn't stop it or push it away or slow it down or speed it up, then I had no choice but to let it explode within me, run riot through my body, pour out of every part of me. I was totally owned by Illana and what she could do.

And the boxing. There was always the boxing. It seemed to be the pivotal point around which our lives revolved. Illana constantly returned to boxing like a junkie to a fix. She became more skillful at ducking my punches and returning blows I couldn't seem to escape no matter how hard I tried. Nothing I said or did could diminish the passion of her blows and the explosive sex that would follow. I began to tell myself that it didn't hurt when it did. I began to make excuses for Illana's behavior when there were none. In a way that was subtle but definite, I began to lose control over my life with Illana and the direction it was taking. In short, everything began to unravel.

And so it began: the end. I began to notice that my time with Illana was chopped up, sporadic and without any firm ground under it. She would come and go but never stay very long. Usually she would show up late in the evening, talk vaguely about her day, and listen to me in a distracted way when I tried to tell her about mine. Before you knew it, it would be late; we would realize we were hungry and frantically order takeout to be delivered. We would eat, fall into bed, and make love until 3 or 4 A.M., at which point we would crash: Illana into a deep bottomless sleep and I into an uneasy slumber.

The weekends were no different. Illana would disappear into the world of her friends or family or darkroom, and when I saw her it would be another late-nighter. Illana had many friends, most of them ex-lovers.

I never understood this lesbian dictum of hers, that you should become good friends with your exes. I had no desire to see mine and preferred to leave the past behind me. Illana's life was cluttered with everyone she had ever known; my life was relatively clear. I had time I could give her, yet she had little time to give me. I felt like a thief when we were together, as if I were stealing her from a larger, more important world that awaited and needed her. She made little effort to bring me into that world, almost as if she needed to keep me separate from that entire part of her life. I would try to make plans to do something or go somewhere with her, only to discover that she already had plans to go out of town to visit one of her many close friends. I was never invited and spent many a weekend in a state of anger and frustration that was becoming an all-too-familiar feeling.

Illana resisted even the smallest token of commitment. Ask her to come over at a certain time and she would arrive hours later. Ask her to make a decision and she would have a full-blown panic attack. Ask her about the future and she would quickly remind me that she was not ready to settle down yet but then would add that if I would just be patient, she would be ready soon, and she knew it would be with me. I chose to believe her, and I would try to be less demanding of her. Much later a friend reminded me that what Illana perceived to be demanding behavior was nothing more or less than my desire to be loved by someone who would still be there the next day.

We had now been together seven months, and the sex and boxing were no longer cutting it with me. I was beginning to look and act like a boxer who had lowered both gloves in defeat and exhaustion. I knew the final blow could not be far behind. Illana left me many times in those months, but like a boxing match she would always return for the next round.

Did I forget to mention that Illana had a very recent ex, a woman named Elise, living in San Francisco? When I would confront Illana, asking her if Elise knew about us, Illana would fire back that Elise was fragile and didn't need to know everything. Idiot that I was, I felt sorry for Elise, with her history of family abuse, willing to accept whatever bone Illana tossed at her. I was arrogant enough to feel pity for Elise, as though my situation were different, somehow better than hers. I have no doubt that each of us felt more special than the other: Elise trying to win Illana back and I trying just to win Illana at all. And I now have no doubt that we were both much too "fragile" to know everything. Illana had convinced Elise and me that what she needed most was time and patience. Having done so, she now had the door open to have her cake and eat us too.

By now any sane human being would have been wondering why on earth I tolerated this madness. I am not ashamed to admit it. I was a willing victim. I ignored the obvious and threw myself into this chaos with abandon. You must wonder, What did I see in Illana? What kept me there waiting for her? Perhaps it was the small but vital gestures that would come just as my doubts would begin to overtake me. There were the moments when Illana would caress my face and speak to me lovingly in coded endearments. There were the times when Illana would turn to me impulsively and say, "My God, I really love you," and I would glimpse the potential in those words, daring to dream a future that included us both. There was the way her face would deepen with concentration as she worked in her darkroom while I sat on a stool in the corner smiling and drinking her in with my eyes. Illana and I both saw the world as images to be transformed into photographs and stories. We had the same vision, and I believed that the same blood coursed through us both.

And there was yet more that held me. There was Illana, looking at me over candlelight dinners in countless restaurants. There was the way she would grip a corner of my T-shirt tightly while she slept as if she feared that I would be the one who would leave her. There was the music and the thoughts and the desires that she, a much younger woman, would share with me. I felt lighter every time she breathed in my direction. There was the way Illana taught me to wear boxer shorts: the underwear kind. Slung low, my slightly rounded stomach and female hips catching them at just the right angle. I still have the first pair of boxers that she ever gave me, green with purple eggplants and red bell peppers. I bury my face in them from time to time, trying to recapture the memory of her laughter the night she put them on me and pronounced me her girl and a true lesbian. And finally there was my desperate need to be loved by her. A simple, childlike desire to be held and loved, to have a friend and lover to play with and grow up with. To want that so badly that I was willing to overlook the abuse, to forgive the chaos, to endure the unbearable.

Can any of this explain why I stayed? Can words piled one on top of the other ever explain the effect she had on me? It was the most dangerous of times, and yet I believed my love would settle the gypsy in her and make her want to stay.

The day Illana left me for good was no different from any other day. The only clue was that she seemed more subdued than usual. We had arrived at an impasse in the relationship, where we had to either move forward and make a commitment or let go and move on. By the look on Illana's face as we sat down to talk that night, I knew that for her it was time to move on. Still, I clung to the hope that I was wrong, that she was about to tell me that she was ready to settle down and that she wanted to be with me the rest of her life. Wasn't that what I had waited for all these months? The next seven words that I heard shattered that hope forever.

"I have decided to return to Elise."

I had a sudden image of a beautiful, delicate vase that had been falling endlessly all this time and had finally hit the floor, exploding into a million irretrievable pieces. I had no words to offer. I could only nod briefly, afraid that if I moved, I would become that vase and knowing that if that happened, it would change nothing.

Illana looked at me sorrowfully for a long time. Then she said softly, "I never told you that I was ready for a relationship. I was always honest with you. I'm sorry." Again my brief nod. Then silence. I don't remember her getting up to leave, only that at the door she paused and said, "I hope that maybe someday we can be friends." And then just as quickly as she had entered my life, she left it, taking a part of my heart that I would never see again.

I don't know how long I remained seated. At one point I noticed that my whole body was trembling, and then suddenly, without warning, huge heaving sobs rose from deep inside. The pain was so intense that I raced to the bathroom just in time to lose my entire dinner. I remained there for some time, with only the cool tile of the wall to ease the burning ache within me.

The months went by, and even though I swore I would not survive I did. But I did not survive intact. I think of Illana now and then, but instead of wild pain I now feel the ghostly dull ache of a long-ago loss.

I don't ask for much these days. Sometimes I wish I could have just one night back that we had several years ago. It was my birthday, and we had sat across from each other in a restaurant by the ocean, our faces glowing in the soft light as we drank a cherry-oak wine, our eyes never straying from each other. Just before leaving the apartment, Illana had wrapped her arms tightly around me, molding her body to mine, and a moan of simple, pure pleasure had escaped her. The sheer joy of loving and touching and feeling had caught up with her, and that moan had come from the deepest part of her heart.

Later, at the restaurant, I could not believe the beauty of Illana's smile, the mystery of her bottomless black eyes, the sheer sensuality of her presence. I remember that I shivered when her fingers touched my wineglass. It was as if she were giving me a preview of touches to come. I wanted the night to both hurry up and never end. I didn't know then that she was already beginning to leave and that the night would end in the saddest of ways; that Illana would never be there in the morning despite all the nights she would spend with me.

I'm a ghost now, insubstantial and dim. I survived but not without paying a terrible price. Now I too wander through the restaurant I once sat in and listen to lovers sitting where I once sat and saying what I once said. I remember all the promises we made as we joyfully raced to our undoing.

I never saw Illana again after that night, and the longing I once had to see her has now transformed into the dread of ever seeing her again. And yet, oh, Illana! At times I miss her so. I am struck, like a crushing blow to the temple, by all that could have been. The kisses that were never kissed. The love that was never made. The laughter that was never laughed. The whole rest of our lives that will never be lived together.

To those who say to me that she was not good enough, that I deserved better, that she was bad news from the start, I have only one response: "I know. Now shut up and take care of your own heart. You never knew her like I did."

I don't box anymore. I don't have the heart for it. But somewhere in what's left of my heart beats the knowledge that to know love once is to know that you can love again. And I still believe in love. So I wonder, and I wait to be loved. Who will love me again? Somewhere in this world she exists right now. She could be anywhere. In this city or in some other city. I can only hope that with every step she takes, she is walking to me.

Crushed
by Janet Mason

Alicia slowly unfastened the hard blue buttons of her shirt. In the center of her gaze, Susan's brown eyes shimmered. All around them women were sitting on blankets spread on the grass. Magic carpets. A sparkling green sky. Alicia's fingers slid down, undoing button after button.

A warm breeze caressed her erect nipples. It blew through the women's music festival and circled back, heady with the scent of massage oil, jasmine, almond delight, lavender. Strains of Tracy Chapman wafted from some distant radio. At the bottom of the hill in the crafts area, colorful fabrics, woven shirts, wide-legged pants, yellow, red, purple, brushed the air.

Alicia's indigo shirt fluttered to the ground. Susan's eyes widened. On the corners of Alicia's lips, a smile played, laughing silently, her nipples hard as the buttons of her cast-off shirt. She removed her shorts and panties in three motions, a snap, a zipper, a brushing downward, palms of her hands against her cool thighs and buttocks.

She lay on a terry-cloth towel and closed her eyes. The mirage between her and Susan washed over her, a warm wave, leaving her salty, glistening. The blades of grass were smooth, cool against her fingertips.

"Take a minute to clear your mind; breathe in." The woman leading the massage workshop sat nearby, but her words hovered far away, entering only part of Alicia's mind.

The rest of Alicia floated free, her magic carpet sailing across a green sky, breezes parting her pubic hair. The sun's warmth spread through her. Susan's hands on her shoulders sent electricity to her toes.

Susan's shadow fell over Alicia's face, and with it the warmth ebbed momentarily. From a faraway place, thoughts of Roz edged in, guilt, another life; nothing to do with Susan's hands on her shoulders, soon to be kneading her arms, fingertips lightly stroking the sides of her breasts.

Roz, the woman she had lived with for eight years, her lover, her life partner—as Alicia often said to women whose flirting threatened to go further—was doing her work shift registering latecomers at the front gate.

Alicia had known Susan for almost as long. Seven years ago they met at a women's studies conference, Susan presenting her dissertation, Alicia doing a karate demonstration. The first thing Alicia noticed when she walked into the morning plenary session late was the large double woman symbol circling Susan's breasts. Above the T-shirt, cropped hair, a face plain to the point of boyishness, and mischievous brown eyes that followed her from across the room.

Susan presented her paper on a panel against pornography. She was highly intelligent. Alicia understood only about half of what she said. But she did understand the central motif—pornography was the flip side of puritanism.

Alicia's ears perked up when Susan mentioned sex toys. "Lesbian feminists who use such things," she said, "are in danger of being co-opted into patriarchal modes of thought."

After the panelists finished, Alicia went to the front of the room to talk to her. Susan's ideas were interesting but nowhere near as fascinating as the promise in her brown eyes.

Alicia didn't have to wonder what would have happened if Roz hadn't joined her at the conference that evening. *How it would have happened* fueled her imagination with endless variation: slow dancing at a women's bar, hands on the small of the back drifting down toward buttocks, cheek to cheek moving into lips and tongues. Urgent, half-clothed sex in the women's bathroom, back pressed to the wall, thighs draped over shoulders. The more realistic, tamer, version—switching roommates in dorm rooms, a night of unbridled passion, wanton, steamy.

All of this from a few intimate encounters. Susan's knee pressed against Alicia's under the table at dinner. Shared laughter. A casual touch on the hand. Breasts meeting in a parting embrace. A light kiss that in the holding back promised the world.

Alicia never thought she'd want anyone else but Roz. Six months after becoming lovers, they moved in together. She still remembered the first night in their Park Slope apartment. Candlelight. Unpacked crates. The futon spread open on the floor. Roz, naked, soft, pulling passion from the pit of Alicia's belly. Voices and bodies so intertwined, they became one. Whispers: *I will love you forever, you and only you.*

Six months later there was Susan. After the women's studies conference, Susan returned to Madison and Alicia and Roz to Brooklyn. Alicia tried to push all thoughts of Susan from her mind. But in the quiet moments of night, when Alicia lay awake with Roz beside her breathing evenly, Susan crept in and stayed.

A postcard—"Hope you're doing well, would be great to see you again"—was all it took for Alicia to bring up the subject.

"Why?" was Roz's only response. Why would Alicia want to be nonmonogamous; why this betrayal; and finally, "Who?"

"No one special," lied Alicia. "I'm just not sure I want to be tied down. You're only the second woman I've ever been with." The excuses were hollow, but the tears Alicia cried, whispering "I never wanted to hurt you" as she held Roz, were not forced.

Dark circles gathered under Roz's eyes. "If you have an affair," she said, voice small with resentment, "I just don't want to know about it."

It pained Alicia to see what she was doing to Roz. She loved her more than anything. *More than your freedom?* her consciousness asked. *More than your passions?* One look at Roz—her once-vibrant lover now moping around—and Alicia knew the answer.

She pushed Susan out of her mind, thinking only of the beautiful, soft, sensual woman she shared her life with, making love, cleaning their apartment, practicing karate. But when Roz went away to visit relatives, as she frequently did, Alicia missed her too much to fantasize about her. Thoughts of Susan smoldered in her mind. She remembered their parting kiss, light and sisterly, with a concentration that burned her lips.

The following year Alicia went alone to the women's studies conference. When she saw Susan's name on the list of presenters, a tingling chill filled her. At the opening reception she caught Susan's eye, nodded hello, and worked her way across the room. Alicia moved forward to embrace Susan and was met with a handshake.

"I'm Mary," said the woman attached to the hand, "Susan's lover."

Susan and Mary had been together for nearly ten years. *Too long,* thought Alicia, *for Susan not to have mentioned it. Unless the attraction was mutual.*

Susan and Alicia met five times in seven years at feminist conferences. Always one or the other was with her lover. Alicia's attraction for Susan condensed to the point where one glance, one touch, one thought sent a bolt of heat through her body, the inner lips of her vulva opening, contracting.

It had been two years since Alicia had last seen Susan. Thoughts of her faded, then flared up like an old wound demanding attention. *If I ever see her again,* Alicia promised herself, *there will be no holding back.*

Now Susan's hands were traveling the length of Alicia's torso, waist to shoulders, fingers fanning under her back, thumbs caressing her sides. Feather fingers alighted on the base of her throat, danced lightly between her breasts, nestled in the folds of her stomach.

Time came for switching places. Alicia, pupils contracted in the afternoon sunlight, watched as Susan undressed. Her T-shirt disappeared in a flash, revealing small round breasts, crimson nipples. Susan unzipped her khaki shorts to reveal a triangle of underpants, black and low cut, just as Alicia had imagined.

Massage oil glistened on Susan's thighs and Alicia's hands. Alicia kneaded her way down the outside, up the inside, the triangle of pubic hair a distraction from the flesh, muscles, and bone under her fingers. Was it her imagination, or did she hear an audible intake of breath, a slight moan, an invitation for more?

When the workshop ended Alicia folded and refolded her terry cloth towel while waiting for Susan to finish dressing. She tucked her towel under her arm as Susan stepped into her sandals. The two women stood looking at each other silently, as if beyond their revealed nakedness they had nothing else to say.

Susan glanced at her watch. "I'm meeting Mary for dinner."

"Wait. I...I wanted to talk to you." Alicia felt dizzy.

Susan smiled, eyes widening. Quickly, almost furtively, she looked in the opposite direction. "I'm already late. How about tomorrow afternoon? Mary's taking a West African dance workshop from 1 to 4. Why don't we meet in the cabin by the lake?"

Alicia watched Susan walk away. She barely remembered answering, except that the word "sure" echoed in her mind. She walked back to the cabin she shared with Roz and six other women, looking forward to a shower before dinner.

"Hi, sweetie!" Roz was sitting on the porch.

Alicia bent down, kissed her quickly on the lips, and stood up again. *Sweetie*—so much was in that word: eight years of loving, living together, oneness, possession, guilt.

Alicia mumbled something about being tired, needing a nap before dinner. No, she didn't need company. She was fine. She'd meet Roz at the dining hall.

Roz kissed her, hugged her, felt her forehead, and, saying, "It must have been all that massage," grabbed her mess kit and went to dinner.

After her shower Alicia sprawled across her camp bed, pulled up against Roz's to make a double bed. Rolling onto her back, she put her forearm over her eyes. What did Roz mean by that last comment? Did she know more than she let on?

Roz, her trusting gray eyes flecked with green, her curly salt-and-pepper hair that Alicia loved to run her fingers through, even as she remembered her lover's last words on nonmonogamy: "I just don't want to know about it."

Alicia groaned, her emotions twisting her from head to toe.

That evening at the concert, Alicia and Roz sat on their blanket in the "chem-free" section of the audience. From the stage Suede crooned a jazzy love song, velvety as the night sky above them. They sat in a sea of women, some on blankets, others sitting on low-slung chairs. Alicia nestled her head in Roz's lap, smiling into her lover's eyes, twinkling with the stars.

When Suede finished, the emcee returned to the stage, attempting jokes, wearing a sequined hat with a veil on it.

"Let's take a walk," whispered Alicia to Roz, pressing her hand lightly.

The two of them waded through the crowd carefully. Hand in hand they wandered down a dirt road lined with shadows that in daylight were ferns, large rocks, fir trees. Roz turned off the flashlight. Moonlight shone on the path. Rounding the bend they saw a sky full of stars reflected in the luminous silver lake, endless and brilliant.

The dock creaked beneath their feet like the oarlocks of a rowboat. The lake was silent except for an occasional splash, a jumping fish, the croak of a bullfrog.

Alicia wrapped her arms around Roz. "Kiss me," she whispered, brushing Roz's hair from her face, tracing moonlight with her fingers.

Alicia wanted Roz to fill her, every crack and crevice, to leave no place wanting. Their mouths came together in a kiss that melded their yesterdays and tomorrows, swirling around them in a finely spun mist.

Their lips drew apart. Alicia looked over Roz's shoulder and shivered. The cabin where Alicia was to meet Susan tomorrow afternoon sat at the edge of the forest, its white paint a shimmering ghost in the moonlight.

They walked back up the path past the stage to their cabin so Alicia could pick up a sweatshirt.

Inside the cabin Alicia lay across their bed.

"Come here," she said. Roz sprawled out next to her. "I wasn't really cold—I just wanted to get you back here alone."

Roz giggled, slipping her arms around Alicia. "Why didn't you just say so? I've been horny all day. Who wouldn't be after looking at all these naked women? I've seen every type of breast there is."

They wriggled out of their clothes and slipped into their double sleeping bag, Roz's hands moving to the inside of Alicia's thighs.

Alicia giggled. "What if someone comes back?"

"They won't," replied Roz. "They're at the concert. And if they do, who cares?"

They slipped into the cadence of kissing, touching, licking, sucking. Between moans Alicia's mind drifted. *This is enough,* she argued with the image of Susan that welled up in front of her, naked, beckoning.

She traced the outline of Roz's nipples with her tongue. *How could this woman ever have been a stranger?* She first knew Roz as an interesting-looking woman in her karate class, then as a co-organizer for the women's self-defense street fair. But since their first kiss she was just Roz. Roz of languid Sunday mornings. Roz with the goddess body. Roz whispering sweetly in her ear.

In their lovemaking was eight years of passion, eight years of daily routine. It was good. Alicia slipped deeper into their rhythms, knowing that what she had with Roz she would never willingly give up.

The next day Alicia walked down the fern-lined path to the cabin by the lake. That morning, waking next to Roz's even breathing, the scent of their lovemaking still lingering, she wrestled with herself. Alicia finally decided that the least she could do after seven years was to meet Susan.

She planned to just talk, to confess her lust for Susan through all the years, but to tell her that she was happy with Roz, happily married, happily monogamous, and intending to stay that way. But as she walked down the path, watching the sun filtering through the trees into the downy green undergrowth where moss held granite and ferns unfurled, she found her thoughts elsewhere.

Her mind undressed Susan, a smoldering kiss, hard buttons opening to soft, the zipper on her jeans cold as ice in Alicia's fingers, underneath a rain forest that was all Susan, lush, tropical, steamy.

Putting her foot on the first step of the porch, Alicia began to feel foolish. *She probably just wants to talk,* she thought. Then pausing at the door, hearing only silence, she added, *Maybe she's not even here.*

Alicia knocked lightly. Hearing a faint "Come in," she pushed open the door.

Inside Susan was naked, sprawled on top of a sheet on a mattress lying on the floor.

Alicia's breath was shallow, her heart pounding in her ears as she turned around and pulled the door shut behind her. She walked uncertainly toward Susan.

"So much for small talk," said Alicia, standing over Susan, her eyes running up and down her body, resting on her face.

"Care for a drink?" Susan motioned toward the flask that sat on the floor next to her. When Alicia shook her head no, Susan poured herself a shot, throwing back her head, bolting it down. She leaned forward and took Alicia's hand.

Alicia knelt down on the edge of the mattress, put her arms around Susan, and lost herself in a kiss that left her wanting more. Her right hand caressed Susan's face and neck, swirled around her breasts, rested on her stomach.

Alicia drew back, pulled her T-shirt over her head, stood up to unzip her shorts.

"Wait a minute." Susan reached toward her knapsack, pulling out a lavender drawstring bag. Inside was a large pink dildo complete with artificial veins and foreskin and a black leather harness.

Alicia looked at Susan with disbelief. "You want to stick that thing in me?"

"Actually, I had the opposite in mind." Susan licked her lips, handed Alicia the harness. "Put it on over your shorts."

"But, I thought…" Alicia wasn't so shocked by the dildo as she was by the fact that Susan was handing it to her. Wasn't this the same Susan who had condemned sex toys at the women's studies conference where they met?

Alicia found dildos intriguing but since Roz wasn't interested had never used one before. With some help from Susan, she figured out the configuration of snaps and buckles. Alicia stood there, dildo protruding from her pubis, and looked around the cabin. "Whose cabin is this, anyway?"

"It's empty except for us. It helps to have friends in the right places. I brought a mattress down early this morning." Susan looked Alicia up and down. "C'mon down here."

Alicia knelt between Susan's legs. She leaned forward to kiss Susan again, her fingers lightly brushing her pubic hair.

Susan pushed her hand away. "I'm ready," she said, pulling Alicia toward her, guiding the dildo inside her. Alicia moved slowly, gripping the sides of the mattress, getting used to the rub of the harness, the push of the dildo.

"Harder. Faster." Susan's cupped hands strained against Alicia's ass, clamping down, pulling at her shorts.

Alicia's clitoris had never throbbed like this. Susan moaned, her mouth open, hips gyrating, head thrashing. Alicia slowed down, her knees chafing, arm muscles trembling.

"Keep going," commanded Susan. "Hard as you can. Harder. Now tell me where we met."

Alicia wondered how much Susan had drunk. Between her own heavy breathing, the slurp of the dildo, and the mattress rubbing against the wooden floor, Alicia answered, "At a women's studies conference."

"No, we met at a truck stop." Susan's head was rolled back, her eyes shut. "We're fucking in the back room."

Alicia stopped humping, resting with the dildo inside of Susan. She looked at Susan, this sweaty, naked woman lying under her. This stranger. She thought about getting up and leaving, but she never was a quitter. In karate class she always finished her push-ups, even once when her teacher was in a foul mood and made them do a hundred.

"OK. OK." Susan squeezed Alicia's ass. "We met at a women's studies conference. Now fuck my brains out."

Alicia took a deep breath, gripped the sides of the mattress harder, her knuckles turning white. The dildo pushed into her clitoris, exciting her into a frenzy but not to orgasm. She wasn't sure whose brains were being fucked out.

Throwing her head back in a long moan, Susan stopped moving.

She kept her eyes closed. Alicia struggled backward, the dildo slurping out of Susan. Alicia sat on the edge of the mattress, catching her breath. Several minutes later, which seemed like an eternity, Susan opened her eyes and smiled.

"That was wonderful." Susan looked at her watch. "My God, we've been here an hour. We should leave separately, with some time between us."

"Leave? What about me?"

"I thought that was for both of us." Susan looked a bit miffed. "But you could wash the dildo off. There's soap in the bathroom."

"No, thanks. It's too big. Besides…I thought you were opposed to sex toys."

Susan looked uncomfortable for a second, then waved her hand in front of her face. "That was years ago. You can't believe everything you hear. Besides, it's an agreement Mary and I have."

"Mary knows?"

"Of course not. I'm very discreet. But the dildo is part of the deal. I use it with whomever I'm with. We don't exchange bodily fluids, so it's safer. And Mary feels better, knowing I'm having more contact with Matilda than with the other women."

"Matilda?"

Susan gestured toward the dildo, erectly pointing at the floor from between Alicia's legs.

"Oh, Matilda. Do you use her with many women?"

"I hope you're not counting." Susan raised an eyebrow. "I lost track years ago."

"You lost track!" Alicia's face was flushed. "Does Mary know how much you screw around?"

"She knows but not who, where, or when. We've been together more than 15 years. She can't expect me to have sex only with her."

"Why not? Don't you love her?"

"Of course I do." Susan's voice was quiet. "But I need the excitement of other women. There's nothing wrong with a roll in the hay in other stables. You just did it yourself." Susan picked up the flask. "A toast to next time?"

Alicia scrambled to her feet, breasts bobbing in unison with the dildo. *Why was I ever attracted to her?* she wondered. All those years thinking I was special, and here I am, just one in a cast of thousands.

She unbuckled the harness, throwing it and the damp dildo into Susan's lap. "I hope you and Matilda have a great life together. My condolences to Mary."

Alicia put on her sandals, grabbed her shirt, and strode out of the cabin. On top of feeling stupid, she felt cheap, dirty, used, betrayed, and most of all guilty for betraying Roz.

When she got to the lake, she kicked off her sandals, unzipped her shorts. Leaving her clothes on the dock, she plunged into the lake, its icy shock welcome.

She churned her limbs furiously until she arrived at the huge boulders, half submerged on the far side of the lake. She sat down on one, rough granite against her bare ass. She pushed against it harder, stretching and flattening her body as if it could erase the acidic aftertaste of her illusions.

She swam back across the lake. By the time she climbed up the metal ladder on the dock, she began to feel a sense of relief. Her obsession with Susan flowed away with the rivulets of water streaming from her naked body. She stepped into her shorts, then back out of them.

She needed to be naked. To walk with stones cutting into her feet, wind whipping through her thighs. She bundled her clothes under her arm and walked up the trail to the grassy field in front of the crafts area.

She ran into the field, throwing her clothes up into the air. Arms outstretched like a child playing helicopter, she spun around and around, laughing as the hill and the woods swayed and circled around her. She fell down, her head filled with tiny stars spiraling into the sky.

The grass, the breeze, the afternoon sun were the fingers and tongues of many women against her skin. Winged fairies in the circumference of the light. But in the middle, there was one woman and one woman only, standing clearly, beckoning. In every feature—the planes of her face, the contours of her hips, the song of her voice—it was Roz.

Kolu, Revisited
by Cat McDonald

Around midnight on the second night of their Christmas
holiday back home in Washington, D.C., Celeste and her
sister, Lauren, walked up two concrete steps into a steamy,
crowded bar. A mellow jazz quartet played on a small stage at
the end of the long, narrow room. Pushing their way through
the crowd of mostly brown and black faces, the two sisters
headed for the bar and ordered cocktails. No sooner had they
paid the bartender than Lauren recognized someone across
the room and sashayed off to get reacquainted.

Peering across the smoky room, Celeste watched as Lauren leaned over to speak with a man who seemed to recognize her immediately. He introduced Lauren to the group of
people with whom he was sharing a booth. Soon enough
they all shifted around to make room for Lauren to sit
down. Celeste figured she wouldn't be seeing much of her
sister for a while, which was just as well. She was happy
enough to sit at the bar soaking up the atmosphere, rocking
gently in time to the music.

Celeste was thinking about ordering another Manhattan
when someone tapped on her shoulder. She turned to face a
tall brown-skinned woman dressed in black from the frames of
her wire-rimmed glasses to the tips of her cowboy boots.

"Munchkin?" said the woman with a sly grin on her lips.

There was only one person in the world who had ever called her that. Celeste glanced at the woman's smile, the shallow cleft in her chin, the narrow bridge of her nose, and instantly recalled the awkward, pretty girl she had known in high school.

"Kolu!" Celeste shouted above the din and reached up to kiss her on the cheek.

"Was that Lauren who came with you?" Kolu asked as she leaned against the bar.

Celeste nodded and glanced across the crowd to where her sister was sitting. Kolu and Lauren had been in the same class at school, but it was Celeste whom she'd befriended.

When she first came to their school, Kolu had seemed so distant and fragile. Having fallen off the roof of her family's summer home in August, Kolu made her first appearance in school in October with her arm suspended in a sling, gripped by a cast that curled her fingers straight up and back. That winter the air around Kolu always seemed sharp and shaky, like thin ice crackling. Whenever she was the least bit anxious, she'd break out into jagged laughter, gasping in and in, like someone drowning. For lunch she'd eat a heap of lettuce topped with croutons and raw red onion hoops too big for her mouth. Then she'd pour herself a Styrofoam cup of coffee from the teachers' silver urn and go smoke a cigarette on the concrete stairs overlooking the soccer field. She'd sip the lukewarm mudwater as her eyes followed the pattern of the white lines around the field. Then she'd blow a long silk stocking of smoke and sip and stare some more.

After her cast was removed, Kolu got stronger. The nervous laughter receded, but even then no one told Kolu that it was time for her to take a gym class or to curb her smoking habit. Not even the teachers seemed willing to take anything away from her, as if they too were all wary of ever seeing her so vulnerable again.

"You look exactly the same," Kolu said.

"Is that good?"

"Like a night flower," Kolu said.

"And you look less like a gazelle than you used to."

Kolu wore her hair shortish and natural, and she stood like a dancer, grounded, with her head and shoulders erect, heels apart, toes turned slightly outward. What had transformed the girl with the brittle laughter and stumbling walk into this statuesque woman with a slow-burning smile?

"Do you live in D.C.?" Kolu asked.

"Vermont," Celeste said, shaking her head. "But probably not for much longer."

"Why's that?" Kolu said.

Celeste shrugged and raised her glass to her lips.

"Heart trouble or work trouble?"

"Both," Celeste said and crunched on a sliver of ice. She told Kolu briefly how recent budget cuts were decimating the educational program she worked for, but she couldn't bear to go into the gruesome details of her war-torn love life.

"Sounds rough," Kolu said. "I bet you're glad to be home for a while."

"Very," Celeste said. "Where are you living these days?"

"Oakland."

As Kolu spoke Celeste remembered the blurb about Kolu that had appeared in their school's alumni magazine.

"Doing medical research, right?"

Kolu nodded, that smile of hers reappearing.

Celeste was so glad that Kolu had lived up to her potential. At 15 Kolu had been a diligent student who prepared her research papers long weeks in advance, spoke French and German, and was on her way to winning the upper school science prize.

After Kolu and Celeste had become friends, Celeste learned that shortly before Kolu was born, her parents had come to the States from Jamaica and had scraped by while her father finished medical school. By the time Kolu showed up at prep school, her parents' hard work had landed them squarely in the middle class. But despite her home comforts, Kolu had feared that she somehow lacked essential social skills, that everybody around her would always know something that she didn't know. For this she blamed her formative years, which had been spent sharing an efficiency apartment with her parents and older brother. As a result, Kolu had spent so much energy catching up to her peers that she'd never appreciated the ways in which she'd surpassed them.

Sitting at the bar Celeste and Kolu talked for a while about people from school. They discovered that neither of them had really kept in touch with anyone from those days. The fact that most of the people who'd once been a central part of their lives were now completely absent was both sad and exhilarating, like the death of a neighbor's dog.

"I couldn't wait to get out of that fishbowl," Kolu said.

"Wasn't it a shock," Celeste said, "going to college and realizing that nobody there knew a single thing about you?"

"It was a revelation," Kolu said. "I came out as soon as I set foot on campus."

Celeste nodded.

"I grew up so much, especially in the first two years," Kolu continued. "I'd always studied hard, but then I started taking ideas more seriously. And I met a lot of really smart, really intense women."

Celeste didn't quite hear Kolu's last few statements. She had been watching Kolu speak, marveling at how strange the familiar girl had become and how familiar this strange woman still was. As in years before Kolu's imbalance of skeptical wariness and sudden intimacy had begun to draw her in, making her wonder if once again Kolu would keep her at a distance. And then, even though it happened years ago, hearing Kolu state that she had waited until college to come out had caused a deafening ringing in Celeste's ears.

Their friendship had had a strange beginning. Before Celeste had ever spoken to Kolu, she'd told a friend that she thought Kolu's haircut was cute. This friend had told someone, who told someone else, and by the time the comment got around to Kolu, who knew what it said?

One afternoon between classes Kolu had sidled up to Celeste in the empty locker room. Planting her hands on her hips, she said, "I hear you've got something to tell me."

Celeste saw immediately that there was no way of wriggling out of this. She was relieved to have the chance to bring her feelings out into the open. And yet she couldn't figure out what it was exactly that she felt. Something to do with the nape of Kolu's neck and how soft Celeste had imagined it would feel against her lips. Something about wanting to be the center of Kolu's attention. Something soft and enticing that made the pit of her stomach feel empty of breath. But what?

Celeste found herself formulating sentences in her head over and over: *I really think you're cute; I think you're really cute; I'd like to be friends with you; I want to kiss the nape of your neck; I'm attracted to you; I have a really big crush on you; I like your hair...*

Celeste stood there so long that Kolu must have gotten fed up with waiting and quickly kissed Celeste on her half-opened mouth, just once. Kolu's breath tasted of onions and cigarettes from lunchtime. In the moment it took for Celeste to register what was happening, Kolu pulled away. The afterimage of Kolu's eyes up close made Celeste gasp softly.

"Whatever you do," Kolu said, "don't start dressing like a diesel dyke."

Then she turned and left Celeste standing in that dark mildewy room alone, as speechless as she had ever been in her teenage life.

After that Celeste's daily life continued to revolve around soccer practice, arguments with Lauren, endless hours of homework, basement keg parties, college admissions decisions, and make-out sessions with her boyfriend, Rich. Celeste still kept getting grounded for staying out with Rich past her curfew. She still cried sometimes for no particular reason. But while she went on mostly as before, in the still moments of her day Celeste would find herself dreaming of how perfect her life would be if she could spend all of her time with Kolu. As the weeks and months went by, Celeste had to admit to herself that that would probably never happen.

Celeste and Kolu didn't share any classes, so they met at in-between places and in-between times: in the lunchroom, in the girls' locker room, on the front lawn when the weather was good. Celeste remembered standing in the hallway between classes, the frayed canvas edge of her three-ring binder rubbing against Kolu's shoulder as she whispered gossip into the tender vortex of Kolu's ear.

A few times during free period, Celeste had perched on the seat of Kolu's bike with her hands around Kolu's waist while Kolu had pedaled them to her house. They'd gone up to Kolu's bedroom, and while Kolu went to change her tampon or look for her lost homework assignment, Celeste had tried to memorize every detail of Kolu's room: the orange comforter, the angled walls, the pale wood floor, the cracked slab of marble that served as a night table, the gray light sifting in through the low windows.

Celeste remembered the time she'd stood in front of Kolu's locker, carefully spinning the black knob so that the little white marker lined up with the correct numbers. First to the right, once around to the left, then twice to the right. Heart beating in her palms, Celeste had eased up the silver metal handle until it clicked. On that day Kolu had saved a seat for her in the cafeteria, had brought banana bread for them to share, and on top of that had entrusted Celeste with her locker combination. As Celeste pulled open Kolu's locker, she swore that she'd remember this moment forever.

The bar was closing, and Lauren was off to another club with her newfound posse. Kolu had her mother's car for the evening and offered to give Celeste a ride home. Walking down the block Celeste decided to ignore the cold and focused instead on the slightly sloshy warmth inside her. As Kolu and Celeste waited for the car to warm up, their breath curled in silver tendrils from their lips.

"Remember the way to my father's house?" Celeste asked, warming her ears with her palms.

"Of course."

As Kolu pulled out into the Saturday-night traffic, Celeste said, "So don't you think it's ironic that you're the one who told me not to turn into a dyke?"

"When did I do that?"

When Celeste reminded her of the incident in the girl's locker room, Kolu laughed out loud.

"I hope my warning didn't stop you."

"No..." Celeste said. "In college I managed to crawl my way toward an enlightened community. I grew up a lot then too. I had two longish relationships with two very different women."

"But..."

"But college was ten years ago," Celeste said. "Now I feel so isolated. I've just gone through an awful breakup..."

Kolu turned and gave Celeste a questioning look.

"With a man," Celeste said. "I still sleep with men too."

"That's good to know," Kolu said.

"When I was younger, women I went out with didn't seem to mind this as much," Celeste said. "They called it experimenting. But now that I've reached a certain age, most would prefer that I make up my mind one way or the other. Like my emotional life has to be as well-packaged as my career." Celeste sighed, "Now you're never going to speak to me again."

"Don't assume."

"Was that why you didn't want to be with me in high school?" Celeste asked. "Because I went out with boys?"

"Everybody went out with boys in high school."

"Not you."

Waiting for the light to change, Kolu said, "I was afraid of hurting you."

Kolu turned onto the street that led downhill into Rock Creek Park, and the streetlights grew sparser. Celeste stared at the beams of light the car threw onto the black road ahead of them. She thought of Kolu, the young loner, and of herself as a girl surrounded by her friends. She'd always assumed that Kolu was the fragile one, that Kolu had kept her distance out of shyness. But Kolu had recognized that she had a certain power over Celeste. Had she kept her distance out of disinterest or because she had understood, even as a girl, that Celeste was capable of being completely unarmed by her own desire?

Coasting downhill, Kolu said, "I remember this route. I used to drive you home in the Blue Bomb. Remember that car?"

"The brakes were always failing at really inconvenient times."

"Yeah, like at the bottom of this hill!"

They laughed, and Celeste clutched the dashboard as Kolu coasted through the yellow traffic light. When Kolu pulled up in front of Celeste's father's house, the two women lingered as the engine idled.

"Here you are," Kolu said.

"Will I see you again before you leave?"

Kolu nodded. "I'd like that."

Kolu was about to say good night, but Celeste moved closer. Kolu sat still and silent for a moment. Finally, Celeste moved closer, and they kissed briefly, as if casually. But after they kissed they didn't pull apart.

As Celeste looked into Kolu's eyes, she wanted to tell her that her heart was still fragile, wanted Kolu to promise to treat her gently. But Celeste was afraid that if she exposed her damaged self, Kolu would tell her again that the timing was wrong. So she took a deep breath and said, "My head is spinning."

"What did you expect?" Kolu grinned.

Another brief kiss became a longer kiss, which could no longer be mistaken for a chaste good-night. Celeste opened her lips a little wider. She felt Kolu's hand on her cheek, another on her shoulder. The car was still running.

Celeste's breathing became thicker as she ran her hands over Kolu's shoulders, down her back. She slid her cool hands under Kolu's sweater to feel the smooth, warm skin.

Kolu pulled away from Celeste. "I hope you don't have nosy neighbors."

"I do," Celeste said.

"I'm staying with my parents," Kolu said. "In my brother's old basement apartment. It's very quiet and very private. Can you come there with me?"

Celeste nodded, "Yes."

They kissed again; then Kolu put the car in gear and drove them back across the park.

Celeste sat on the edge of Kolu's bed, waiting for her to hurry back from the bathroom. As she stared absently at the bowl of whole walnuts sitting on the nightstand, Celeste gave herself permission to enjoy whatever came next.

She couldn't believe her luck in having found Kolu again. Celeste welcomed time spent with an old friend to whom she didn't have to explain every little thing about herself. Because the changes in her personal and professional life were making her feel exposed and unsteady, Celeste needed friendship as much as passion.

Kolu didn't enter the room so much as burst into it. She leapt from the bathroom door directly onto the bed, knocking Celeste onto her back. Celeste let out an involuntary grunt as her head hit the thick down pillows. Her arms wrapped around Kolu as Kolu moved on top of her. She wanted to feel Kolu's skin and rolled Kolu's shirt up until it was bunched under her armpits. Kolu, meanwhile, was unbuttoning Celeste's shirt so that soon their breasts were pressed together, and the skin covering their hearts was exposed to the cool air.

Celeste wanted to devour Kolu's body with her eyes, but at first she was so shy that she looked at Kolu only obliquely: the glowing brown skin wrapped taut around her body, the full breasts with tight dark-chocolate nipples. She saw this from the corner of her eyes in the bedroom where the only illumination came from the streetlight beyond the window. Then she began to explore Kolu with her tongue and her hands. And when Celeste saw Kolu's eyes appreciating her body, her shyness dropped away.

"Does this feel good?" Kolu said as she licked the outer edge of Celeste's breast.

Celeste assented with an "Mmm…"

Kolu's mouth moved down Celeste's body, and Celeste was excited for what would come next. What she didn't expect was for Kolu to reach up to the nightstand and pull out a little rectangular piece of latex and a small bottle of lubricant. Celeste looked down and saw that Kolu had already put a latex glove on. When had she done that? Then she felt Kolu's safe lubricated finger—or was it two fingers?—slide into her cunt. She leaned back with a moan, lifted her pelvis in a slow rhythm.

Then Kolu placed the square of lubricated latex between her lips and Celeste's cunt and began to work her tongue around Celeste's clit. Using her lips to massage and suck, Kolu Frenched Celeste's cunt as she had done to her mouth.

Celeste longed to hear Kolu call her name and lose control. She turned Kolu's body until her head was resting between Kolu's strong thighs; then she reached over to the nightstand for a fresh square of latex.

"Where's that lube?" Celeste asked. And Kolu handed her the little bottle of clear, scentless liquid, which Celeste squeezed onto the latex. Before putting it in place, Celeste buried her nose in Kolu's muff.

"You smell delicious," Celeste said, running her nose gently along the ridge of Kolu's clit, breathing in the strong scent.

Kolu moaned and lowered her head again and began tonguing Celeste more vigorously. Celeste moaned and struggled to put the latex in the right position, then searched with her tongue for Kolu's favorite places.

Kolu was not beside her when Celeste opened her eyes that morning. A narrow shaft of sunlight fell through white curtained windows. The pale salmon walls, melon green trim, and oval mirror hanging over a pine dresser gave the room a calm, unhurried feel. Celeste felt languorous. She wanted Kolu to return from wherever she was so she could smell her body again: the sharp celery scent of her tangled armpits, the smoked salmon of her cunt, the cocoa butter of her nappy hair. Where was she?

Celeste got up and threw on the terry-cloth robe she found hanging on the back of the door, then walked through the French doors to the little kitchen. There was Kolu, standing at the stove, transferring oatmeal from a saucepan to two small blue bowls. A teapot sat on the kitchen table flanked by two hand-turned mugs. Kolu looked up from the stove and smiled. Much to Celeste's disappointment Kolu was completely dressed, in jeans and a white T-shirt.

Celeste swallowed hard. "Morning."

She sat down at the kitchen table and looked out the window at the back garden, at the roots of a large tree twisting through the earth.

"Did you sleep all right?" Kolu asked, pouring Celeste a mug of milky tea.

Celeste nodded. She was worried about Kolu going all formal on her when what she wanted to do was kiss her. Hadn't they just spent a brazen, slippery night together? Was that ancient history now? Or maybe it hadn't been as great for Kolu as it had been for Celeste. Had she been too selfish, too clumsy? Was Kolu just waiting for Celeste to leave so she could have a good laugh about her?

Kolu sat down with two bowls of oatmeal. "How are you feeling today?"

Celeste picked up her spoon and said, "Good." Her voice caught in her throat and tripped over her windpipe. She took a sip of her tea, which was warm and spicy.

"Would you like some honey?" Kolu said, nudging a spoonful of oatmeal into her mouth.

"No, thanks."

They ate in silence, not looking at each other directly. Why did it feel so damned awkward? Celeste was scared by this silence that Kolu was putting between them. Instead of embracing Celeste, Kolu was serving her breakfast and talking like a stewardess.

Celeste put down her spoon. "Last night was wonderful."

Kolu raised her eyebrows. "But…?"

"What do you mean?" Celeste said. "What's wrong?"

"Look," Kolu said, "for all I know you could be thinking this was just some little adventure. You were on the rebound. You were lonely. You had a few drinks. You fell into bed with a woman…" She ended with a shrug.

Celeste's heart was pounding. "Don't you know how long I've waited for last night?"

"And what about today?" Kolu said. "Now that you've gotten what you wanted."

"I want more."

Kolu's hands were resting on the table. Celeste found it difficult to move, but she found the courage to place her fingertips against Kolu's.

Kolu said, "No regrets?"

"My only regret," Celeste said, looking directly into Kolu's eyes, "is that you live 2,000 miles away."

"Good," Kolu said. "Because the next time we make love, you're going to be completely sober. It's going to be deliberate and intentional. There's not going to be any excuses."

"I'm sober now," Celeste whispered.

"Are you?"

"Yes," Celeste nodded.

"Eat your breakfast," Kolu said. And she watched until Celeste picked up her spoon and began eating her oatmeal. Then Kolu slid down in her chair and disappeared under the table. Celeste felt her warm hands on her ankles, sliding up her calves to her thighs. She pushed her chair back from the table as Kolu rose to part the robe that clung to her warm body. Kolu's tongue slid up her thighs, along the crease that ran between her thigh and stomach, past her navel, between her breasts, up her throat and her chin to her lips. Kolu's warm, slippery tongue circled Celeste's lips until Celeste could no longer sit still. She slid the robe down from around her shoulders and ran her hands up under the T-shirt that separated Kolu's brown body from her own.

The Doctor's Wife
by Nilaja A. Montgomery-Akalu

Doctor's Wife was not happy. It was another cold, lonely, horny night. He had been called away for an emergency cranium operation or some shit like that. She could not have cared less. It would be hours before The Doctor's Wife saw him again. That was the life of a doctor's wife, always on hold. It had been her life for the past 20 years. It had gotten old. She had no idea how she ended up at the bar, especially a bar like this. It was one of those women's bars, with lesbians. She took a seat at the end of the bar and ordered a rum and coke. She wanted something light 'cause Lord knew the last thing she wanted was to get wasted in a place like this. The Doctor's Wife looked around her surroundings. She had no idea there were so many of them. Some were actually kinda pretty-looking. Not like what she was brought up learning about women like them. They were all dancing and grinding their bodies into each other. Their skin shone with perspiration. The Doctor's Wife fanned herself with a napkin. She was starting to feel the heat.

"Hey, pretty lady." The Doctor's Wife turned around to see who was speaking to her. She looked up into the face of a rather large woman. *Must be one of the masculine types,* she guessed from the array of tattoos that adorned the woman's flabby arms.

"Hello," The Doctor's Wife said stiffly.

"Why are you sittin' here all by yo' pretty little self?" the tattooed woman asked.

The Doctor's Wife blushed.

"Let's dance," the woman said, pulling The Doctor's Wife from her stool at the bar before she had a chance to protest.

"I don't think so," she said.

"One dance and I'll leave you alone," tattoo woman said.

"Sure, whatever," The Doctor's Wife agreed as the woman led her to the dance floor.

After an hour and so many drinks she lost count, The Doctor's Wife had loosened up. She had danced with four women and was working on her fifth. The fifth woman was a beauty. She was a gorgeous black woman with salt-and-pepper hair. She had eyes that were a dark, sexy brown, and her lips were full and kissable. She was the color of honey. *Probably tastes just as sweet,* The Doctor's Wife thought. She blinked twice. What the hell was she thinking? *He* was probably at home waiting. *Let him wait.* The Doctor's Wife smiled at her companion.

"You got a name, darlin'?" her drinking partner asked.

The Doctor's Wife thought about it. She didn't have a name. She was always Dr. So-and-so's wife. That is how everyone referred to her. No one ever knew her name. She was just The Doctor's Wife.

"D.W.," she said.

"Macalynn," Macalynn said, holding out her hand. She had a strong, firm grip.

"Nice to meet you, Macalynn."

"What's your story, D.W.?" Macalynn set her brown eyes on The Doctor's Wife.

"Story?" The Doctor's Wife took a long sip of beer and swallowed. Her hazel eyes met Macalynn's, unflinching. "I got no story. Just wanted to drink and relax."

"Of course you have a story." Macalynn motioned around the room. "We all have a story."

Macalynn leaned closer to The Doctor's Wife. Her breasts peeked out from under her silk blouse. The Doctor's Wife pulled her eyes back to Macalynn's. "Your story is, you're a lonely housewife. Your kids have all left the house. You spend your days watching the soaps...make that the talk shows. Your husband's an accountant...no, a doctor. You look like a doctor's wife. He's off performing some major surgery, the fourth one this week."

"Go on." The Doctor's Wife smiled, amused.

"He hasn't touched you in weeks."

The Doctor's Wife's eyes narrowed.

Macalynn smiled. She had hit a nerve. "Maybe even months."

The Doctor's Wife's jaw tightened.

"So you got in your car, a silver Mercedes, and decided to see how the rest of us like to play. Am I right?"

"I should be going." The Doctor's Wife placed a ten-dollar bill on the bar and stood. Macalynn's brown hand covered hers. The Doctor's Wife saw she wore no rings on her hands.

"What's the rush, gorgeous? We're just getting to know each other," Macalynn teased. "I'll bet you're just dying to know what it's like to have another woman's tongue in your mouth, her soft naked breast against your skin." Macalynn stood. "Come with me." She held out her hand to The Doctor's Wife.

"Where are you gonna take me?" Doctor's Wife played along. She was starting to feel bold. *Why the hell not? Couldn't be any worse than with him.*

"I'm going to show you how I like to play."

The Doctor's Wife let herself be taken slowly. She knew her seducer wanted to prolong the moment. The Doctor's Wife was going to be begging.

The Doctor's Wife accepted the hungry mouth that was attacking hers. The thick tongue tickled her own. Hot, wet kisses were drenching her face and neck. Macalynn grabbed both of her ass cheeks and squeezed...hard. The Doctor's Wife winced. Her moist panties were being pulled down. She stepped out of them. Her butt pressed against the cold door of the bathroom stall. Macalynn slid a long finger in The Doctor's Wife's creamy center. She was already wet. The Doctor's Wife sucked in her breath, her fingernails digging into Macalynn's shoulders.

"You like that?" Macalynn asked, her voice low.

The Doctor's Wife nodded.

"Say it. Say, 'I like it,'" Macalynn said.

"I...I like it."

Macalynn slid her finger out. "Open your mouth."

The Doctor's Wife parted her lips slightly and sucked. She ran her tongue over the length of the finger.

Macalynn took her finger out of The Doctor's Wife's mouth.

"That's what you taste like. Sweet, I bet. You like the way you taste?"

"Yes."

Macalynn stepped back and sat on the toilet. "Take off your blouse slowly. One button at a time."

The Doctor's Wife did as she was told. She unbuttoned the first button, her fingers easily slipping it out of its hole. The others came out just as easily. She dropped her blouse on the tile floor, revealing large round breasts. She straightened her posture to make her breasts look perky and firm. The Doctor's Wife's round large tits had began to sag as the years rolled by. She held Macalynn's gaze, hoping the woman wouldn't see her sudden self-consciousness. The Doctor's Wife had skin the color of coffee, no cream. Macalynn licked her finger and circled a chocolate nipple until it stood erect.

"Beautiful."

"Thank you," The Doctor's Wife said.

"Don't speak unless I tell you to." Macalynn focused her sexy brown eyes on the ripe nipple that stood at attention, ready for the plucking. She took it in her mouth and sucked hard, grazing it with her teeth. The Doctor's Wife stroked her hair. She gave Macalynn her belly, and Macalynn accepted. The Doctor's Wife was delighted in the pleasure of the tongue on her belly button. Macalynn withdrew her mouth, leaving a trail of saliva on The Doctor's Wife.

"Take off your skirt."

The Doctor's Wife let her skirt fall to the floor. She stood completely nude save for her black heels and wedding ring.

"So beautiful," Macalynn murmured. She ran her hand down the length of The Doctor's Wife's slender body. She grabbed The Doctor's Wife's hips and brought them inches from her face. "You want this?"

"Yes, please. Now."

Macalynn pushed her away and stood. She got behind The Doctor's Wife and bent her over the toilet. The Doctor's Wife gripped the back of the seat, her round ass in the air. She felt Macalynn's hand slap her butt like it was a basketball. She bit her lip but didn't make a sound.

"Good girl." Macalynn stroked her hair as if stroking a kitty.

The Doctor's Wife heard a snapping noise. She looked over her shoulder and saw that Macalynn had taken out two white latex gloves from her purse. She was pulling the second one over her hand. She squeezed a big glob of lubricant over a hand, oiling it well. She whispered into The Doctor's Wife's ear.

"Relax."

The Doctor's Wife tensed. She had expected to feel the force of a hand pushing its way into her body. Instead, she was rewarded with the cool stroke of a quick tongue sliding up the crack of her ass, lips sucking on her asshole. She felt the pinch of teeth biting her moon-shaped butt cheeks. Macalynn ran her tongue up the length of The Doctor's Wife's arched back.

She hovered over her ear, whispering, "Hold on."

The Doctor's Wife held her breath as the hand invaded her delicate virgin membrane. She felt the muscles of her sphincter contracting, trying to accommodate the raid into previously uncharted territory. Her eyes rolled back in her head as the hand balled into a fist. She felt her ass opening wider as it moved deeper inside of her. There was a spot a few inches up her ass that made The Doctor's Wife moan with delight because it felt divine as Macalynn probed her. It hurt, but *fuck*, it was feeling so *good*. Macalynn must have been in up to her elbow.

Her pleasure surged when, with her other hand, Macalynn glided a long finger up and down the shaft of her engorged clitoris, playing roughly with her.

She could feel the pressure of Macalynn's body on her back. Her breath was hot on The Doctor's Wife's neck.

"Want me to stop?" Macalynn asked in a throaty voice. She was teasing her. The Doctor's Wife knew she wouldn't stop now.

"No, please don't," The Doctor's Wife begged.

"Play with your nipple," Macalynn said.

The Doctor's Wife let go of the seat and gently fondled her nipple.

"Harder," Macalynn ordered.

The Doctor's Wife pinched her nipple between her fingers. She rolled the hard black button as if she were kneading dough. Macalynn's body pressed into hers. Her ass and cunt were on fire with pleasure. She could feel the wetness of her lubrications as she was fucked harder and faster. He would never do this to her. She wanted to come.

"Oh, God. Oh, God." Her heart raced. "Feels so good," she said through gasps. "I wanna come."

"Come, baby." Macalynn pumped The Doctor's Wife's delicious butt and juicy pussy.

The Doctor's Wife was in a frenzy. Her ass ground against Macalynn's hand. "I wanna come. I wanna come now." The Doctor's Wife spread her legs farther, allowing Macalynn's hands to go deeper inside her openings.

"Come on, baby. Come on," Macalynn urged, pumping harder. Her mouth sucked on The Doctor's Wife's neck. She bit gently.

"Now!" The Doctor's Wife felt the rush of the orgasm coming on.

"Yes, now!" Macalynn hissed in her ear.

The Doctor's Wife's grip on the toilet seat was so tight, her knuckles turned white. Her body jerked and convulsed in spasms. The muscles in her ass and cunt squeezed and contracted as Macalynn pounded intensely inside her. Her body shook like Jell-O. She came all over Macalynn's hands.

Macalynn slowly slipped her hand out of The Doctor's Wife's bottom. The Doctor's Wife gasped as the hand slid out of her tender ass. Macalynn pulled off the glove and tossed it into the waste can for sanitary napkins. The hand that had been in The Doctor's Wife's cunt went to Macalynn's mouth. She sucked each of her gloved fingers like they were lollipops. "Turn around," she said to The Doctor's Wife. "Good?"

"Yes." The Doctor's Wife's chest heaved up and down as her breathing settled. There was a tingly sensation in her asshole.

Macalynn bent down and picked up the clothing on the floor.

"Get dressed." Her eyes never left The Doctor's Wife as she got dressed. "So, now you know how I like to play."

"I wanna play again," The Doctor's Wife said. She hoped she didn't sound like she was begging, which she was.

"Hmm." Macalynn's dark brown eyes rested on The Doctor's Wife. "Maybe."

She leaned in closer to The Doctor's Wife and kissed her on the lips. Her tongue tickled the roof of The Doctor's Wife's mouth.

The Doctor's Wife pulled Macalynn's lean body closer to hers, their crotches grinding into each other. Macalynn pulled away and kissed her on the cheek. With that she turned on her heel and left the bathroom stall and the bathroom.

The Doctor's Wife went to the sink and splashed cold water on her face. Her face was still flushed. She washed her hands and grabbed a paper towel. Two younger women entered the bathroom. They ignored her as they entered an empty stall together. The Doctor's Wife closed her eyes and listened to the sounds of heavy kissing and the beginning of what was going to be fierce sex. She tossed the paper towel into the garbage and left.

The Doctor's Wife's husband had not returned from the hospital when she got home. She headed for bed, skipping her shower. She stripped to her birthday suit and climbed into bed. The black satin sheets were cool against her skin and tender ass. She could still smell Macalynn on her body. Her hand went to her breast and played with her nipple, hard. With her other hand she slipped her middle finger into the garden between her thighs, running it over the head of her clitoris. She was still wet. The Doctor's Wife slid her finger out and sucked on it until it was dry.

Sweet.

Showtime
by Lesléa Newman

I love to watch them watch you. I stand in the back, leaning against the wall, with one foot crossed in front of the other, arms folded, left over right. You are up onstage, of course, warming up the crowd in a fitted black jacket and tuxedo pants with a sexy silk stripe running down either side. You're wearing a white shirt and a burgundy tie, which you tied yourself this evening. Remember, it was I who taught you how to tie a tie. It was I who untwisted the knots your clumsy fingers made, who laughed as you cursed every time you didn't get it right. It was I who taught you to perfect your butch look, to swagger across the stage, to smile at the crowd and wink with one eye.

Your brush cut stands tall, short on the sides, long in front, stiffened with pomade. Only I know what it feels like to run my fingers through your crowning glory. Only I know how that stiff hair feels against the inside of my silken thigh.

Music fills the room, and you open your mouth and begin the first song. Women gasp, they swoon, they inch closer to the stage in one hungry wave. I can practically hear the disbelief churning through their minds: "A woman as gorgeous as that can sing too?" A femme in tight black Lycra wipes her chin with the heel of her hand as if she's drooling over you. She wouldn't be the first. Another femme sticks her tongue out as if she's panting like a dog.

You work the mike like it's an oversized clit, drawing it close to your lips, your tongue, caressing it with your hands, all the while singing words of love. I can feel all the butches in the room break out into a sweat. They know they're in deep, deep trouble. How many of their femmes will wish they were going home with you tonight? How many of them will imagine it's you kissing them, you undressing them, you laying them down softly on the bed, or you taking them roughly against the wall? How many of them will actually say, "Why aren't you more like *her*?" and gloat at the hurt the question brings to their butch's eyes? And how many of the butches will say to their femmes in a moment of self-doubt, "Am I as butch as *she* is?" knowing that the answer, "Yes, dear," is as transparent as Saran Wrap, an out-and-out lie.

I watch you flirt with a femme in the front, close to the stage. You pretend you're singing to her, only to her. You drop down on one knee and extend your right arm. You pretend she's everything you've ever wanted and more. You will never hurt her. You will never lie to her. You will never leave her. You will fuck her into ecstasy each and every single night of her entire life. You will never fight with her over stupid things like money or the dishes. You are beyond all that. Your life is pure and simple lust. Nothing else matters. You will never say things like "I'm too tired" or "Honey, do you have to be so goddamn loud?"

The femme is dripping wet, watching you. Her eyes are as big as nipples. She's wondering if you mean it, if she should go backstage afterward and rap on your dressing-room door. Every girl in the room wishes she were that femme in the front. You take her to the edge, reaching out with your fingertips as if to stroke her face, and then in a split second you turn and focus all your attention on someone else in the crowd. Every girl thinks she has a chance with you. Every girl is wondering, *Could I just ditch my butch for the night, let her fuck my brains out, and then go home in the morning with everything just like it was before?* Only everything won't be like it was before. Believe me, I know.

You finish the set and promise to return. As you disappear backstage I wander through the crowd, listening. I like to hear what they say about you.

"I'd drink her bathwater," sighs a femme with a Southern accent.

"I'd die to lick her shoes," says another.

I notice the butches standing up a little taller, being more assertive, jostling each other as they wait at the bar for a beer. They don't fool me for a second, or their femmes, who are still mooning over you, the stage a magnet for their eager, impatient eyes.

The houselights go down, and the music goes up, promises you are about to appear. All the femmes jockey for position near the front of the stage. The butches roll their eyes at each other and hurry to claim their turf, to stand behind their femmes with their arms around their waists as if to say, You belong to me, baby, a fact that many a femme would just as soon momentarily forget.

This is the part of the show I like best. I'm almost drooling with anticipation. You make them wait for it. First they're standing quietly, politely; then they begin to clap and cheer; and then, just before that split second when their eagerness turns to annoyance, you emerge. Like everything else about you, your timing is perfect.

As always there's a pause, a heartbeat of silence, and then they gasp. Is it really you? It's really you, my darling. You, transformed in a tight, black, glittery gown that shows off your to-die-for figure, complemented with elbow-length gloves and three-inch heels. Your hair is brushed out and fluffy, and there is a hint of mascara on your eyes. You are not a parody of yourself, not an exaggeration like Dolly Parton or RuPaul. No, you are truly, utterly beautiful.

Now it's the femmes who are getting nervous as their butches relax. The butches puff out their chests, hold their chins high, surge forward as their femmes hold them back, hooking their hands into the crook of their butches' arms, as if to say, You belong to me, baby, a fact that many a butch would like to momentarily forget.

You begin to sing, and as you do you slink across the stage, perfectly at home in those three-inch heels. Only I know how many weeks it took for you to master that walk; it was I who taught you, who nursed your twisted ankles, who laughed as you cursed every time you fell. It was I who taught you to wiggle those hips; it was I who taught you to bat those eyes.

You pick a butch from the audience and wag your finger at her. She tries to step forward, but her legs are shaking. Her pals clap her on the back; even her femme, who's frowning, lets go of her arm. She's being a good sport, but they'll have words later, you can be sure. You hold out your arm, an invitation, and bring the butch up onstage. You place her behind you and wrap her arms around your waist. You sway as you sing, and she sways with you. You move one of her hands up to your breast and let it linger there for a minute before you slap it away, pretending indignation.

But you got your point across by the look on the butch's face. It tells the audience what they want to know: You're just like Coca-Cola, baby. The real thing.

You indulge the butch for a minute more and then shove her offstage with a playful push and reach out your arm, beckoning to another, all the while singing words of love. The new butch bounds up onstage and takes her position behind you. You turn your head to gaze into her eyes through half-closed lids and pretend to sing to her, only to her. Your eyes and your body are saying that you will never hurt her. You will never lie to her. You will never leave her. You will fuck her into ecstasy each and every single night of her life. You will never fight with her over stupid things like money or the dishes. You are beyond all that. Your life is pure and simple lust. Nothing else matters. You will never say things like "I'm too tired" or "Honey, do you have to be so goddamn loud?"

And now it's the femmes in the house who are getting nervous. The ones who wore pants tonight are cursing themselves for not wearing a skirt. They pat their hair, wipe their thumbs around their mouths to clear away any smudges of lipstick. They know they'd better keep their big mouths shut tonight. The question "Why aren't you as butch as *she* is?" can now easily be answered: "I don't know. Why aren't you as *femme* as she is?" For the butches are enthralled. Every one of them is dripping wet, watching you. Every girl in the room wishes she was that butch standing behind you, who is wondering at this very moment, *Could I just ditch my femme for the night, fuck* her *brains out, and then go home in the morning with everything just like it was before?* Again, the answer is no.

After several encores you bid the audience good night.

That's my cue, and I hurry through the crowd, for I'm the lucky one who gets to go backstage and help you out of the dress. I'm the one who gets to watch you wipe all that makeup off your gorgeous face and slip your perfect body into a T-shirt and jeans. I'm the one who gets to go home with you, make love with you, sleep next to you all night long. I'm the one who gets to see you looking less than perfect with sleep goop in the corners of your eyes, your hair all sticking up on one side, the side you slept on, like a baby bird. I'm the one who gets to argue with you about the grocery bill, the clothes left on the floor, the letter you forget to send to your mother. I'm the one who gets to hear about your insecurities, your fears, your desires. I'm the one who gets to see through the illusion, who knows you are so much more than they think you are.

But not tonight. Tonight you are the star, and the real show is about to begin. That show in the bar is just foreplay, after all. The minute we're in the house, we're all over each other, wet with the power of desire. All those women wanting what they can't have. You, my darling, neither butch nor femme tonight. Only mine. We kiss each other hungrily as we make our way down the hall to the bedroom, shedding clothes as we go. Your jacket lands on the kitchen table, my sweater on the living room floor. My breast finds your mouth; your fingers find my thigh. You lift me onto the bed and lay down gently beside me. Finally we are together, naked, a little breeze ruffling our skin through the open window. We touch each other everywhere, fingers stroking, mouths caressing, skin on fire. When we enter each other, as if on cue, you sing out to me, and I sing back. I'm the only one who gets to croon a duet with you. And even though I can't sing to save my life and your voice is a gift from on high, our fingers find their slippery rhythm, and our songs meld together in one long chord of perfect harmony.

After we catch our breath, I ask for an encore, and as you comply I clap my thighs around your beautiful head while you sing a song my body loves. I want to give you the standing ovation you deserve, but my legs are too weak to hold me, so I pull you up to look at your face, so close, so naked, so dear. I stare into your eyes and see my own tiny reflection mirrored there; I know you also see yourself in me. Our mutual-admiration society is more important to you than a thousand fans will ever be. But that little secret is safe with me. Basking in each other's love, we draw the curtain of darkness around us tightly and sleep.

Disco Nights
by Mariana Romo-Carmona

Neny was a timid girl, especially each time she walked
into the Evergreen, the new bar where the jukebox was
stocked with all the latest disco and a woman might ask her
to dance as soon as she took off her coat. She'd have to
shrug and smile and pretend she was sore from playing softball to slide away from all the glittery women, the after-
work crowd in their two-piece office suits that so easily became disco skirts. It wasn't that she didn't like disco; it was
easier to dance than salsa anyway, and she was the only
Latina west of the Connecticut River who couldn't do salsa,
lead or follow. But she was shy.

She almost wanted to return to the old bar, The Lib,
where the jukebox had hardly anything she'd want to hear
except maybe Patsy Cline, but when Neny walked into the
dark hovel nobody even looked at her, and she was safe.
There was no dancing at The Lib anyhow, except maybe by
the pool table in between games, when all the butches
would take a break and hold their femme girlfriends tight,
their cigarettes lining the edge of the table, burning a hole
into the wood. And that wasn't dancing—it was hugging,
making out; it was feeling the length and breadth of the
woman they loved for a few minutes, before getting back to

the interminable tournament. Not a bad way to be, but Neny had been lured to the new place too like all the other younger dykes: to the bigger space; the frozen, pretty drinks; the bathroom with a big mirror in it; and the friendlier atmosphere. The new bar made everyone feel like the dark ages were over and people could be young and queer if they wanted to, without having to hide in some joint where the bouncer was a man. At least at the Evergreen, the bouncer was a woman too: Marylou, with her pack of Camels rolled up into the sleeve of her T-shirt.

So this evening, Neny rode around on the bike once more, once around the block, feeling her legs getting crampy since she'd been riding for two hours already, waiting for it to get dark so she could get to the bar. It was the summer days, so long since she had nothing to do but work at the bakery with her mother, play softball with the jock girls, and then go to the bar. And fantasize about somebody, because Neny had decided she'd never fall in love for real again. It hurt too much. She was too easy, too soft, with her baby face, freckles, and black spiky hair that no amount of dippity-do was going to tame; and her big hands, brown arms, all achy for a girl to hold, a woman. She had to stop this fantasizing and riding around at the same time, though; it didn't take much for Neny to get all excited on the bike, riding over the Hartford streets, making her underwear so wet she'd have to go home and change before going into the Evergreen.

She locked her bike on the fence and took her cigarettes out of the seat pouch. Neny didn't smoke much, but she was tall and lanky, and what was she going to do? She had to smoke to hold something, since she looked horrible in a disco dress holding a purse. She fixed her purple bandanna in the back pocket of her jeans and prepared herself to saunter in. Marylou was watching from the door.

"That's $2—" she told Neny.

"What?" Neny's heart nearly stopped.

"Just teasing you, kid! You're never here late enough for me to charge you cover. Get in there and watch you don't eat all the peanuts off the bar before the customers arrive."

Marylou could be cruel. She slapped Neny's behind as she walked in. Neny tried to play it cool, peering inside for someone she knew, but then she could hardly see anything, since her eyes hadn't adjusted to the darkness of the bar.

By 11:30 the place was so crowded there was a constant line by the bathroom and nobody could move more than five inches in any direction on the dance floor. There was a choice of standing or dancing in line, which worked well when everybody was doing the hustle, and there was no difference between the women dancing and the ones just standing there, holding a beer, watching. That's what Neny waited for, when there would be no pressure and she could pretend to sway while trying to learn the steps, pushed by the feminine wave that carried her to and fro.

Meanwhile, the music had reached the level when conversation is impossible except in short bursts. Donna Summer crooned about getting some hot stuff this evening, along with everybody else in the bar, including Neny, who was nursing her second beer and beginning to feel bold.

Mouthing the words to the song, Neny was suddenly enveloped from behind by Alma, the hottest dancer and the nattiest dresser in the place. Even the jock girls acknowledged that Alma cleaned up good when she got out of work and headed for the bar.

One song glided into another, and everybody oohed and sighed in unison.

"Come on, dance with me, Neny!" Alma was wearing a pale blue polyester dress that shimmered and hugged her body like a glove—a pair of them, one over each breast, thought Neny, feeling a little dizzy. Alma had three long gold chains around her smooth neck, which twirled when she did and then nestled conveniently when she shimmied, golden-brown arms by her side, a little salsa shake of the shoulders for good measure. Neny lost her mind and did what Alma told her, letting herself be led until the last echoes of the famous Donna Summer orgasm had stopped ringing in her ears. Alma twirled Neny one last time and seizing her by the shoulders, placed a coral kiss right on her lips, saying, "Thank you, Neny, that was great!" before disappearing toward the bathroom line. Neny was heartbroken but elated, and now with nothing to do she decided to head for the bathroom.

This time she got in surprisingly quickly. Alma wasn't there, and one stall was actually free, the other full with seven girls sniffing coke and gossiping. And the only woman sitting on the bathroom vanity, looking into the mirror to apply more mascara, was Evelina, who acknowledged Neny with a weak "Hey" and went back to the tissues and makeup.

Neny used the bathroom and considered she'd done all right for the evening. She might as well go home and fantasize some more.

"Hey, Neny, *pásame un poco de toilet paper, por favor.*" A hand reached out under the stall to her right. Neny wadded up some to give her.

"Why don't you speak English—you're in America now." Neny recognized Karen's voice, the pitcher from her softball team.

"Listen, *gringuita,*" came the response. "You're in here doing coke with us, so you gotta speak Spanish, OK?"

"OK."

"Hey, Neny, you wanna do a line, *m'hija?*"

"No, *gracias,* Quela, you know that stuff makes me nervous." Neny zipped up her jeans and went to wash her hands. Evelina was still there, blowing her nose.

"Evelina."

"Neny."

"Evelina, you crying?"

"Nope," said Evelina, tears streaming down her face and ruining her mascara. Her round face and full lips were all flushed and pouty, making her look like a sad little girl. Neny wanted to hug Evelina, to comfort her somehow, but she wasn't sure if she should.

"Well, where's Carmen?"

"At work. She'll be here soon," Evelina sniffed.

"OK, don't cry. Coming to the game on Sunday?"

But the answer was obliterated by the magnificent seven exiting the stall, high as kites and ready to party.

"Ooh, girl!"

"Tell me about it—"

Neny decided she was hungry and decided to make one last pass by the bar to see if there were any more peanuts or Chex mix. It was before 1, and she knew that things were just beginning to get good, but she couldn't hang with it. The jock girls called her over from a table to sit with them, but she just gave them a practiced smile and took refuge by the barstools. The black girls had arrived, and there was some hot dancing going on between them and the Italian regulars. The peanut bowls were empty, and Neny felt deflated. She didn't belong anywhere. She could run and steal bases; that was her calling in life.

Just then the music ended and there was a lull in the heated night. Neny looked up and saw Carmen, Evelina's girlfriend, walking in the bar. Alma and Quela joined her.

"Awright! The Latin mafia is here!" one of the regulars yelled near the bathroom. "Now we're gonna get some music!"

Indeed, Carmen and company squared shoulders and sauntered to the bar to talk to the manager. Carmen, with her square face and square haircut and square manners, who always got exactly what she wanted. Alma and Quela simply crossed their arms and waited patiently by the bar. A new bowl of Chex mix appeared magically on the counter. Neny knew that even though the manager, Gloria from Peoria, the toughest dyke in the free world and loyal fan of Barbra Streisand—hence the name of the bar—would dig in her heels for a while, claiming that salsa was too new and nobody really knew how to dance to it, eventually Carmen would prevail. If Gloria authorized the playing of three Latin tunes, it was a major victory. It was also the only time Neny felt proud, and giddy, even if she couldn't dance.

Neny stayed for as long as her growling stomach let her. It was a three-tune night, and Carmen was soon holding her adorable girlfriend, Evelina, and twirling her, leading her in an increasingly complicated set of erotic passes and sweeps that showed off Evelina's curves, generous and graceful, and Carmen's own practiced, steady moves that drove all the femme girls crazy. There was Alma, dancing up a storm with Quela, who came a close second to Carmen in terms of being *muy* butch and impenetrable. *And to think I got a kiss from Alma tonight*, thought Neny. Then everyone else lost their fear and joined in, swinging, shaking, and shimmying their booty for all it was worth, until Gloria deemed it was time to bring back the Bee Gees and calm everybody down.

"Wow, Carmen is hot!" someone said to Neny's right.

"Nah, it's Evelina who's hot!" said the woman to her left. Neny was stuck in between a serious gossip session, because as usual people didn't even know she was there. She stood still.

"Yeah, but Carmen knows what she's doing: She calls the shots."

"When they're dancing, OK, I agree with you. But when you get them in the sack, I hear she's a yawn."

"You're kidding!"

"Nope. She's the kind who rolls over and hands her lover a vibrator."

"No!"

Neny's ears were burning. Is that why Evelina was crying in the bathroom? *Enough,* she thought, *it's late and Mami's going to wake me up at 6 to go to the bakery.* Time to go home.

The afternoon light streamed in and bathed the room in waves from the rain on the windows. Evelina slid her hips a little farther under Carmen's hands, raised her right thigh a little higher, and waited for her girlfriend's breathing to get a little more rapid. She thought this might be the time; she felt excited and wet, all elastic with desire and tenderness. She felt generous and open, but then everything about her was that way; her spirit, her body, rounded, soft, from her breasts to the smooth heels of her size 5½ feet.

"Evelina?" Carmen was happy, her square jaw and her shiny black hair nestled in the curve between Evelina's neck and the rising line of Evelina's breast. Carmen grasped Evelina's hips and gently turned her over on top of herself, sighing languorously at the silky impact of their skin blending together. Carmen closed her eyes and let Evelina take over. Evelina opened hers and took in Carmen's features, smiling placidly, her dark eyebrows perfectly shaped against her light skin, turning her head against the pillow and showing off the profile that Evelina had once thought noble. No, it wasn't going to be this time.

Everyone thought Carmen was such a butch and envied Evelina for having it so good, but there was much more to it than having it good, thought Evelina as she initiated the familiar journey down Carmen's body. First here, then there, then some kissing around the belly button and she would be screaming with those short little yells. Damn it, why did it have to be so easy? Evelina wrapped her arms around Carmen and lost herself in the moment, feeling again open and giving. It was, after all, something in her power to give and to do it well: to slide her breasts on Carmen's, to let her hair down to tickle the inside of Carmen's well-toned thighs, to tease along those legs with her tongue until she herself was ready to dip her tongue in the right place and move it fast, slow, sideways, up and down, then still, then push once, twice—that's it.

She placed her head slowly down on Carmen's breast, feeling satisfied but still excited, waiting.

"Mmm, baby, that was so nice," whispered Carmen.

Evelina slid up on the bed, brushing against her lover's body, opening her brown eyes and reclining her face on Carmen's shoulder.

"Carmen?" She cooed, placing Carmen's right hand against her mound.

"Oh, Evelina, you know I can't get into that now. I gotta get to work, babe." Carmen slid out of the bed and headed toward the bathroom.

"But, Carmen, I want—" Evelina began.

"You want me to pay the bills, don't you, honey? Come on, you know where the vibrator is. I'll see you tonight."

Slam, went the front door, and crash, went the vibrator against the full-length bedroom mirror.

"Pay the damn bills," yelled Evelina to herself, because Carmen was gone and there was no one else to yell at. "Well, maybe I should quit the damn Wilbur Beauty Academy and enroll at Trinity College; then she can really pay some damn bills." Evelina put on her white terry-cloth robe and went to the kitchen to get herself a piece of Italian bread and butter. She pulled the butter dish out of the refrigerator, then sat on the counter as was her habit, dangling her feet, reaching for the bread and the fresh smell that came out of the paper bag. She opened the pink butter dish so it would soften, but she couldn't wait. She thought she'd call Alma to talk about her troubles, and she picked up the green wall phone but realized Alma wouldn't be home. She herself should be at the school, practicing the Vidal Sasson bob, but she'd stayed home, hoping... Evelina got down off the counter, stuffing a soft piece of bread into her mouth, thinking she should go in the bedroom and clean up all the glass from the broken mirror, then maybe take a bath to calm down.

It was completely dark out, and the candle had burned all the way down. Evelina didn't know how long she'd been in the bathtub, but the water had cooled considerably. She thought she'd get out, yet she wanted to lie there a little longer, spreading the droplets of water and bath oil over her cinnamon knees, her rounded belly, the breasts that spilled easily over her rib cage and got tickled by the edges of the warm water. She had cleaned the apartment, picked up all the glass and tried the vibrator even, but it was busted. *Good,* she thought. Ever since Carmen had gotten to be the manager at the steak house on the Silas Deane highway, there was no point in going to bed with her. *What was the point?* Evelina asked herself. Her girlfriend got more of a kick from getting people to do things than from sex. The guys at the grill, the wine steward, the waitresses, even Gloria from Peoria at the Evergreen. She just liked to give orders, play the butch, but when she got into bed…nothing.

But Evelina had felt sorry too for breaking the mirror. She'd started to make zucchini bread from scratch; a special corn dish, *pasteles;* and beef stew Cuban style, just to please Carmen. She sat up in the bathtub, thinking about the mess she'd left on the kitchen table, on the counters, all the plantains, corn husks, and the zucchini. She squeezed off the water from her hair, wrapped the long curls into a towel, and stepped back into the white robe. Just then, the doorbell rang.

"Who is it?" She ran on her bare feet, calling toward the door.

"Um," said Neny when Evelina opened it.

"Oh, it's you. What's wrong?"

"Nothing, I thought I'd see if, I mean last night, and you know, well, practice was rained out, I can come back if you—"

"Oh, get in here—I don't care. Come in, keep me company."

"Where's Carmen?" Neny asked, looking all around.

"Is that all you can say? She's at work, where she always is. Come in the kitchen; I'm making bread."

"What's with all the *guineos?*" Neny took off her leather cap, adjusted the lace on her sneakers, then plunged her hands into the pockets of her shorts. Evelina's robe was opening, and Neny could see the cleavage that existed only in her fantasies.

"That was going to be *pasteles*. Sit down, I'll make you some *café con leche*."

"Why were you crying last night?" Neny thought she'd gone crazy. What else would she be doing asking a question like that?

Evelina stopped on her way to the stove. She turned around and looked at Neny, who looked back at her with concern in her sweet, freckled face. "Ay, Neny!" She rushed into Neny's arms and hugged her, gratefully. "You're so sweet!"

Neny held Evelina for the longest time, smelling the bath oil on her neck and the shampoo from her hair when the towel fell off and feeling the warmth that came through Evelina's robe. Without knowing why, Neny started to kiss Evelina's hair, saying softly to her, "It's OK, Evelina, I'm here, I'm here."

Until the phone rang. Evelina jumped out of Neny's arms to get it. Neny wanted to apologize for something but she didn't know what. Maybe there was nothing. She watched Evelina spring up on the counter to get the phone. It was Alma. Neny sat down on a chair and watched.

After a few minutes Neny was intently watching Evelina on the phone because it was a beautiful sight to see. Evelina was completely absorbed in the call, looking away, twirling her hair with her left hand while she held the phone with her right. She had raised her left knee up, and her small left foot was planted flat on the counter. Her left arm rested on her knee, and the robe had slipped down the side of her leg, but nothing, nothing showed. Neny couldn't see how this was possible. She looked again. Nothing. *The robe was open at the neck and at least Evelina's breasts must be in there,* thought Neny.

"Alma, why didn't you tell me about this?" Evelina was saying. "Oh, wow, that's crazy!" And then she saw Neny looking at her, realizing that she was sitting on the counter the way she always did. But now she was in her robe, naked. A rush of her upbringing invaded her momentarily, then left her. She looked at Neny, eyes half-closed and those long eyelashes shading the girl's pretty, freckled face. Evelina switched the phone from one hand to the other, stretching, letting the robe fall a little more open until her right breast was completely visible. Neny froze on the chair. Evelina stretched her back and started to raise her right leg up the counter. Neny almost fell off her chair then.

"Oh, please, you don't expect me to believe that!" Evelina said into the phone. Neny got up and walked toward her. Evelina kept talking. Neny looked into Evelina's eyes and waited.

"Mm-hmm…?" said Evelina and switched the phone back to her right hand, leaving her neck exposed. Neny bent to kiss it, and she was hooked. There was no way she could lift her face from that neck, from Evelina's shoulder, any more than she could deny her own name. So she steadied herself by reaching for Evelina's breasts and trying to be as quiet as she could. It was a tacit agreement.

"Ooh, no!" cried Evelina into the phone, because she didn't have to be quiet at all. She felt Neny's hands gyrating slowly over her breasts, the girl's thumbs and forefingers pulling gently on her nipples with such precision, Evelina was amazed she couldn't remember ever having looked at Neny before, not this way, definitely not this way.

"Oh, stop!" she gasped into Alma's ear, who chattered on, unconcerned and totally uninformed.

Neny felt she was about to start moaning loudly, so she bent down lower and began to roll her tongue over Evelina's breasts, wrapping it around each nipple and sucking as though the nipple was a raisin protruding out of a cinnamon roll. On the phone, Evelina was talking fast, God only knew about what, but it seemed to steady her, and Neny kept licking and sucking until she was too dizzy to stand up.

"Girl, you better tell me everything!" Evelina commanded, and Neny knelt on the floor and undid the robe, quickly, taking hold of Evelina's left leg and placing it over her shoulder in case she got tired.

"Go on—" said Evelina, and Neny didn't wait to bury her face in paradise. Evelina's black pubic hair was wet, very silky, and tasted and smelled like a cornucopia of flavors. Salt, bath oil, tangy wetness.

"Oh, my god! I can't stand it!" said Evelina weakly, supporting herself on Neny's shoulders. "Hurry up, get to the point!" And Neny did, twirling her tongue again, only more gently, to find Evelina's clitoris.

"That's it, *muchacha,* you're killin' me!" cried Evelina, and then she was quiet for a long time while Neny applied pressure and long strokes on the sides of her labia, her clitoris, the edges of her vagina. Evelina was so turned on she wanted to explode, and yet she didn't want the moment to end. She felt every part of her body sizzling in an erotic vibration that sent her higher each second, and she wanted to play it to the hilt, but she knew she was either going to have to stop or lose consciousness or come and end everything right there. She slammed the phone in the cradle in the middle of Alma's question about her state of mind and hoisted herself with both hands to get closer to Neny's mouth. Except her left hand landed in the butter dish and sent the cover flying across the kitchen floor.

"Uh?" said Neny, her mouth moving kind of slow.

"It's just the butter," Evelina told her, contemplating the gob of it she had on her fingers.

Neny got up again and kissed Evelina, who tasted her own juices and decided to spread the butter on Neny's face and neck, then her own breasts. Neny's knees buckled watching the spreading of the butter, pleading, "Evelina, I have to make you come!" She picked Evelina up in her arms and stumbled to the table, where she tried to make some room, but Evelina didn't care. The robe served well enough, and she laid her head carefully on an ear of corn, while Neny straddled her and held her steady with those long legs of hers. Evelina now moaned and sighed freely and let Neny spread the rest of the butter all over her until she got to licking again, gasping for air because the girl was too excited for words.

"Faster, faster, Neny!" sighed Evelina, and Neny obliged, considering at the same time one of the zucchinis on the table, but since she already had so much butter on her hands, she easily pushed three fingers into Evelina's vagina without taking her mouth off her once. *It was amazing how a table facilitated matters,* Neny thought, but she didn't have much time to ponder, because Evelina was coming in waves and she wanted to make sure she caught every one with her tongue.

After a few seconds Neny lifted Evelina off the table and held her on her lap, both of them sitting on a chair, each stroking the other's face, kissing, and sighing slowly.

"Evelina?"

"Hmm?"

"Nothing, I just wanted to say your name."

"Mmm."

"Neny?"

"Yeah?"

"You're going to have to go, baby. I gotta clean this place up."

"I know."

"I'm sorry, I wanted to…" Evelina started to say, because she knew how it felt to be left wanting.

"Oh, don't worry about me; one turn around the block on the bicycle and I'll be off!" Neny laughed. Evelina joined her. Maybe tonight was her night, after all.

When Neny left, Evelina stood in the kitchen for a while, surveying the mess. She wanted to laugh, to dance perhaps. She went into the bathroom to take another bath.

Carmen's turquoise Datsun turned into the driveway with the wipers on. The headlights went off and the door opened as Carmen got out. She'd had a good night at the steak house, and she was in a good mood. She looked up to see that the outside light was out and made a note to change the bulb while she jangled the keys to her first-floor apartment in her hands. But inside, the lights were off in the living room too and in the kitchen, so she turned them on.

"Evelina?" she called. There were corn cobs on the table. Zucchini on the floor. *That's odd,* she thought, and went to get a beer. Then she saw the counter. "Evelina?" she called again. "What happened to the butter?"

The rain had stopped, but the seat on Neny's bicycle was all wet. She retrieved it from under the skinny tree where she'd locked it up a block from Evelina's apartment and wiped the leather with her sleeve. She headed home, taking the long way around down Asylum Avenue, and then deciding to do a turn around Bushnell Park. The streetlights had a haze of moisture and moonlight glowing around them, the park benches glistened with raindrops, and the puddles on the brick sidewalks splashed when the tires of Neny's bicycle rode over them. Her legs felt warm, not cramped at all, and her hands felt powerful somehow, as she watched her fingers gently squeezing the brakes and changing gears. There was a smile on her face.

Shine

By Stephanie Rosenbaum

"The queen," Johnny says, turning over a card. "She's the one you gotta watch for, Mink. Bust your balls every time."

Johnny's trying to teach me to play poker, but so far she says I'm a slow learner. I'm a Libra, see, and we're not big on games of chance. We know too much about the trials of tempting fate.

Lately, though, I haven't been doing too much tempting—of fate or anything else. See, I'm not the kind of girl you'd picture to have a name like Mink. Johnny's girlfriend, Vikki—now that girl could be a Mink. Nails, lips, curves you could get shipwrecked on; Vikki doesn't walk so much as ooze. Her bones just get all liquidy, and she floats into a room like a smoke ring.

Me, I'm small and dark, with skinny wrists and a small, pointed cat's face. My real name's Delilah, and believe it or not my brother's name is Sam. Back in the early '70s when I was born, my parents were on a back-to-the-land trip, living in this Jewish commune in upstate New York. It was considered very righteous to give all the babies Hebrew names, but my parents just went biblical instead. Luckily, my last name is Minkowitz, so I've been called Mink just as long as I can remember. I don't mind, actually; it saved me a lifetime of haircut jokes, and every once in a while I try to live up to it. But growing up with Sam, my uncle Max who lived upstairs, and a mother whose idea of hell was having to get out of her gardening clothes, I'm not exactly up on the fine points of femininity. I'm not built to be looked at. That's a role for the Vikkis of the world, not me.

Johnny's built to be looked at but in a different way. She wears her coppery hair cut short on the sides and spiked up on top, although sometimes she doesn't bother to gel it stiff, and then her head looks close-cropped and velvety. She's got that peachy skin that lucky Irish girls get, just this side of pink, with only a few freckles. But the best part about Johnny is her size. Johnny has some meat on her bones, and those bones are generous. She doesn't apologize for taking up space. In fact, she swaggers, especially when she's decked out in cowboy boots and the kind of pale blue ruffled tuxedo shirts popular with unsuccessful lounge singers in the mid '70s.

Right now she's wearing her favorite boots, which are black and shiny, with a hand of cards—hearts, naturally—fanned out in white and red leather across each side. She's drinking a beer and leaning across the kitchen table to riffle through the cards spread faceup between us. I'm drinking iced tea and chewing on the ice. I usually drink bourbon, but I don't want to scare anyone. Outbutching her would be a bad idea, I think.

Johnny's crowd divides pretty evenly along butch/femme lines. Not that everyone always paired up with their opposite; there was always a couple who liked the boy-boy thing or the girlie girls who didn't mind getting two shades of lipstick all mixed up. I liked what I'd seen of her friends: They had style, and although they took their identities to heart they had a sense of humor about the whole thing. One girl even had a dog collar with a little bone hanging off it that read BUTCH on one side and FEMME on the other. She flipped it around depending on her mood.

But somehow I always felt like the kid sister around them, little Skipper to a roomful of Kens and Barbies. Like today, for example: I was wearing an old green schoolgirl kilt that was unraveling along the edge, a T-shirt that had shrunk and a dark blue sweater that had stretched. And I don't go to Victoria's Secret, OK? I wear white cotton underpants, and I wear them till the elastic stretches out and I can't keep them up around my hips anymore. Vikki wears tiny black lace thongs, I'm sure of it.

But Vikki's not here, and Johnny is. Or rather, I am, since we're sitting in the kitchen of the house Johnny's house-sitting this week, taking care of the plants and five-month-old puppy belonging to the two guys who run the landscaping business where she works.

In front of me Johnny's gathering up the cards. Her fingers wrap around the red-and-black pile and shuffle, cutting and recutting the deck better than any blackjack dealer. Johnny used to play blackjack—not professionally, she'll tell you, but for profit. The cards are snapping and riffling, and I can't seem to take my eyes off Johnny's hands. Her palms are wide, and her fingers are long, with nails cut short. There's a callus on each thumb from the yard work she does, and when I look at them my own hands seem to develop a mind of their own. But quickly I yank my hands back under the table, trapping them under my thighs before Johnny can notice anything.

"OK, we're gonna try five-card stud. That's the basic game. Now, the first rule of poker is, if you have nothing, fold. But if you have something—anything—then milk everyone for everything they're worth. Remember that. Don't bet unless you're willing to soak your partners for every penny they've got. If you can't take money from your friends, then don't play. Or just play for chips." She shrugs. "But chips are for pussies."

My hands are working their way up around my knees again. I slide my chair back to get some more ice. Yes, it's true: I've got a big Vegas-sized crush on Johnny. Every time she pins those turquoise eyes on me, my spine vibrates and I'm acutely aware of every inch of her. Especially her breasts. She carries them carelessly, not like she's shy but like she's just cool with them. Like, yeah, she's got this gorgeous chest, and she knows it, but she's not going to make any big deal about it. At least that's how I read her. Still, it was hopeless. She had Vikki, who looked like Rita Hayworth in thigh-high boots. Why would Johnny need to look at me?

The worst part about this crush is that I haven't got a clue about what to do. What would get her to treat me like anything besides a kid brother? I didn't consider myself butch, exactly, but it seemed like Johnny did, punching me on the arm like she did with her other butch buddies, advising me about boxer shorts and motorcycles, and even, like tonight, going out of her way to teach me things she thought I ought to know.

That's what we were doing tonight: Johnny and five other women played a regular Thursday poker game, and I was being groomed to join them. Like I said, I'm not much of a card player, and gambling is not my forte. Still, this was the first time Johnny had asked me over. She could have been teaching me how to swallow fire or walk on a bed of nails; I didn't care so long as we were alone together, in private.

So far, being across Roy and Bob's kitchen table was much worse for my cool than seeing her and all her friends in a crowded bar. Every minute was like wobbling a loose tooth around with your tongue. It hurts, but you don't exactly want to quit, either.

I sit back down and start chewing on my straw. Johnny flips the cap off another beer. We've gone through the various merits of the royal flush, the royal straight, and both the inside and outside straight.

"See, here you've got a four, a five, and seven and an eight. Alls you need is a six to make an inside straight, which is pretty good." Even though I've had nothing to do with picking the cards in my hand, I'm impressed with my luck. "Except there's only a 4-in-52 chance that a six is going to turn up in your hand when you draw again." Oh. I hadn't thought of it like that. "Now, if you were to do an outside straight, looking for a three as well as a six, then you'd double your chances." She's looking straight at me as she says this, and one hand is rubbing at a spot on her T-shirt, just at the place where the kitchen table meets her ribs.

"What about bluffing?" I ask her, looking right back. "Isn't that the big thing in poker?"

"The way you bluff depends on who you're playing with. Everyone's got their own way of protecting what they've got and letting slip just what they're really holding. You play long enough, you can read that easy. The rest you'll just have to pick up by doing it. So let's play." She shuffles the cards again, the red and black shuddering through her fingers with a snap. "Poker's not really good with just two, but you won't remember any of this unless you play. Here, you deal. Remember, dealer chooses the game." She slides the pack across the table.

OK, Mink, I say to myself. *Let's see if you can bluff through this one.* I push my glasses back up. Out loud, I say, "Seven-card stud. Three rounds." She nods and lifts her beer for another swallow. I deal. Three up, one down.

I glance through my hand. An ace down, a two, another two, and a ten up. "What are you betting?" I ask Johnny. There are no chips on the table. My pockets are empty. Johnny keeps her eyes on her cards, carefully rearranging her three cards, frowning, then moving one card carefully from one side to the other. "Got any money?" she asks, and for a sudden moment I think she's going to offer to lend me a handful of change. But Johnny's a gambler, and gamblers don't bet against their own cash.

I shake my head. There's a long pause. My fingers are unraveling the edge of my skirt.

"Guess we'll just have to play for strip." For a second I don't think I've heard her right. Strip? Strip poker? It's so silly, so frat partyish. But then I catch her cool gaze and understand about bluffing. Is she testing me, seeing what I'll risk, what kind of guts I have? It can't be because maybe, just maybe, she wants to see me naked. I don't want to think about that. Somehow, in all my fantasies about Johnny, my being naked—and looked at—is kind of glossed over. It's not that I just want her to like me for my mind or anything. It's just that scrutiny makes me nervous.

"Sure," I agree. "And the winner? What does she get?"

"Anything she wants," Johnny answers, fingering the queen of spades lying faceup in front of her.

"It's a deal." I look down at my ace of hearts, then over at her queen. Aces are higher than kings, or they can be lower than twos. It just depends on what you need in your hand.

"I win this round, you take off your sweater," she says. Easy. I look at my ace again, then back at her. "And if I win, you take off your shirt," I answer. She's wearing a faded blue work shirt with the sleeves cut off and pearl snaps that gap slightly in the middle. I deal. One up, one down. A king for me, a ten for her.

She takes another pull off her beer and glances over at the clock, looking rattled. This is a girl who's used to winning. But this betting was her idea, and she can't chicken out now without looking coy or, worse, a poor sport.

Toughness wins out, and she unsnaps the first little square white button, taking her own sweet time. Now I know why guys will spend their whole paycheck, dollar by dollar, just to see some woman take off her clothes. I've never watched anything so hard in my life. When she gets to the last snap, I stop breathing. Underneath she's wearing a man's white ribbed undershirt, but no man, not even Marlon Brando in *A Streetcar Named Desire,* ever filled out an undershirt like she does. She's not wearing a bra. Mangos, melons, pomegranates: My mind is a cascading tumble of tropical fruits, and she is ripe for the picking. I want to bounce their taut weight in my hands, feel her warmth, her heart beating faster, brush my lips against the apricot skin at the base of her rounded throat. I want to twist the thin fabric of that undershirt harder and harder, pulling it into a tight knot between her breasts, watching how her nipples prod through the stretched cloth. I want to yank that knot hard and slam her against me, my teeth against her lips, my hand gripping her back. I want to drive every thought of Vikki right out of her head, at least for as long as it takes.

Oblivious to the effects her magnificent butch breasts are having on me, Johnny bets again. "Your sweater—and your shirt." I raise one eyebrow. What cards is she holding?

There's no way to tell; you can't count cards when you're only playing with two.

"Your belt," I counter. Now it's her turn to consider my motives. Her pants—black denim Ben Davises—aren't going to fall off if she unbuckles her belt. In fact, they won't budge. If I really wanted to get an up-close-and-personal view of her boxer shorts, getting that belt off won't do it, and she looks relieved. She won't be breaking her stone stance over a hand of cards, that's for sure.

What she doesn't know is that I have a terrible, terrible hand. A couple of twos, a seven, and a ten. Nothing matches; even the pair is practically worthless. But I've got a king down, and now I've got an ace down as well.

I deal Johnny her last card. She gets a six. I get a seven. She reaches down for her belt. The kitchen is so quiet I can hear the space between the ticks of the clock. The leather slips against the denim, making a sound like water. She rolls the leather strap up in her hand and places it on the table between us. It's warm from her, so lately pressed up against her back, her stomach, the generous curve of her waist.

Last bet, but it's not for clothing this time. I'm still fully dressed. Johnny's breasts are rising and falling, a little faster than they were five minutes ago. A faint line of sweat beads her upper lip. One at a time I lay down my cards. A seven of clubs. A ten of hearts. A couple of twos. A four of clubs. The king of spades. The ace of hearts. Johnny rubs her hand across her mouth. She lays down her cards. A royal flush. The jack of hearts. The queen of spades. Johnny has beat me, but good.

She looks at my cards. She looks at her cards. I look into the dark hollow between her breasts across the table. Johnny gets up and puts her beer bottle on the counter. She puts my iced glass next to it. Then she walks back a few steps until she's leaning up against the stove. She crosses her arms over her chest. She looks at me. I stop breathing again. "Get up on the table," she says.

I don't make her ask me twice. I pull her chair out away from the table, pushing it off to the side. I hoist myself up on the edge of the table where her breasts had been resting just a minute ago and face her across the wide expanse of black and white floor tiles. White, black, white, black, white. Twice. She's ten tiles away. It feels very far. The clock ticks, then ticks again. My breath is still caught in my chest.

"Now," and her voice falls into the silence of the kitchen like a stone sunk into a still river, "now, spread your legs."

What game is this? Here was Johnny, and here I was, but she wasn't kissing me or wrapping me up in her arms or getting into any of the sweaty tangles I'd been imagining in my teenage make-out fantasies. She wasn't even near me. The only thing that was on me was the one thing I didn't want: her eyes, running over me inch by inch. Was this some kind of poker game initiation? I couldn't quite imagine Johnny telling Jesse or Lee or C.J. to spread their legs for her, though. They'd have decked her first. I want to do something with Johnny—I want it desperately—but what I really need to know is just what she wants to do to me. What does she want? A boy? A girl? Someone to flex her muscles over?

There's only one way to find out. My knees open up a few inches. It's not enough. She keeps up that unsmiling stare until my knees are splayed open, pressed flat up against the edge of the table on both sides. She smiles at me then, just a flicker of teeth; then her eyes drop from my face to travel down my body to rest on the hem of my skirt hanging unevenly over my thighs. I hate her doing this, and she knows it. "Pull up your skirt," she says, and her voice is cool, even. She's in control. She doesn't really care; it's all one to her whether or not she gets to look up my skirt. But she's got her belt back in her hands, snapping it taut, then unrolling it again to dangle along her leg. I tuck the hem of my skirt into my waistband. Her eyes slip down to the triangle of white cotton between my legs, and she sucks her breath in sharply.

"Baby butch, my ass," she says. "That's what Vikki and all the girls say about you, you know. Cute little baby dyke. 'Teach her a few things for us, Johnny. Give her a little butch training, and we'll do the rest,'" she says, mocking the femmes of her group, who were always lamenting the lack of what they called "good" butches. "But I think that would be a waste of your talents. Talents that you don't even know you have." Her eyes come up to my face again, and for a second her tough-girl stance drops completely. Her eyes blaze out blue as the pilot light burning in the stove behind her, and suddenly I get it: It's Christmas morning, and I'm the biggest box under the tree.

"Now, little girl," she says, and this time her voice is all butter and honey, the voice of a stranger who rolls down the window of his big air-conditioned car and holds out a handful of licorice and lollipops and all-day suckers. "Pull down your panties for me."

My cheeks burning, I lean down and pull the white pants down, letting them slide over one foot to lie in a heap in the center of a black tile, my knees still wide open to her steady gaze. The tip of her tongue flicks out, and she licks her lips, just a little. Which of us is bluffing? Does she know what comes next? Do I? An ace, a queen, a ten. Her draw.

"W-e-e-ell," and I can hear her Texas roots all of a sudden. "So pretty," she says, and I flush. I don't care if she's just playing out some fantasy script of her own; no one ever calls me pretty, and hearing her say it, especially in that drawl, hits me harder than a double shot of bourbon. My throat stings, and if my knees weren't already pressed against the edges of the table, I'd be clenching them together to keep my legs from shaking.

Johnny takes a step closer. "So pretty," she repeats, and I bite the inside of my lips.

Sucker, I tell myself furiously. *Don't be such a sap, Mink*, but it doesn't do a lick of good. "Might as well be hung for a sheep as for a lamb," my uncle used to say, just as he was about to do something bound to get him in hot water with my mom. If you're going to get yourself into trouble, he taught me, you might as well have as much fun as possible getting there.

I lean back on my hands and look Johnny deep into her baby blues. She holds my gaze for a second, then takes another step closer.

"Such a pretty little girl," her voice dropping to a breath. "With such a pretty little pussy. Why don't you show me what you've got there, baby?" Half commanding, half cajoling. The belt wriggles across her palm like a snake. "Let me see you touch yourself." My skin crawls around the back of my scalp. I have never done this for anyone, not in the heat of passion, not with anybody.

When I don't respond she takes another step. "Can't you do that for me, baby? No?" Her voice is still low. She folds her arms again. "Then I guess I'll have to do it myself." And in one swift step she is standing in front of me and the belt is wrapped around my wrists, tight, the buckle jabbing hard edges into my thin skin. Johnny's hand is grabbing my hair, yanking my head back. "Is that what you want, baby girl? 'Cause that's what you're gonna get."

My eyes are watering as she twists a handful of hair between her fingers, and I lean my head back into her hand, submitting not out of fear but desire.

Keeping her hand wrapped around my hair, she lets the other slide down the side of my cheek, across my lips, tracing the pointed edge of my jawline, sinking from just beneath my ear, down my throat to rest on the damp skin stretched over the hollows of my collarbones. Then lower to unbutton my sweater.

I can see the reddish curve of her eyebrows, almost invisible against her flushed skin, the three silver rings encircling the curve of her ear. She is so close I can smell the tobacco on her fingers, the honeysuckle in her shampoo.

Then finally, finally, she puts her hand on me. Or more accurately, her fingertips. The tips of her fingers brush up and along my leg, following the line of my thigh to pause just before the triangle of dark silky hair. She turns her hand so her knuckles brush so lightly against me. Then again, back and forth, soft as a handful of feathers. Her mouth is inches from mine, but she's not looking at me. My breath is coming choppy and faster, and every time she grazes my skin it's like a little electric shock, like the tiny crackle of static electricity that shoots up your arm when you go from touching a doorknob to someone's fuzzy sweater. Snap. Snap. I'm breathing so fast, the room is starting to go black and fuzzy at the edges, and finally I have to, I have to, and my voice tears out the back of my throat, and I say, "Johnny, kiss me." And she does.

She kisses me wet and sweet and sloppy, and I want to sink into it, to roll around in her kiss like it was molasses. "Baby," she says, when I finally let her come up for air. "Baby," she says like a caress, but her eyes are wicked again.

"Baby needs a little attention, doesn't she?" and she leans in to kiss me again, harder this time, pushing her tongue into my mouth.

Each movement of her tongue sends a quiver of heat down my body, a spark of heat down between my legs, and then her hand is slipping between my legs again, tracing the curve of my thigh, flickering at the edge of my pussy, beginning to stroke, gently at first, teasing at the opening, rubbing her knuckles to and fro while with her other hand she is pinching my nipple softly, twisting ever so slightly, then twisting a little harder, and with each twist my clit jumps under her hand.

She pulls up my shirt, ducking her head to take my whole breast into her mouth; she is sucking and licking, teasing my nipple with the edge of her teeth, pulling and sucking, while her fingers are still playing around the outside of my pussy, sliding up and down, easing between the lips.

"So wet," Johnny whispers, lifting her mouth from my breast. "Aching for it. Baby needs a good fuck, doesn't she." It's a statement she's making, not a question, but still she doesn't fuck me; she keeps touching me, my breasts, my thighs, my stomach, till just when I'm ready to blow her top cool, she slides two fingers into my cunt, smooth and easy but not slow. I don't want slow. I want fast, I want rough, I want a lot of attention. "Velvet," Johnny murmurs. "Silk," and she slides her hand back and then in deep, again and again. "More?" She breathes, and I breathe back, "More." I can't tell how many fingers she's got inside me now, just the rhythm, pushing down against her hand, the slippery filling and emptying.

But it isn't enough. I open my eyes and look up at her, at her arm pumping in and out, sweat beading again on her lip and around her hairline. "Please," I whisper, "please." It was like having to touch myself in front of her, only worse, because I couldn't do without it. "I want, I want, I want your whole hand inside me," I whisper, my eyes closed.

Then I feel her breath hot on my cheek and then her lips on mine, kissing me, flooding my heart. "Give it to me, baby girl. Give it up to me," she is saying, and I lie back feeling the weight of her body pushing against me, the whole power of her behind that solid arm, the burning flush of my cunt swelling around her hand as she rolls her fist around the mouth of my cunt, rolling it wet and slick as she slides inside and as I breathe, deep and deliberate, willing my body to open up for her, take her in, be filled.

A wincing shard of pain; I suck in a sharp breath, and she stops, retreating. We hang there for a minute, joined, my feet pushing against the edge of the table. I breathe again, and there's a rush like water gushing down to fill a dry streambed after a summer of drought, and I reach down and feel her slippery wrist at the mouth of my cunt. Her whole hand is buried inside me, so deep, and I put my hand on my stomach to feel the lumpy shape of it down low. Slowly, she starts rocking her hand from side to side, just the smallest bit, and I can feel waves rolling through my body, waves of heaviness and sensation. I am impaled, pinioned, my whole body wrapped around her fist.

"Oh, girl," she is moaning now, caught between wonder and amazement. "Delilah, what a girl you are," and I can't even think of answering because my head is floating somewhere up near the ceiling, up near the lazily turning fan and the dim glow of the yellow light making a sparkling copper halo around Johnny's head. With her other hand Johnny starts rubbing her thumb in circles over my clit. It's like being in a forest fire and a flood at the same time, and I think, *If I come like this, I'll die.* Which is, of course, just what Johnny wants, and she doesn't stop with either hand, and I can feel the flames of her fingers licking around my clit while her other hand sinks deep inside me, like metal, heavy and molten, until all the flames come together and I slam my hips up against her over and over until everything explodes. A volcano, a rocket. It's like that. There's no other way to describe it.

Later, much later, I turn over and look at Johnny. She is a hump of blankets next to me, deep in the sleep of the righteous and the just. Across the room daylight is glowing at the edges of the dark green shades. Softly, so as not to wake anyone, I slide out from under the sheet. Then, putting one bare foot lightly, carefully in front of the other, I walk down the hall and begin—with slow, tender strokes— to polish the table.

ISO Gräfenberg
by Elisa Ross

I have to find it. She doesn't know about my search. But I'm gonna find it. They say it's there. I know it is. It has to be.

If she knew, she'd probably laugh me right out of her bed. She'd consign me directly to the rubbish heap of ex-girlfriends, do *not* pass go, do *not* your golden labrys, do *not* et cetera. My photo would turn up on a milk carton: lesbian last seen crawling from love nest covered in complete shame and dressed in utter mortification.

But if I have my way, she won't find out until it's too late. Until it's just right. Then it won't matter.

I first met her in a bar. Easy enough to do, right? She was hanging out by the pool tables, cigarette dangling, making those killer shots with cocky grace, wrapped in wreaths of smoke and laughter. Her tattoo blazed on her biceps like a trophy.

I hate that tattoo now, that winged Pegasus she sports that never takes flight. It smirks at me, whispers of other lovers, of cool liaisons in the shifting quiet of the night. It has fed on the breath of other sighs against her shoulder; it has drunk from an endless stream of bedmates who once teased and sucked, stroked and licked, challenged and pleased. That tattoo is a score sheet in my mind, tracking every kiss, every stain of others on her skin. It stands watch over her body like a sentry, the peerless champion of her soul, hoarding the loot of legions of past lovers.

I bit it once. It winked at me, I swear it did, and I couldn't help myself. She thought that was sexy, and that's just fine with me.

She sent a drink over, followed by herself. Her tattoo heralded her. While an ex of hers hissed in the corner, she sauntered over to me and shook my hand, tattoo preening over her skin. My friends who had mouthed caution, my friends who knew her all too well, my friends who kept me constantly under their collective wing and watchful eye couldn't help but be amused and begrudged her an inch to maneuver in. Maybe they needed new entertainment; I could already hear the sound byte on the 11 o'clock evening gossip. "Big Bad Bull Dyke Makes Moves on Blushing Baby Dyke."

She took the opening and sidled in, then sat down for a conversation, flexing her lesbian muscle, expert con artist that she is. Once she had elbow room, she quickly made herself comfortable, straddling a barstool like a rancher mounting her favorite horse. I wanted her to straddle me like that; I wanted her to take me for a ride. To ride me hard and put me up wet, as they say.

So I charmed her, I really did. I'm good with my tongue that way. I know how to tease that way and stroke and lick and challenge and please that way. Words are my playthings.

Unfortunately, women's bodies are a different story altogether. I'm so afraid of them; they make me awkward, make me clumsy, make me weak. They're a language I can't seem to master; their power is too much. She knew this right away. She knew she had all of the advantages.

She walked me back to the car that night, made a show of dancing between the raindrops, then lounged jauntily against my car door. Blocked my escape.

"So, you wanna hang out sometime?" she challenged me casually. Ransom for my freedom. I paid her price, gave her my number. Satisfied, she leaned in and snuck a kiss. A surprisingly soft kiss, a disarming kiss, a potentially lethal kiss. How she loves to be bad! I had a vision of the two of us dancing on the edge of a precipice: dashing love vigilante and her lovelorn muse. I guess you could say that's when my search actually started. The softness of her lips, the taste of smoke on her breath, the press of her body taunted me. So I kissed her back, on full alert for every murmur, every sigh that might indicate her pleasure. Searching for the weakness that might show me how to make her mine.

She knows I'm pretty new at this, and to be fair she's been patient. She wants to protect me, she says. I make her laugh, she says. I let her be who she wants to be.

Oh, but there's so much more I want to do.

I want to find that spot. The one that will make her shake and moan, the one that will turn her to quivering jelly in my bed. The one that will make her ejac-u-late. I'll find it, and she'll be so shaken, she will never want for anything else. She'll be my prisoner, held captive forever by my sorceress fingers that know just how to get her there. Get her off. Get her.

I saw a film of it once. Two women fucking, and the woman getting fucked just shoots across the room when she comes.

G spot. Gee, Spot. See Spot. See Spot come. C spot. C spot come. Come spot. Come, Spot, come!

Who the hell was Gräfenberg, anyway? An impassioned scientist with a desperate fascination for female fixtures? A wanderer of wombs? An ogler of ovaries? A fool for fallopians? Was he just some lecherous mercenary with the happy ability to plumb for treasure? Did he conduct his research with the scalpel or the skin? Why didn't they name the great discovery after his girlfriend instead? Did he drive her crazy with endless experiments at night, collecting empirical data, magnifying glass and flashlight in hand? Did he work for love, or did he work for money? Did he get rich from her ecstasy? Is it all a hoax?

Maybe I'm just as crazy, chasing my lover with my relentless whims. But I want to find it anyway.

There is, of course, a tactical problem. You could guess. She is always on top.

That's the way it's been since the beginning, ever since the first time. I didn't mean for it to happen the way it did, but then I never meant for her to happen to me the way she has either. Certainly I didn't mean for it to happen so quickly. She carbonated my hormones right from the start, though, and I just couldn't help myself. I think she knew it too. She came over to pick me up for our dinner date and just picked me up instead. I didn't have a chance. She followed me into the bedroom as I was getting my coat, and she ambushed me from behind. That was it. She wrapped her arms around my waist, she nuzzled my neck, and I was hers. It was all I could do to breathe as she slowly undressed me, breathe as her strong fingers traced over my skin, breathe as her lips brushed over my nipples, breathe as she slipped off my jeans and explored me, breathe as she peeled layers of me away like an onion, as she worked her way into my body, my mind, my heart. I was hers. She touched me in a way that left no ground for resistance.

And really, what *was* there to resist but the pleasure she gave me? A pointless struggle indeed. So for the first few times, I'm embarrassed to admit—the first ten, the first hundred, the first thousand—I didn't notice the disparity. Only gradually did I begin to wonder why her clothes never came all the way off, why I never remembered how her skin felt, why her sighs and moans of desire never reached my ears. Awareness came late to the party, blushing a flimsy excuse, too late to join the game.

I've been maneuvering to change things. But it's not easy getting a 175-pound butch to turn over and take it just because you're a little worked up and want to reciprocate. Try it sometime. No one moves until she's done. Until *I'm* done. She takes a long time too: She whispers enchantments, she romances every inch of skin, she charms every cell into submission, she shares secrets of my body with me that I never even knew. Until I'm done. And when I am, when I'm soaked and panting and spent, when she has drawn all the cries from my throat and all the wet from my body, she turns away and goes to that private place of hers, the one that has a sign posted outside: NO TOUCHING, NO TASTING, NO TALKING, NO TELLING, NO TRESPASSING. In short: KEEP OUT.

Nothing is as terrifying to me as the silence that follows my ecstasy, the silence that should be filled with the rustle of her body moving with mine, the murmur of her voice to my touch, the protesting whine of bedsprings.

My first attempts to breach the distance were unspectacular. I would lie there in my exhausted passion, in my tears, and stroke her skin, murmuring praise, murmuring sweetness, hoping to lull her off her guard. I would move surreptitiously toward her mound, sneaking closer. Ever vigilant, she would deter my trickery: She would roll over and

241

proclaim herself tired or get up and busy about. I *did* get her to catch her breath once. But I couldn't keep from getting excited, and she, no fool, casually brushed my hand away and mounted me again.

So I altered my strategy and began to let my fingers wander as she rode me, as she drove me toward that sweet place. It was rough, I tell you. A gargantuan effort of will was required to concentrate on my plans through the delicious sensations she showered upon me. But the tactic has been more successful. I have actually gotten to touch her wetness, to explore just a little bit. Inevitably, though, she redoubles her efforts to tame me, and try as I might my resistance always crumples under the onslaught of her skillful manipulations, her magical fucking.

Sometimes I try to get into her head, hoping it will help me. Maybe her G spot is in her brain. She's patient with this. She has given me her credentials—she's a card carrier if ever there was one—she has shared her history and suffered through almost every notion of psychotherapy I can dream up. She has dared to *process*. She knows this is not courtship; she's a practical lady. She told me once, "If this mental masturbation bullshit is better foreplay for you than the usual stuff, hey, I'll try it. 'Codependence' and 'intimacy'—ooh, stop; I'm getting hot!"

That's the closest we have gotten to talking about sex too. She will not discuss it. We talk around it, as I scan every word, every reaction for a hint. But she remains impenetrable. So none of this has gotten me any closer to the Holy Grail either. Oh, sure, I can identify our issues and harp on them when we fight. I can explain why sometimes I get needy and why she's so aloof. I know exactly the right things to say about her mother and exactly the *wrong* things to say at the right time. Frankly, I also know her well enough to be surprised that she is still with me. But in defiance of all this processing, she's as hidden from me as ever...the golden cup still eludes me.

Meanwhile, we romance as if by accident. I read poetry to her and play my music for her, while she fills my house with flowers and silly toys. It's as if we live politely with two other people who are trying to carry on in secret even though everyone knows. We never speak of this; it just happens that way.

At my wit's end, I even tried a little honesty.

"Babe," I finally whispered into the dreadful stillness of the dark as sleep was about to ambush us both, "I want to make you come." And I cowered motionless in the bed, waiting for her response. Would the heavy artillery open fire into the night? Would she call her armies into retreat, a mass exodus from my lair? But nothing happened. She was quiet for so long, I thought she had already fallen asleep.

"Why?" Her unexpected whisper.

"Because I want you to feel the same kind of pleasure you give me."

She dismissed this. "Watching you works me up so much, I couldn't get any more excited." Jocular.

"I have a hard time believing that. Don't you even want to try?"

"Baby, I can't."

"Can't try?"

"Can't come,"

"Can't come!"

"No. Believe me, I have *tried.*"

"Can't *I* try?" Didn't believe her.

"I don't want you to touch me. Not like that."

Was that a weak note I heard in her voice? I sent out the scouts, wrapped an arm around her waist. Such a slim, vulnerable waist for such a fortress of a woman.

"But I just want to touch you."

"Go to sleep." Her voice held a warning.

So the troops backed down and dug in for the night.

In the morning, though, her whisper was warm and close. "Mornin', doll."

Never one to give up a fight (or, more accurately, a whiner at heart), I ignored her and fretted. "I still can't believe you don't want me to touch you," I pouted.

She laughed. "You can touch me in other ways, baby. You *do* touch me in other ways."

"There's no 'other way' that compares to how you touch me. Don't you get frustrated?"

She traced a finger along my cheek. "Well, I wonder. Sure, yeah, I'm curious about it." The finger moved to my hair, then to my neck, then snuck back and forth. "But I feel you, and I feel your muscles, I feel your juice, and it's like when you come, something inside me shakes too, and I go there with you."

And she smiled that bad-girl smile. "Let's go for a ride right now…"

She leaned down to kiss me, such a soft kiss. I am utterly defenseless against a good kiss; she knows this all too well; she always has. She kissed away my resistance, she kissed away the tear that gathered, she kissed me to nakedness, she kissed me to want. Even as she kissed me, this time she let me undress her; she endured my trembling fingers, and she gathered me in her arms. I sneaked a glance at her tattoo, stalwart symbol of her honor. This time, at last, it was quiet. I traced it with my fingers; in my mind I saw it bow

to me. I closed my eyes, I bowed back, and this time I gave
her my unconditional surrender.

She took me slowly like she always does; she took her time.
But this time her lips were a prayer over my skin; this time I
felt her offer herself to me with her touch. Her hands molded
me in the shape of her pleasure; her fingers danced over me,
through me; her tongue frolicked over me, in me. I was my
body, succumbing to the pleasure she gave, but I was also her
hand, feeling the softness of my own skin. I was her mouth,
tasting the nectar of my passion. I was her gentle gaze, drinking in the sight of our dance and reflecting the joy of it back
to me. Behind closed eyes I saw her, a knight on prancing
horse, lone on a desolate plain, swearing her allegiance, a surrender of her own, welcoming me on our journey.

And then she was inside me, coaxing me tenderly, guiding me so sweetly, driving me home.

"Take me with you, love," she whispered.

So I tried to feel her riding with me. This time I flew on her
fingers; this time she carried me. She became my charger, gal-
loping across a barren desert to an oasis where the parched
thirst would at last be quenched. Yes, it was close now. I tried
to touch with my heart the gathering energy inside her that I
couldn't touch with my fingers. I felt her; I almost felt her...

And then a stream of wetness broke from me and covered
her hand, her arm, her belly. I became a fountain, repleni-
ishing myself. It seemed to last an eternity.... I became her
orgasm. I became her smile.

"Jesus." Her hand slowed; she bent to kiss me. "Jesus,
love, that's just what it felt like to me. How did you do that?"

I couldn't answer her. I was too moved to speak and too
spent to do anything but laugh. She repeated, through my
laughter, as she moved into my arms, "How did you do that?"

So I guess maybe I found it, her G spot that is. Which is also mine. Which is what I suppose I was really looking for all along.

Now, is that codependent or what?

Chapter 18
by Anne Seale

Juliette blew lightly across Mrs. Vanderpool's black-mixed-with-gray pubic hair, then stuck out her tongue and traced its moist tip among the follicles, wickedly delaying the inevitable dip into the nearby fragrant depths. *Will she be sweet or salty?* she wondered.

Mrs. Vanderpool suddenly arched her back and shoved the depths down onto Juliette's startled face.

"Yee-hah!" Mrs. Vanderpool shouted as she rode Juliette's tongue to glory.

"Salty," decided Juliette.

"Alexandria..." I hear Georgie say. I pull my attention from the computer screen and look at her, blinking to refocus, then blink a couple more times to be sure I'm seeing what I'm seeing.

Dressed only in black satin panties and a matching push-up bra, Georgie stands at the bottom of the staircase holding a glass of red wine in one hand, caressing the newel ball with the first two fingers of the other.

"I'll be upstairs," she says, sounding like Marilyn Monroe in *The Seven Year Itch*, "—if you *want* me." Not waiting for an answer, she turns and climbs leisurely, dragging the two fingers behind her on the handrail. Soon afterward

Celine Dion's "Falling Into You" floats down from the guest room.

All of a sudden the import of the thing hits me. My lover's visiting ex-lover just propositioned me! I shake my head vigorously. No way! No way am I going to jeopardize my relationship with Moira by doing it with Georgie while Moira's off earning our bread, even if Georgie does have a gorgeously plump body and just showed me most of it. No way!

I shake my head, to clear it this time, and turn my attention back to chapter 18, the final chapter of my latest novel about Juliette Renfrew, lesbian detective. Juliette is in bed with the woman who stabbed her best friend, Carrie Ann Prentiss, to death. Of course, Juliette doesn't know yet that Mrs. Vanderpool is the murderer. I resume typing.

Mrs. Vanderpool finally stopped bucking and lay splayed on the mattress, limp as a wet dishrag. Juliette reached for the glass of wine on the bedside table and took a sip. She was about to replace it when Mrs. Vanderpool took it from her hand and pushed Juliette flat on the mattress, slowly tilting the glass. An icy drop escaped, landing smack on Juliette's left nipple. Juliette yelped in ecstasy.

The phone on the wall by my left ear rings loudly. I yelp. It's Moira.

"Hi ya, sweetums," she says. "How's it going?"

"More than halfway through chapter 18," I brag.

"Good for you! Georgie been giving you any trouble?"

"What d'ya mean?" I say too quickly.

"I was afraid she'd play her music loud or something. Distract you."

"Nope. Music's no problem."

"Good. Listen, hon. I have to work late tonight. You and Georgie can go ahead and have dinner if you like."

"Oh, no, not without you!"

"It's been hard on you, having her here, hasn't it? I know I'd just die if an ex of yours came to visit."

"I don't think that'll happen, since you're my first," I point out.

She gives a happy laugh. "Good thing. You know how jealous I am."

Actually I don't, since I've never given her any reason to be jealous despite the fact that our monthly vanilla sex hardly satisfies me. I look at the desk calendar and silently calculate the number of days to the next encounter. Twenty-three.

Moira yaks on.

"Hang in there, hon. Georgie will be gone in a day or two. When did she say she has to be back in Detroit?"

"I don't know. She doesn't talk to me much."

"It's soon, anyway. And then there'll be just the two of us again." Her voice has become playful, flirty. "You and me, babe. Whooping it up."

Yeah, sure, I think. I'm not falling for that one. It'll be 23 days and eight hours from now. Exactly.

After we say our good-byes with the usual audible smooches, it occurs to me that it would be polite to inform Georgie of the postponement of dinner, in case she wants to have a snack or something.

I climb the stairs and knock on the wall without looking in the open doorway.

"Is that you, Alexandria? Come in."

I stay where I am.

"Moira just called. She'll be late for dinner."

"Come in. Please."

I peer around the jamb. She has taken off her underwear and is sitting in the navy upholstered chair by the window, one leg flung over the arm, holding a paperback. The glass of wine is beside her on the antique cherrywood table, the one that Moira inherited from her maternal grandmother. Moira!

"Moira just called," I repeat calmly, as if I chat with naked women every day. "She'll be late for dinner. So maybe you'd like to get yourself a snack or something."

I bolt down the stairs.

"Why don't you bring me one?" I hear as I hit the carpet and dash for the Mac.

Mrs. Vanderpool licked the wine from Juliette's nipple and on down around the breast where it had run. Then, still holding the stemmed glass, she took Juliette's hand and pulled her up and off the bed, leading her to a velvet chair by the fieldstone fireplace.

"Sit!" she commanded.

Juliette was too weak from lust to resist. She sat on the edge of the chair and opened her legs hopefully. Mrs. Vanderpool kneeled between them and raised the glass of wine, tipping it about five inches above Juliette's clit.

"The carpet!" Juliette protested weakly.

"I'll buy you a new one," said Mrs. Vanderpool.

"OK."

Juliette closed her eyes and braced herself for the shock.

My stomach surprises me by growling with hunger. I look at my watch. 2 o'clock! I forgot to eat lunch. I stand and let my feet take me to the kitchen.

The refrigerator is well-stocked, as usual. Moira's very generous with food and other necessities of life, all except sex, of course. Actually, I don't know what I'd do without her. The income from my mystery series, along with the occasional sale of a short story, would buy me a tent and a weekly can of Bush's baked beans. And that's in a good year. Even the Mac belongs to her.

As I assemble a corned beef on rye, it occurs to me to make one for Georgie too, so I make another and arrange them on Moira's everyday plates, garnished with a handful of potato chips and some olives. I carry one to the foot of the stairs.

"Georgie," I call. "I made you a sandwich. Corned beef."

"Bring it up, please," she calls back.

"No, you come down and get it."

I'm expecting an argument, so I'm taken aback when she appears at the top of the steps and starts down, still totally bare.

She smiles innocently as she approaches me and asks, "Where's yours?"

"Uh, in the kitchen."

"Good, we'll eat there."

She brushes past me and glides into the kitchen; she's very graceful without clothes. After grabbing a can of Pepsi from the Frigidaire, she sits at the table, in Moira's place. I follow like a zombie, setting the plate in front of her, fetching mine from the counter. I sit across from her, and we work on our sandwiches. Her foot rubs my ankle now and then, but I ignore it.

"I'm driving back to Detroit tonight," she says around a chip. Her voice is pretty much back to normal, thank goodness.

"Tonight…" I echo stupidly, intent on keeping my eyes on my plate. Unfortunately, two olives pointing their pimentos at me do nothing to divert my mind.

"Yes, my business is done, almost. I really appreciate your letting me stay here."

"Well, you know. Any friend of Moira's—"

She interrupts. "Ah, yes, Moira. How are you handling the once-a-month nooky?"

I gape at her for several seconds, then leap up, grab the plates—hope she's done—and throw them in the sink. When

I turn around Georgie's standing close in front of me, reaching with her right hand toward my hair.

"I'd like to have some dessert now," she purrs, "wouldn't you?"

The voice is Marilynesque again, her eyes narrow, sparkling. The hand strokes my hair, touches my ear. A shock runs through my body, hitting every vital spot. I find myself wanting her more than I've ever wanted anyone, even Moira. Moira!

"I don't *like* Bush's baked beans," I cry, sliding out from between Georgie and the sink and running from the room.

"What?" I hear her say as I hit the desk, but I don't answer. I am typing crazily.

Juliette was nearly swooning from the pounding in her groin brought on by the cool drops of wine, when suddenly everything stopped. She lifted her head to find Mrs. Vanderpool standing in front of the library table, rummaging furiously through her giant black leather handbag.

"Aha!" Mrs. Vanderpool said, emerging with a pint of strawberries and an aerosol can of whipped cream. She turned and waggled them in the air. "Bring yourself over here, my dear."

Juliette rose as if mesmerized and crossed the room. Mrs. Vanderpool swept the handbag, three books, and a vase of flowers to the floor, directing Juliette to lie back on the table. She inserted several large strawberries into Juliette's trembling valley, then filled it with a mountain of whipped cream. She licked her lips slowly, lasciviously, and dived in.

Hands grip my shoulders, *firm* hands that begin moving, caressing, kneading.

"Alexandria, you're so stiff," says Georgie softly. "How about letting me give you a little rub?"

I grunt. It's the best I can do. Georgie takes my hand, leads me upstairs to the guest room, and motions for me to lie down. Undressing me as she goes, she applies fragrant oil from a cobalt-blue bottle, expertly working it into my body.

When she has finished my back and as far under the front as she can reach, Georgie tells me to turn over while she puts on some music. She selects some reggae, turns it way up. Fine-tuned by the massage, I begin vibrating to the beat, feel myself pulse with energy, inspiration, creativity. Before she can turn back around, I am downstairs again, my oily bottom sliding precariously on the wooden desk chair.

Juliette grabbed handfuls of whipped cream and smeared it across her breasts, rubbing in time with Mrs. Vanderpool's tongue until her body began to throb. Then she relaxed, abandoning herself to the intensity of the climactic moment. When the throbbing finally subsided, she lifted Mrs. Vanderpool's strawberry-smeared face, kissed it thankfully, and slid off the table.

She went to the kitchen, took a bottle of Wesson's from the cupboard, and headed back to the bedroom, stopping in the living room only long enough to turn on her favorite soft-rock station. Natalie Cole's dulcet tones merged with the charged air.

Mrs. Vanderpool met her at the bedroom door. They fell together and danced. Without missing a beat, Juliette removed the cap of the plastic bottle and poured oil on their crushed breasts. It cascaded in rivulets, down, around, between. They massaged each other with their bodies, drowning out the music with gasps and moans. They danced over to the bed and into it, still slipping and sliding against each other in time to the music.

I hear the front door open. I spin around to beg Georgie not to leave—to tell her that I *am* almost finished with chapter 18 and that then I'm hers.

It's Moira.

"Surprise!" she calls, taking off her boots and putting them and her coat in the closet. "I couldn't do it, sweetums, couldn't leave you alone to entertain my guest when you're working so hard to finish that book thing. I mean, just listen to that loud, awful music. How can you think?"

Finally she looks in my direction, but I don't give her time to react to my oily nudity. I fling myself across the room and onto her. As we fall to the floor, I pull up her sweater, reach under her skirt. She gives a shriek of surprise, then astounds me by getting into it. Her hand slips between my legs, rubbing, plunging.

"Oh, Georgie, Georgie," I groan.

The hand freezes. Moira pulls away, stands up, straightens her clothes.

"So it's Georgie, is it?" she says very loudly.

The music stops.

"OK, fine. I'm leaving now, for one hour. I want both of you out of this house by the time I get back!" After grabbing her coat and boots, she stomps out the door and slams it behind her.

Georgie comes downstairs looking incredibly sexy in a terry-cloth robe.

She smiles and says to me, "Well, Alexandria, think you're going to like it in Detroit?"

"Might," I say. "By the way, do you have a Mac?"

"IBM," she says.

"I'll adjust." I turn back to the keyboard. "Be with you in a minute."

"Yes, yes, it's good, so good," groaned Mrs. Vanderpool. "Don't stop! Whatever you do, Carrie Ann, don't stop!"

With difficulty Juliette aborted a pass across Mrs. Vanderpool's slick body.

"Did you just call me Carrie Ann? As in Carrie Ann Prentiss?"

"No!" Mrs. Vanderpool sat up. "Goodness, no. What I said was 'Carry on!' Yes, that's what I said, dear, 'Carry on!' "

But Juliette had already found her fanny pack, had retrieved her pistol, and was aiming it directly between Mrs. Vanderpool's shiny breasts.

"So you're the one who was Carrie Ann's secret lover! Then you're the one who stabbed her that night in the middle of having sex! Were you going to do the same to me?"

Mrs. Vanderpool didn't answer, but the involuntary shift of her eyes to the cheese knife on the bedside table told Juliette she had guessed right.

With her free hand Juliette tossed the knife into the corner of the room and picked up the phone. "God, could I use a shower!" she said as she punched 911.

Visit to the Seamstress
by Jess Wells

I was surrounded by packing boxes, feeling like a chipped cup wrapped up in the newspaper of another divorce. My bowls and glasses were my heart, smothered by a lover's protection, and I tore the wrappers off them as if the coffee mugs were gasping for air. I had gotten too involved again, so I had run away in the hopes of regaining myself. Disgusted, I pulled a beer out of a paper bag and sat on a box marked TANQUERAY.

That's when I saw the seamstress across the driveway, downstairs in a bay window. She was a small woman with a skullcap of straight black hair. The sleeves of her white shirt were rolled up, a yellow tape measure around her neck and a pincushion strapped to her wrist. She walked very slowly, looked very closely at a woman in a tight blue dress who stood on a platform with her arms straight out, her eyes closed. I liked the way the seamstress walked. I watched her with my lips on the edge of the bottle.

The seamstress held each end of the tape measure as if it were a lapel and crossed in front of her client, whose chest was slightly above the seamstress's eye level. I shifted in my seat at the thought of her inspection, ran my tongue along the inside of the bottle. The seamstress looked the woman up and down, reached out and ran her fingers along the neckline of the dress, then down the darts, cupped the woman's breasts, smoothed the bodice. She gathered a tuck of the bodice between her fingers as if to tighten the fit but pinched the cloth at the nipples with such a steady grip that I smoothed the front of my own shirt. What sort of fitting was this?

The client tilted her head back, dropped her arms, and reached for the seamstress, but the woman quickly moved aside and disappeared into the shadows of the room. The woman in the dress dropped her head in disappointment and stepped off the platform. I put down my beer, entranced.

After I had unpacked the kitchen, I approached the window from the side rather than boldly face the front, and the seamstress was there again, same pincushion, same tape measure, but different client. This woman was standing on a chair on the platform, and I could see only her legs and the hem of a full-skirted flowered dress. The seamstress circled the client, bouncing the hem in the palm of her hand, checking for stray fabric. Standing to the client's side, she stopped, then turned her face up to my window. I backed away. The client didn't see me. The seamstress continued to look in my direction; then she lifted the flowered material and slid her face inside the back of the woman's skirt, her hands up the woman's thighs. The woman crouched slightly and seemed to sway dreamily into the seamstress's grip. I stepped all the way into my kitchen, my back pinned against the wall.

As dusk fell and most of my boxes were unpacked, I crept back to the window with what felt almost like envy. Who would be with her this time? It was so unlike my life. I had tolerated a string of women who curled into my breast pocket, pressing on me with their demands until I couldn't breathe. *The seamstress slid under a woman's skirts, then sent them home,* I thought longingly. I could almost smell the fresh air that must rejuvenate their faces as they stepped freshly fucked into a solitary night. The seamstress's freedom made me pace the floor. I imagined her strutting, satisfied with her performance, inhaling the scent of cunt from her fingers as she washed her hands and peeled off her clothes in blissful solitude.

Tonight the seamstress was alone, boldly facing the windows and my apartment, standing near enough to the glass to show me her unbuttoned shirt. When she knew she had my attention, she produced a needle and thread, snapped the thread taut, and slid the needle through the button panel of her shirt. With a long, expansive gesture, she reached over her shoulder and slipped a stitch into the back of the shirt, pulling it open to expose her breast and a tight brown nipple. The seamstress stitched the side of the shirt to reveal her torso, the black thread pulling across her ribs. With each motion I inhaled and watched the cloth. I pressed my hands against the glass, drawn to her as if gliding along the thread. She stitched a sleeve to a collar to expose a shoulder, gathered the buttonholes to frame her belly, and as I leaned forward against the glass she stitched the hem of the shirt through the darts with motions so slow, I thought the metal must be grazing her skin. She stepped back from the window and raised the cloth to show a sculpted hip and a fiercely dense triangle of hair. Bound now with thread and stretching cloth, she held the glinting needle as if asking for direction. I picked up my house keys and headed across the street.

After she opened the door to my demanding knock, the seamstress simply let go of the door handle and strode back across the room. I closed the door behind me and watched the black threads taut over her back, cupping her buttocks and disappearing between her legs as she walked.

"My name is Carla Forester," I said, slipping one of her business cards from a holder by the door into my pants pocket.

One large studio, her entire quarters were set up for business. Her brochures sat by the front door, signs that declared her policies festooned the wall, and the huge bay windows that dominated the place were painted with her company name. Her bed, undone I noticed immediately, was a pullout sofa that sat between a walk-in closet and a tiny kitchen and bathroom. Bolts of cloth were piled on bookshelves; boxes spilling tassels and zippers sat on the floor next to tin canisters of buttons. A ridiculously tufted sofa circle sat in the middle of the room with a potted palm arching toward the ceiling from the high peak of its center. It was something from a ladies powder room or a high-class hotel of the '50s. A dress form in the corner seemed like a voyeur.

"I was so afraid of who might move in," she said quietly. "A very old couple had been living there for years, and now it's such a pleasure to leave my curtains open." She sat lightly on the edge of a table and crossed her naked legs at the ankles. Her skin was the color of new butter. The black threading and black muff were journey and destination to me.

"It's a joy to meet you," I said softly and started across the room.

The seamstress leapt off the edge of the table and stepped into a puddle of black watered satin that lay on the floor. She picked it up by a collar and, whirling in a circle, brought the black fabric above her head. I was held at bay by the wide sweep of cloth, entranced by the quick flip of her triangle, her buttocks, her triangle. The black cloth cascaded over her body and covered her from a wide expanse at her feet to a high-standing collar at the tips of her ears. I gathered the voluminous fabric to me, struggling to find the reed of her body inside it. She pulled me to a tapestry-covered chaise longue and took off all my clothing.

By the morning I had glimpsed a length of leg. I had found the softness of her breasts behind their shiny black shield; I had made love to bits of skin that peeked out of the corners of the cloth. I had writhed with her amid the ocean of fabric, me entirely naked and white, she entirely hidden in black.

As she made coffee, emerging from the other room in a white shirt and black jeans, it was as if our sex had taken place in my dreams, broken into snatches as dreams are, as the black mantle had done. It left me wanting to begin again, and I sat twisting nervously on a wooden stool.

The coffee she brought me was scalding, and as I carefully held it in my mouth, the seamstress put her lips over mine. The coffee spilled from my lips down the front of my shirt, and I writhed under its heat. I grabbed her legs, wanting to see all of her, to strip her naked and pull her close enough to inspect. It was a very different sensation. In all my relationships—and there had been too many, I felt today—my lovers thought it was their duty to eliminate the skin between us, to become so imbedded in me that they were like pollen up my nostrils. I spent the relationship sloughing them off, keeping them at bay.

Now I was faced with a woman whom I couldn't decipher, couldn't seem to even get my hands around. I didn't care that women came through her shop in an endless stream. I had to know who she was. Earlier in the morning she had deflected questions of her upbringing, city of origin, previous professions. Every question was met with lips over mine or with the silencing effect of heavy duvet covers and the seamstress rooting between my legs.

I opened my mouth to ask her about herself. She gripped my lips, slid her clean morning teeth across them, and bit down. The seamstress grabbed the coffee urn that had been sitting on the table behind my head and slowly poured the hot liquid down my collar. I moved into its heat, warming inside and out as it coursed between my shoulder blades. Her mouth covered my chin, and she sucked my flesh as the brown coffee soaked through my white shirt, my nipples standing erect and clinging to the warm gauzy fabric. She bit the soft flesh of my neck, dug her teeth into the hard ridge of my collarbone. She was panting, sounds coming from her throat that made me think of a cat with its face sunk into a little bird's chest. I tore at her belt, her fly, massaged her clit until her sounds changed to a snarl. She rode me as she bit the skin between my breast and armpit, and we descended to the floor.

By the early afternoon I was exhausted from fucking her, unfocused in my mind as one becomes when one's body takes over. I wandered through her workroom, thirsty, out of breath, the feel and smell of coffee now mingling with last night's glimpses of flesh peeking through the yards of black cloth. My shirt left little splatters of brown on the floor with every step. I heard the shower. It was still Sunday, wasn't it? I didn't have to leave.

This sex was like a long drink of water. Sex always fell away too fast in my relationships. Information would replace intimacy; consensus would quickly masquerade as closeness. As time went on the lust was replaced with an irritating, parched feeling, and desire denied further became anger. As my relationships fell apart, both of us ventured out and screwed like thirsty women. The seamstress was wet and satisfying, yet the thirst remained. I followed her into the bathroom.

The steam nearly obliterated her, blurring the outlines of her tiny body. I hadn't noticed how much shorter she was than me until I stepped into the shower and held her against me. Toe to toe we were an entirely different matter. The water poured over her head, her face, making her close her eyes and concentrate on breathing. She looked more vulnerable to me than even when she came, like a cat pitifully soaked to the skin by rain. I held her tenderly, running my hands down her warm, wet back. She rested her head in the space between my breasts, her arms quietly still. Suddenly an idea, a desire started building in her: I could feel it in the slight tensing in her arms, in the way her cheek almost imperceptibly lifted off my chest. In retrospect I think perhaps she had reached the limit of her ability to be vulnerable, to be ordinary. She stepped out of the shower and disappeared into the other room.

I stood for a long time letting the hot water soak into me, leaning out of the shower over the sink to drink long drafts of cold water. When I shut off the shower and stepped into the steamy room, I heard big band music blaring. Walking into her room with a white towel around my waist, I felt as if I were walking naked into a department store.

The seamstress stood in the corner by her stereo, dressed
in a midnight-blue cocktail dress with a skirt that stuck out
farther than her shoulders. She had on cat glasses, and her
skullcap of hair was somewhere underneath a little slanted
cap of the same color as the dress. I expected her to put on
elbow-high gloves. I chuckled. She turned and brought me
a mimosa.

"Care to dance?" I asked her.

She smiled grandly and glided away from me with an exaggerated step.

Although I tried to take her in my arms, she whirled and
danced in front of me, only our fingers entwined. I wanted
to reel her in and hold her. I admired her dress, comment-
ed on her perfume.

"What's your name?" I asked, thinking perhaps this fantasy of hers was reserved for strangers.

"I'm the woman of your dreams," she said.

She would not hold me close. She eluded me at every
turn and dip. I succumbed to asking about astrological
signs and her taste in music but got no reply from those in-
quiries either. She whirled in front of me, a mysterious little piece of midnight sky, and I smiled.

She pushed me onto the circular sofa. My towel fell open
as she used her own legs to spread mine. Wetness surged
over my labia as she undulated in front of me, the rigid
bodice of her dress scraping my nipples and the net of her
underskirts scratching my thighs.

"A woman just for you," she said and suddenly thrust into
my wet cunt a dildo she was wearing under her petticoats.
She lunged like a man, with her skirts bunched around her
waist. Her dress covered her buttocks, covered her cock and
her pussy. The sound of her was like a debutante, all rustle

and swish, but she pounded into me with a cock that was hard and fast and deep. I shuddered from the tight response of my body and wrapped my legs around the scratchy waistline of her dress. I scooped her breasts from the top of her bodice and fell into a dark, glorious dream, finally arching off the side of the sofa onto the floor.

From deep within my mental well, I heard her unsnapping herself and straightening her skirts.

"Now that I'm dressed we must go somewhere," the seamstress said. "I never have anyone to go anywhere with me."

I opened my eyes.

"Let me dress you, darling," she said, using a term of affection for the first time. "I want to decorate you." She kissed my knuckle.

Please let her be serious, I thought. *Don't make me leave with just a job ticket for a shirt to be mended,* as I imagined all the other women had done.

She moved to a box at the far end of the room and brought back yards of tassel on satin rope, draped one over my neck, brought the soft length over my shoulder. I wanted her to wrap me up, to pull me into her life hand over hand up the length of rope. She lifted my breasts to position the cord, pulling me to my feet and turning me around and around, with the dark purple cord crossing my waist. She regarded me and her handiwork, then tied a knot at my navel and let a series of large tassels fall between my legs, where their satiny fingers stroked my thighs. She attached another tassel between my breasts and one under each arm until even my breathing caused a tassel to brush against skin somewhere.

"And now this," she said, helping me into a camel-hair coat and holding me upright as I struggled into my cowboy boots. She buttoned up the coat, picked up her purse from the side table, and opened the door. "Promenade?" she said, the gentle night air rushing under the coat.

"Whatever you'd like," I said quietly.

She took my hand and led me out the door.

Suit of Leather
by Barbara Wilson

Carter's family, her mother's side of it, had been rich for generations. They didn't call it being rich, nor did they talk about how they had made their money and had kept it. They spoke of wealth. They spoke of managing their fortune well. They spoke of being responsible to future generations. As Carter understood it, wealth was not about money but about power. Wealth was noticing how people treated you when you said your family's name. It was not about having actual money of your own to spend or having access to the millions that sat, paper quiet, in banks all over the world.

One of the ways that Carter's family had managed their wealth was to hire a brilliant young lawyer to marry their daughter. The man who would become Carter's father had no more access to the family's actual money than other sons- and daughters-in-law. But he did his job excellently and soon had the family's complete trust. He did not have money of his own, but he had power, and thus he had wealth.

Carter did not remember much about her mother. Slate-blue eyes, an oval face. In photographs she looked washed-out, remote, but Carter had some faint sense memory of orange peels just breaking away from the fruit—her mother's scent?—and she recalled a story about a magical bluebird, the bluebird of happiness, that went together with her mother's eyes.

Her mother had also been named Carter, and she had died—no one had ever quite explained how——when Carter was seven, shortly after Carter was sent from San Francisco to her grandparents' home in New York. She did not return to San Francisco except for visits. Her father never remarried but kept living in the huge house in the exclusive estate and working for the family. Carter hardly knew him. She didn't dislike him, but he frightened her just a little. He was short and quick, rather hairy, and his eyes were clever.

The summer before her 18th birthday, Carter came to San Francisco for a visit. He'd had the cook prepare a special dinner for just the two of them and then had told the cook she could leave early. The maid too. He served Carter himself, explaining about the food, which was light and decorative, and about the wine. At first their conversation was banal, the usual. How was her boarding school and her classes? Carter answered mechanically. He knew her grades better than she did, for they were sent to him regularly; he knew that she would be accepted at Smith, her mother's college, without doing much about it. It would be arranged, as so much had been arranged for her in life.

He asked if she were "seeing" anyone. Of course he knew she wasn't. She didn't mention how she had taken off her clothes once with her friend Sarah's brother on a visit to their house or how afterward she had let Sarah pretend to be her brother and to do the things Carter would have never permitted him to try.

"Not really," she said.

"Good," said her father. "In your position you need to be very careful about the motives of people around you."

She nodded and chewed her barely cooked duck with walnuts and pomegranate seeds.

Her father poured them both more wine, and his clever eyes grew brighter and yet deeper too, more secretive. He told her he would like to get to know her better, to start talking with her more regularly about what would happen on her 18th birthday in January, when, technically, she came into her fortune. Of course most of the money was in trust, and she wouldn't be able to touch it, but she would begin to get a regular allowance that was more than she had now.

Carter felt he was looking at her with a kind of hunger and caressing her with his words. He would, he said, continue to manage the family's fortune, which was her fortune, for as long as she found him useful.

"Why didn't you ever get married again?" she suddenly asked him, and for a second he was shaken; then he said smoothly, pouring more wine, "I made a promise to your mother as she lay dying that I would never marry until I could marry someone as beautiful as she was. I've never found that woman."

Bullshit, she wanted to say. *You probably use an escort service or fuck the cook.*

He looked at her sentimentally. "It's uncanny how much you're growing to look like your mother, Carter. The same blue eyes, the same sweet expression."

That night he came into her room wearing nothing but his boxer shorts. When he woke her up, his erection was sticking slightly out. His voice, oddly enough, sounded as if he were still discussing money. "Just wanted to have a little talk. A man gets lonely. Just wanted to get to know you a little better. You're my daughter and yet not my daughter."

His breath came faster, and he tried, clumsily, to unbutton her pajama top. Carter knew suddenly that the reason he wanted her body was not really about sex but about money and power. She understood that what he wanted to rub his hot flesh against was her fortune, not her cunt. He wanted to possess, through her body, this abstract thing called wealth.

Carter's school, while not progressive, had nevertheless recently sponsored a "self-protection weekend." When she felt her father's hand on her breast, she gave a tremendous roar, poked him in the eyes, and thrust her knee upward into his groin. Then, while he screamed and tried to hobble after her, she ran for the door and down the stairs to the foyer. In the hall closet she grabbed his trench coat and jammed her feet into a pair of spare galoshes.

She heard him staggering down the stairs after her, trying to explain. She slammed the front door and started running.

She remembered the way to the gate, but in the fog the streets were lost and eerie. Several times she heard a car slide by slowly. She was determined not to be found, especially since by this time she had discovered that the trench coat's pocket contained a wallet with $400 in it and some change. She finally found the gate and the guard drowsing in his little sentry house; she dropped the wallet nearby as she slipped past.

Carter used the change to take a bus into the city and the dollars to buy new clothes. Granted, they were secondhand, but her leather vest, pants, and jacket set her back almost the full sum. Why, when she had no idea where she would stay that night, did Carter spend almost all her money on a suit of leather? It wasn't because as a rich girl she was by nature extravagant about clothes; most of her life she'd worn a school uniform or dresses her grandmother picked out for her. It was only that, walking down the midnight streets of the brightest part of the city she could find, she had begun to see men and women wearing leather: leather jackets mostly but also vests and skintight pants, sometimes with the buttocks cut out. Heavy leather and smooth-as-silk leather; black leather and studded leather and leather with painted designs or words. She had never seen so much leather.

It seemed natural, when she passed a shop full of leather clothes (and other leathery things that she did not inspect too closely) to go inside and to ask, "Do you have anything that would fit me?" They giggled at her at first, the two bulky men with their pierced ears and tattooed arms, but they were very kind. They didn't even ask her why she was wearing pajamas underneath her trench coat.

"From sweet 16 to baby butch," one of them marveled when they had encased her in smooth black leather from head to foot. Carter looked at herself in the mirror and for the first time in her life felt completely safe. She was zippered from neck to ankles; they had even found boots in her size and a leather cap that hid her long blond ponytail. She left almost all her money as well as her trench coat and pajamas behind when she ventured back out onto Castro Street, but she felt transformed, both invisible and proudly herself. An hour ago she had been like the girl in *The Nutcracker,* looking at the dance from the outside, still wearing her childish nightclothes. Now she was part of the dance. She was ready to be looked at, knowing that no one could get to her inside her dark, invincible skin.

"What the hell? Hey, wake up, get out of here. Get off our steps, you little junkie."

Carter leapt up. "I'm not a drug addict," she said composedly. "I simply had no other place to sleep."

The woman stared at her and then laughed. She was big and blond, sleepy curls all around her wide face. She was barefoot and in a faded Japanese kimono.

"I get it. You had a fight with your girlfriend, and she threw you out."

Carter had been about to confess, "I ran away from home," but she liked this explanation better. "Yeah, that's it," she said and tried to look both abashed and tough.

"Oh, mama, does it start young! Where'd you learn that look, kid—from old James Dean pictures?"

Carter didn't know who James Dean was. She said, "Around. On the street." She could have added, "Last night," but thought that simple answers might be best when she didn't really know what she was talking about.

"I guess I should offer you a cup of coffee," the blond woman said and glanced behind her.

"I don't drink coffee," Carter said. "Actually what I need is a job."

"And you think I've got one?" The woman looked amused again. "Oh, mama."

"Gail? I thought you were getting the paper. Who are you talking to?" A rapid step came down the staircase, and then the most gorgeous woman that Carter had ever seen, tall with silver and black hair, dressed in running clothes, came to stand behind the blond woman at the door.

"Weren't you telling me we needed a new dishwasher at the café, Nat?"

"Yes, for the evening shift. Why?"

Carter didn't register in Nat's dark eyes the way she had in Gail's blue ones, of that she was certain.

"I'm prompt and reliable," Carter said. "A hard worker."

"Where else have you worked?"

"It was in Los Angeles," Carter invented.

"A queer bar?"

"Of course," Carter lied. And then with that little swagger she was trying to develop, "Who else would hire someone like me?"

"It would be under the table."

"No prob," Carter said without having a clue what that meant.

"What's your name?"

"Ricky," Carter said quickly. "Ricky Carter."

"Well, Ricky Ricardo," said Nat, edging past her, "see you tonight. Gail will give you the details." She set off on her run, straight up a hill. What incredible thighs she had. The silver-black hair gleamed in the sun.

Gail was watching her too. "She's my ex," she said. "Break up, don't talk for two years, then start a restaurant and move back in together as friends. Lesbians, eh?"

"Lesbians," Carter agreed.

It was the first time she had said the word aloud, and she relished it.

Nat and Gail's café was open at lunch and dinner and for coffee and dessert in between. Within a week Carter felt that she had been there all her life and that she was part of the small family of cooks and waitresses at Nightingale's. Nat had introduced her as Ricky Ricardo, and that was what she was always called, which was fine with her because two days after she started work she had seen, to her horror, an article in the *Chronicle* about a missing heiress called Carter. For a moment when Carter saw the article and photograph she forgot that it was her. The newspaper showed a bland,

white-faced, light-haired schoolgirl with a forced smile on
her lips: her junior picture. She was relieved to see that her
father had not suggested that she'd been kidnapped or was
in danger; still it was strange to read her name in print and
that of her family's, "one of the nation's wealthiest."

No one at her new job could possibly connect Ricky Ricardo, the leather-clad dishwasher, with Carter, the heiress,
but just to make sure they didn't, Carter resolved never to
remove her black second skin if she could help it. She had
to take off her jacket of course; it would have been impossible to work with it on, but she always kept on her cap.

They would tease her about it at the café. "Ricky, don't
you ever change clothes? Have you worn them so long that
they've stuck to your skin?" And once Nat took her aside
and said seriously, "If you need an advance for some new
clothes, some jeans or something, just let me know."

She resisted. The leather was what protected her from
anyone seeing who she really was. It was a magic skin over
the powerless little rich girl. In her leather pants and vest,
she strode down the street and looked girls and women
straight in the eye. She watched how other women in
leather looked at her and how girls in little thin T-shirts that
showed their nipple rings watched her. She had never felt
tough before she put on the leather; she had been more like
the girls in the T-shirts, wistful and avid, allowing Sarah to
stick a finger in, then two, then three. Carter knew now that
it was she who should stick in the fingers, if it ever came to
that. For she was butch. Everybody told her so. Everybody
treated her like that.

Her shift was from 5:30 to 11:30. She had all day to
walk around the city and to marvel at it. Outside the Castro she lost a little of her ease but made up for it by

putting on more swagger. Some people looked at her in distaste, tourists maybe, but there were always women who, even though they were wearing dresses and hanging on the arms of men, shot her glances that were not merely curious.

It was a strange new world. Many of her off-hours she spent at A Different Light, poring over books in the shelves and on the tables. There was so much history she needed to know at once. There were so many ideas, so many words, so many stories to absorb. It was like learning a whole new language, a complete anthropology. And Carter needed this rich strange new language not just for herself but to have conversations at work, to invent her past life, and to understand what her coworkers were talking about. Because she couldn't ask them straight out, couldn't ask what *transgendered* meant and how it was different from *transsexual,* couldn't ask how top and bottom were related or not related to *butch/femme* or why *femme* never came first or was sometimes written *fem.* She couldn't even ask the meanings of the simplest words, words like *dildo* or *diesel* or *dagger* or *drama queen.* She simply had to nod and laugh or look knowing and then rush to A Different Light afterward and try to figure things out.

The young waitresses at the café were either bi or heavily into butch/femme, especially the latter. They flocked around Ricky Ricardo, teasing her with their lipsticks and laces and with the tiny jingle of their pierced nipples, navels, and God knows what else. They would have loved to have worn perfume, but Gail wouldn't allow it: The café had to be fragrance-free, just as it was smoke-free. It wasn't alcohol-free, since marked-up bottles of wine made so much profit, but it definitely wasn't a bar.

"Not a bar scene," as Gail said proudly to Carter the first day. "Our emphasis is on food, fresh food, imaginatively prepared."

When Nat and Gail weren't around, the waitresses discussed them endlessly. They all were crazy about Nat and knew details about her daily life. How she ran every day, how she worked out at the gym, how she was totally cool and, like, hardly middle-aged at all. Gail they treated like their mothers. They sighed and rolled their eyes and looked straight through her at the same time as they confessed a grudging respect for how long she'd been politically active. Gail's greatest achievement in their eyes was, however, the number of years she'd been able to hang on to Nat.

"Nat just never *looks* at us," they complained to Carter. "But she's not seeing anyone. We *know*."

"What about Gail, is she seeing anyone?" Carter asked out of fairness rather than curiosity.

"She's over the hill! She's 40!" they crowed. "Why, are you interested, Ricky? Want to work your way up? Oh, look, she's blushing. Our baby butch is *blushing*."

Carter was blushing because there was someone she was interested in, but it wasn't Gail, even though Gail was so nice to her and Nat didn't even know she existed.

"Where's your family, Ricky?" Gail would try probing. "Do they have any idea where you are?"

"Don't know and don't care."

"But surely your mother—"

"My mother's dead."

"Then your father?"

Carter knew all the vocabulary now. "My father tried to sexually molest me."

"Oh, God, I'm sorry."

"That's why I had to leave home."

"Are you...underage?"

But Carter couldn't tell her the truth about her age. Gail might have to fire her if she knew. "I told you already, I'm perfectly legal, 19 going on 20."

"When I was 19 I was in college."

"Some people are smarter than others."

"You're very smart! Every time I walk past A Different Light, I see you through the windows, reading their books."

"I buy some," said Carter, stung. "I'd buy more if I had more money."

"But you must want more from life than to be a dishwasher. You could do so much more."

"I'm happy here just the way I am."

"Oh, mama," Gail sighed.

Other times Gail asked her about her old girlfriend, the one who had thrown her out. To please her Carter made up a story.

"She was a beautiful woman," she said earnestly. "Lots of curves, blond hair. Around 40, I think. "

"Forty! Wasn't she too old for you?"

"Forty's not old," said Carter primly. "Don't be ageist."

"No, I mean, of course 40's not old... What does she do for a living?"

"Money manager," Carter said without thinking. "She advised rich families on their money."

"Money manager!" said Gail in disappointment. "I thought I might know her, since she's around the same...since the Castro is a small world. But I don't know any money managers."

"She was more like a consultant or something," Carter backtracked. "She advised people to put their money into the environment and nonpolluting, nonexploitative industries."

Gail looked at her dubiously. "How did you meet? How long were you together? Were you *comfortable,* moving in such high and mighty circles?"

"I didn't move in those circles," Carter said quickly, and then, to shock Gail, "She just kept me around for the sex."

"Oh, mama," said Gail, turning away. She looked as if her knees were about to buckle.

All this time Carter had been staying in a small room behind the café. It had a small toilet but no kitchen. She usually ate her meals at the café. Breakfast she skipped. She was trying to save money. She'd never saved money before, had never really thought much about the concept. As the weeks went on, Carter gradually began to realize it would take her a very long time to save enough money dishwashing to get an apartment of her own, much less do anything like go to college. She knew that at any point she could go back to the life she'd left, could go back to her boarding school in Connecticut, could go back to a future that included a trust fund and college.

One day she woke up thinking about her grandparents. They were cold and proper people with whom she could hardly have a conversation; still it pained her that they might think her dead. She made up her mind to call her grandmother at least to reassure her, but when she got through, heard her grandmother say in that bitter-hard society voice, "Yes, to whom am I speaking?" Carter quietly put down the phone. It was just as well. They might have been able to put a trace on the call. Might have alerted the private detectives, the FBI, whomever else they had working for them. Better not. At least not now.

Carter had left her father's home in August, and now it was November. One night Nat and Gail closed the restaurant down to have a big party at their house to celebrate the second-year anniversary of Nightingale's. All the waitresses had been in a tizzy about it for the last week, huddling together like so many high school girls to discuss what they should wear. Samantha was even getting some new part of her body pierced for the occasion.

"What about you, Ricky?" one of them asked, and they all laughed. "Will we see you in something different?"

"I might not be able to make it," Carter said coolly.

Samantha in particular looked dismayed. "But we all wanted to dance with you!"

"Maybe some other time."

It was not that she was tired of her suit of leather, Carter thought as she made her way down Castro Street the morning of the party; after wearing it for almost three months, it was soft and flexible and molded to her body. It smelled like her. She even felt peculiar when it was off, when she took a shower, for instance, and more than one night, when street noises seemed too threatening, she had just slept in it. But all the same there was a way in which she could see that safe and protected as she was in her suit of leather, she would never get Nat to look at her as long as she wore it.

She took the streetcar down Market and drifted into the Emporium, to the lingerie department. She could at least get some new underwear. An hour later she left with several packages under her arm. She made another stop, at the drugstore, before she returned home.

The party was going full swing as Carter walked in the door of Gail and Nat's house. She thought she would have to be careful and stay away from the waitresses, but when Stephanie, with a silver chain connecting her lip to her right nipple, passed by her with a casual hi, Carter realized that her new disguise was as effective as her old. Once or twice she saw Gail, splendid in an ivory tunic with strings of beads, glance at her in puzzlement as if trying to recall where they might have met, but Carter kept well away from her. Even in her silky red camisole and semitransparent harem pants over black lace panties, Carter was hardly the most risqué of the younger women there, several of whom were down to their tattoos and jewelry. With her face made up and her long blond hair washed and swinging free, she almost looked wholesome.

At least that's what Nat told her when they bumped into each other in the hallway.

"Mmm," said Nat, looking at her as if they'd never met before, "you remind me of someone I knew in high school."

"The cheerleader probably," Carter said. "You were probably on the track team, and you used to kiss behind the football stadium."

"I wish high school had been like that," said Nat, laughing, and by the way she laughed, Carter could see that she'd been drinking, not enough to be drunk but certainly enough to be slightly red in the face and open to whatever might happen. "In actual fact I was a nerdy science student planning to be a civil engineer. I only dreamed about girls like you."

"Dream no further," said Carter, reaching up to pull Nat's arms around her. "Let's dance."

It was so easy, it was amazing how easy it was. When Carter wore her suit of leather and saw women look at her in the way they did, she was turned on, but not like this. She had to work at her tough look, and she had no idea what she would do if they ever responded. But this was simple. She pressed herself close to Nat and let her fingers trail over her neck and then up her shirt in back, and the whole time she felt amazingly confident that Nat was excited and getting more so.

"I'm afraid to ask, but how old are you?" murmured Nat into her hair. "God, you smell good."

"I'm not going to ask you that question," said Carter. "So don't ask me. Just hold me. Hold me close."

Nat did. Now this was power. Not money power but wealth of a different kind. The ability to make someone want you. The lights were low in the living room; off in the kitchen, where Gail was, a cluster of women were talking animatedly, but here it was murmuring quiet and sweaty warm. Carter could see a few things going on in the corners of the room that made her feel faint. Stephanie, as far as she could tell, was having sex with three women at once behind the sofa.

Carter had a strange sensation; she was sopping wet between her thighs, and she hadn't even been touched. She felt the tips of her nipples tight and hard through the camisole, rubbing against Nat's shirt and hard muscles underneath. The zipper of Nat's jeans caught in the flimsy rayon of the harem pants. Trying to free it, Nat's fingers brushed against Carter's pubis, felt the wetness soaking through the black panties. Her fingers didn't move away; they couldn't seem to.

"I know I am going to make a social faux pas," said Nat in a choked voice, "seeing as we haven't even been introduced, but can I dance you into this bedroom located conveniently behind us?"

"You lead, I'll follow," said Carter. But it wasn't that way at all. How could she have known, based on Sarah's tentative impersonations, so much of what she wanted? How could she have been so ready to arch backward, muffling her need with one of the coats on the bed over her face? "Give it to me, give it to me," she said. She had read those words in a book at A Different Light, had imagined herself, standing there in her suit of leather, cool and in control, hearing her lover beg for more and giving her everything she wanted. But now Carter's thighs parted wide, and she felt herself filling up with practiced fingers until she sobbed and shattered, then floated into a swirl of gauzy particles, a diaphanous shawl or maybe the Milky Way.

"Nat?" someone said. It was Gail's voice, polite and cold. "Are you in there? Our guests are leaving, Natalie; they need their coats."

Nat sprang up. Her black and silver hair was wild, and her pants were down. "Jesus Christ, what am I doing?" she said. She pulled Carter up and pushed her into the bathroom. "Here, I'm sorry, but God, some of these people are my employees. I don't know what got into me...what's your name—give me your phone number?"

Carter said, "I don't have a phone. Don't try to reach me." She went into the bathroom, which led back in the hallway, and let herself out the kitchen door. She did not feel safe going through the night streets in her fragile clothes. She wanted back her suit of leather.

It was only as she fumbled with the door to her small room that she realized she was holding something in her hand. It was a pinkie ring, familiar as Nat's. She must have pulled it off in the midst of everything. She tucked it under her mattress and took off her clothes and got back into the suit of leather, which comforted her with its smoothness and smell of herself. Then she went to sleep.

"Well, you missed a great party," said Stephanie the next day. "I knew Nat had a wild side, but I never imagined that she would actually fuck someone in public at her own house. I thought only sluts like me were into that."

"She...did it in public?"

"Well, practically. She took her into the spare bedroom off the living room, like, where the coats were, and you could hear them going at it like two hogs in heat. 'Give it to me, give it to me,' the girl kept saying. Whew! Hot stuff. I only wish it had been me. But at least we know now what Nat is capable of. Maybe next time."

Carter gulped a little. "Who was the girl? Did anybody know her?"

"Nah. Some straight-looking blond chick with red lipstick and kind of a big butt. Like yours."

"I do not have a big butt!"

"Hey, it's juicy. Come on, Ricky, don't be shy. I had so much sex last night that I'm still horny. How about a little hair of the dog with me in that room of yours off the kitchen? Ten minutes, my butch friend, even five minutes, just suck me off. I'm quick, I promise you."

"That's enough of that kind of talk," said Gail, stomping into the kitchen. "This is a restaurant, not a sex shop. If you want to work at Good Vibrations, Stephanie, I'm sure I could give you a good recommendation." She stomped out again.

"Uh-oh," said Stephanie. "We'll have to keep our heads down today. Gail is going to be in a pissy mood, and I bet Nat won't want to look any of us in the eye."

It was as Stephanie had predicted. The evening was a disaster, with orders mixed up, plates dropped. Gail actually did fire one of the waitresses, the one with blond hair. It was shorter than Carter's, but maybe Gail suspected her anyway.

"It's so incredibly unfair," said the waitresses to each other as they dashed back and forth through the swinging doors. "I mean, Gail and Nat have been broken up for years and years, and now Gail is acting like she *owns* her."

Nat was shamefaced but also moony in that strange trance that sex can produce. Carter knew. She was in that trance too, not that Nat was aware of it. While Carter stood at the sink, getting wet at the very sound of Nat's voice, she realized that Nat was talking to her impatiently. "Can you hurry it up, Ricky? The cooks hardly have a plate to put the food on."

Carter snatched a glance at her. The pinkie ring was gone, and Nat looked dark under the eyes and bruised around the lips. If she couldn't even recognize the woman she'd been passionately making love to when that woman stood two feet away—well, then, let her suffer. Let her wait and suffer. The time would come.

The weeks passed, and things returned to normal. Almost. Sometimes in her room Carter dressed up, secretly, in her red camisole and semitransparent harem pants and lay on her bed and arched backward, using a dildo she had bought from Good Vibrations (another place of revelations). It wasn't quite the same on her own. She stood in A Different Light reading the erotica books and was confused. What did she want? Who did she want? She loved to walk down the street and see women wilt, she loved it (though was also embarrassed) when Gail looked at her with that silly hungry look in her eyes sometimes and said, "Oh, mama." But Carter knew that she could never hope to satisfy Gail or anyone else in just the way that Nat had satisfied her. She didn't understand why, but she knew it was true.

In December, Gail said, "One of our cooks is leaving. Want to take a stab at it? You'd be making mostly breads and desserts. I'd teach you."

"Why not just hire a real chef?"

"Because, if you want to know the truth, I don't want you to leave, and I'm afraid you're going to if you don't have any new challenges."

Dear Gail. Carter loved her for her kindness. And she loved Gail even more because she knew that Gail didn't want to sublimate her desire under layers of maternal kindness. She wanted her desire satisfied or at least appeased, just like anybody else. But she was responsible and shy; she would wait for Carter to approach her, hoping that that James Dean look meant something. She would hope until she found out differently.

Because she couldn't give Gail what she needed, Carter started baking, and she turned out to be a good baker. She loved to mix and stir and roll and shape; she loved sweet things and also the slightly bitter tastes of almonds and dark chocolate. Gail and Nat were happy with her, though Gail once expressed some doubt about the black leather.

"Are you sure you don't want to wear a nice white baker's smock?"

Carter just looked at her.

"No," sighed Gail, "I guess you wouldn't be who you are without your black leather."

It was Nat's 42nd birthday, and Gail was giving her a surprise party, just a quiet one with a few friends and employees after work. Since the anniversary party in the fall, large celebrations had been out, and Christmas and New Year's had gone by quietly. Nat had gradually emerged from the doghouse, though, and she and Gail were on the best of terms again. Neither of them was seeing anyone else. Nat still went around sometimes with a slightly vacant expres-

sion on her face, but mostly she looked either sad or resigned. Lately she'd been given to talking about how old
she felt. She had pulled a hamstring, and it was slow to heal.
Then her knee went out. Carter had overheard Gail and Nat
talking about menopause and Gail assuring Nat that she was
way too young for hot flashes.

To the waitresses, of course, Gail and Nat were practically in an old-age home. Stephanie had resigned herself to the
fact that there would be no action with either Nat or Carter
and had found herself a car mechanic.

Since Carter had begun cooking and baking, Nat had more
to do with her, and sometimes when Nat came into the kitchen
to discuss the menu, she seemed a little bemused when she
looked at Carter and more inclined to linger and to chat. Once
or twice she asked Carter how long she'd been out on the
streets and whether she was in contact with her family.

"I'm sure they think I'm dead," said Carter. For she had
read another little article in the paper. MISSING HEIRESS PRE-
SUMED DEAD. Her father hadn't waited very long. She wondered if the money would go to him, as her closest relative.
In a way she wished it would. It would be so much less
trouble. But on the other hand, if she had it and could find
a way to get at it, she could do a lot of good with it that he
never would. She'd set up a walk-in center for girls on the
street, for one thing. Maybe build them a shelter.

"Do you have any brothers...or sisters?" Nat asked another time and then seemed confused.

"Not a single one."

The night of the celebration, Carter brought out two
cakes. One of them was splendid and three-layered, with
raspberry filling and dark chocolate frosting that fit it like a

suit of leather. It had 18 candles. The other cake was very small and golden-looking, unfrosted and with just one candle. It had a ring baked inside.

Carter brought out the big cake first, all lit up. Everybody laughed. "Did you run out of candles, Rick? Too many to stick on one cake?"

"Oh, God," said Nat, preparing to blow them out. "I'm so old."

"Actually, Nat, that's my cake," Carter said calmly and in one breath took out all the flames.

There was a surprised silence and then a chorus of "Happy Birthday, Ricky! Why didn't you tell us? We didn't know."

Gail was counting the candles. "Eighteen? Oh, mama, I knew it. I knew you were just a baby."

"Not anymore," Carter smiled, handing Nat the plate with her cake on it. It looked small but pretty there, with its golden sheen.

"That looks unusual, Ricky—what is it?" everyone asked, though they were slightly taken aback that Carter had made such a big cake for herself and such a small one for Nat.

"It's a special cake," said Carter. "It's 'specially for Nat. Don't let anyone else have a bite."

Nat sat and stared at it. "I'm so old," she said, and blew out the single candle. "I'll take it home and have it for breakfast."

Early the next morning Carter heard someone come into the restaurant. She'd been sleeping in her suit of leather, and now she put her leather cap on too. There was a hesitant knock at her door, and she opened it. There stood Nat in her running clothes, looking as wonderful as she had on the first morning Carter saw her. She held out her hand with the pinkie ring on it again. "I had cake for breakfast."

"Was it good?"

"Yes. But what was more interesting was what I found in it. I lost this ring one evening a couple of months ago. I don't remember some parts of that evening very well, though most people seem to think I made a pretty big fool of myself. But I do remember the woman I was with, and she wasn't you. Do you know her? Can you help me find her?"

"Yes and yes again," said Carter, pulling off her cap so that her long blond hair fell onto her shoulders. She zipped down her leather jacket, and there was a red silk camisole underneath. Finally she unzipped very slowly her leather pants and pulled them down. She was wearing very wet black panties.

"Don't ask me how old I am," Carter said. "Because now you know."

Some hours later the staff began to trickle in through the front door. Carter and Nat could hear them rattling around cheerfully. They could hear Gail, bustling and scolding. Nat began to look worried, but to Carter it was a homey feeling. Especially now that it was coming to an end.

"You know there's no other way out of my room than through the kitchen," Carter said.

"We're never leaving here," said Nat. "We're just going to stay here until you're 30 or I'm dead, whichever comes first."

"Well, I need to get moving," Carter said, getting up and starting to dress. "I've got places to go, things to do."

"Like what, little girl?"

"Like letting my grandparents know where I am. Like opening a bank account so I can receive the first installment of my new allowance. I'd like to start looking for an apartment, and I want to call the university to see about an early admission. I'd be wasting my time back in high school now that I'm ready for college. And then if I have time, I might do some shopping. I really need a few more clothes, just for variety."

Carter pulled on her leather pants and vest and jacket. It would be hard not to wear these every day, and she thought that in times of fear or stress or when she needed extra courage and invincibility, she would probably always put them on again. For now she left off the cap and let her hair stream down; how good it would feel to let the wind blow through it again. She put her feet in her boots and reached over to give the stunned and admiring Nat a kiss. Then, sexually appeased, secure in her love, confident of the future, Carter strode out of her room in her suit of leather to give her friend Gail a great big hug and to ask, very humbly, for her blessing.

Oh, mama.

Contributors' Notes

Roberta Almerez lives and works in the Bay Area. "A Friend of a Friend of Dorothy's" was originally developed in a writer's workshop on erotica by and for women of color held at the San Francisco Women's Building during the fall and winter of 1995-1996.

Katya Andreevna has had her erotic fiction published in *Best American Erotica 1996, Best Lesbian Erotica 1997, Heatwave: Women in Love and Lust, Once Upon a Time: Erotic Fairy Tales for Women,* and *The New Worlds of Women*. Her work has also appeared in Spain, Denmark, and Norway.

atara is an associate professor of English literature at an institution of higher learning. Her hobbies include writing erotica, watching *Star Trek,* and being an all-around Net geek. A Dodgers fan, she lives in Southern California with her Mistress and spouse, Ruth. "Play Ball!" is for Ruth, even if she is a Giants fan.

Sally Bellerose is the author of *Sex Crimes,* a poetry chapbook, and has been published in numerous anthologies and small press publications. She is currently working on a novel, *The Girls Club,* for which she received a 1995-

1996 Creative Writing Fellowship in Prose from the National Endowment for the Arts.

Louise A. Blum is the author of the novel *Amnesty*, which was a Lambda Literary Award Finalist. She has also had short stories and poems published in the anthologies *Lovers, Love's Shadow*, and *Breaking Up Is Hard to Do*. An associate professor of English at Mansfield University, she lives in Pennsylvania with her spouse, Connie, and their daughter, Zoe.

Rhomylly B. Forbes has had stories published in the anthologies *Tomboys! Tales of Dyke Derring-do, Close Calls: New Lesbian Fiction, Queer View Mirror II,* and *Cherished Blood*. She lives near Washington, D.C., with two gay housemates and several small animals.

Julie Anne Gibeau graduated from the University of Iowa in 1989 and works as a seasonal employee for the federal government. Writing erotica is her favorite vehicle for telling stories of self-discovery and growth, and *"Le Main"* is her first published story. She lives in Kentucky.

Mary Diane Hausman, a native Texan of Cherokee ancestry, is a fiction writer, poet, teacher, and painter. Her work appears in publications nationwide, including the journals *Common Lives/Lesbian Lives, Pearl, New Texas,* and *The MacGuffin* and the anthologies *My Lover Is a Woman: Contemporary Lesbian Love Poems, Writing Our Way Out of the Dark,* and the upcoming *Unsilenced: The Spirit of Women*.

Susan Kan writes stories, poems, and book reviews. Her work has been published in small literary journals. She works as a freelance copy editor and makes her home in Shutesbury, Mass.

Sara King holds degrees in English and creative writing from Cornell University and the University of Arkansas. She has taught English in China and Japan and now teaches English and English as a second language at two universities in northern Virginia. She is also the fiction editor of *The Green Hills Literary Lantern*. A native of Washington, D.C., she lives in Maryland with her partner. "Fantasy Vacation" is for Kim.

Catherine Lundoff has had her writing published in *Lesbian Short Fiction, 1001 Kisses,* and *off our backs*. She is a former warehouse worker and law school dropout turned freelance writer and eternal temp worker. Currently she is working on a book about feminist bookstores.

Judy MacLean has had fiction published in *Love Shook My Heart, All the Ways Home, Lesbian Love Stories II,* and other collections. Her humor and commentary have appeared in *The Washington Post, San Francisco Chronicle, The Best Contemporary Women's Humor,* and *Dyke Life.*

Mary Marin writes a monthly theater column for *Female FYI*. Her stories have appeared in *The Loop* and *Moon,* and a staged reading of her play *Just Say It, Goddamnit!* has been produced at the Celebration Theater. Currently she is working on *Drink Me: A Collection of Erotic Liquor Recipe Stories.* She lives in Los Angeles, where she works as a psychologist.

Janet Mason has had her work published in numerous journals and anthologies, including *Exquisite Corpse, Brook-*

lyn Review, American Writing, Girlfriends and *Lesbian Adventure Stories*. She has also published a collection of poetry entitled *When I Was Straight*. She lives in Philadelphia with her lover, Barbara.

Cat McDonald is a bisexual writer currently working on a novel titled *What Does Not Kill Us,* from which "Kolu, Revisited" is excerpted. She has received support for her writing from the Harmony Women's Fund of Minnesota. She lives on the Atlantic Coast.

Nilaja A. Montgomery-Akalu is an aspiring filmmaker, writer, and bartender who lives in the San Francisco Bay area. She describes herself as a "20-something African-American, girl-crazy chick" who believes that "when it comes to women, the blacker the berry the sweeter the juice."

Lesléa Newman has written 20 books and edited six anthologies. Her most recent titles include the humor collection *Out of the Closet and Nothing to Wear,* the poetry collection *Still Life With Buddy,* and the anthologies *My Lover Is a Woman: Contemporary Lesbian Love Poems* and *The Femme Mystique*. Four of her books have been Lambda Literary Award finalists. A native New Yorker, she lives in Massachusetts.

Mariana Romo-Carmona is a Chilean lesbian writer of fiction in English and Spanish. She co-edited *Cuentos: Stories by Latinas* and *Queer City: The Portable Lower East Side*. Her novel *Living at Night* was published in the fall of 1997. She teaches creative writing in the MFA program at Goddard College and lives in New York City.

Stephanie Rosenbaum is a freelance journalist who writes about food, fashion, and culture for a variety of Bay Area publications. Her fiction has been published in *Beyond Definition: New Gay and Lesbian Writing From San Francisco, Virgin Territory,* and *Tangled Sheets: Stories and Poems of Lesbian Lust.* She is now working on *Angelina,* a mystery novel, and *Cooking With Queen Pearl,* a cookbook for the well-intentioned and faint of heart.

Elisa Ross is a writer, poet, and aspiring filmmaker. Her poetic series, "Seasons of Rebecca," has appeared in *Refractions.* A professional bartender, she currently lives in Washington, D.C., where she is working on a film depicting lesbian lives in the nation's capitol.

Anne Seale writers humorous lesbian songs, stories, and plays. She has performed songs from her tape *Sex for Breakfast* at many music festivals and on gay stages on the East Coast, including the National Lesbians Conference. Her work has been published in *Ex-Lover Weird Shit, Love Shook My Heart,* and *Lesbian Short Fiction.*

Jess Wells has had seven volumes published, including the anthology *Lesbians Raising Sons,* the novel *AfterShocks,* and the short-story collection *Two Willow Chairs.* Her work has appeared in numerous anthologies, including *Women on Women: An Anthology of American Lesbian Short Fiction, The Femme Mystique, Lavender Mansions, Lesbian Culture,* and *When I Am an Old Woman.* She is a two-time winner of the Lebhar-Friedman Award for Excellence in Journalism.

Barbara Wilson is the author of the memoir *Blue Windows* and the novel *If You Had a Family*. She has also published several mysteries, most recently *Trouble in Transylvania*. She lives in Seattle.

About the Editor

Lesléa Newman is an author and editor with 26 books to her credit, including the anthologies *The Femme Mystique* and *My Lover Is a Woman: Contemporary Lesbian Love Poems;* the poetry collections *Sweet Dark Places* and *Love Me Like You Mean It;* book of humor *Out of the Closet and Nothing to Wear;* and the children's book *Heather Has Two Mommies.* Four of her books have been Lambda Literary Award finalists. Forthcoming titles include a book of humorous verse, *The Little Butch Book.*

alyson
books

AFTERGLOW, edited by Karen Barber. Filled with the excitement of new love and the remembrances of past ones, *Afterglow* offers well-crafted, imaginative, sexy stories of lesbian desire.

CHOICES, by Nancy Toder. *Choices* charts the paths of two young women as they travel through their college years as roommates and into adulthood, making the often difficult choices all lesbians will understand. "Nancy Toder's first novel really is a classic lesbian love story. The outstanding thing about *Choices* is that it is a good story." —*Off Our Backs*

A FEMINIST TAROT, by Sally Gearhart and Susan Rennie. "Reading the tarot can be a way of understanding the conscious and unconscious reality surrounding a particular question or circumstance. In *A Feminist Tarot* you'll learn how the traditional tarot can be a women's tarot...a tool for self-analysis. *A Feminist Tarot* gives us entry to knowledge of ourselves that we must never lose." —*The Lesbian News*

THE FEMME MYSTIQUE, edited by Lesléa Newman. "Images of so-called 'lipstick lesbians' have become the darlings of the popular media of late. *The Femme Mystique* brings together a broad range of work in which 'real' lesbians who self-identify as femmes speak for themselves about what it means to be femme today." —*Women's Monthly*

HEATWAVE: WOMEN IN LOVE AND LUST, edited by Lucy Jane Bledsoe. Where can a woman go when she needs a good hot...read? Crawl between the covers of *Heatwave,* a collection of original short stories about women in search of that elusive thing called love.

THE LESBIAN SEX BOOK, by Wendy Caster. Informative, entertaining, and attractively illustrated, this handbook is the lesbian sex guide for the '90s. Dealing with lesbian sex practices in a practical, nonjudgmental way, this guide is perfect for the newly out and the eternally curious.